"The dog is going to decide," said the judge

Mercedes and Cass both gasped. "She wants the dog in court?" Mercedes whispered to her lawyer.

The judge overheard her remark. "That's right, Ms. Delacruz, since the two of *you* can't decide who gets the animal. Plantiff and defendant—that's you and Mr. Montgomery—will each spend two weeks in the other's home. Then you will return to this courtroom, dog in tow. You and Mr. Montgomery will stand at opposite ends of the room with the dog in the middle. Whoever he chooses when you both call him gets permanent custody."

"What kind of test is that? My daughter and I haven't seen the dog for three years!" Cass burst out just as Mercedes protested, "I can't leave my daughter and my job to go to Florida! This is totally unfair!"

"It certainly is," he snapped.

Mercedes looked at Cass, startled. Their gazes locked for a brief moment. Amazingly enough, this was the first thing they'd agreed on. She turned back to her lawyer. "What do we do now?"

The voice that answered was a deep male one. "I suggest, Ms. Delacruz, that you buy yourself and *my* dog an airline ticket." Cass Montgomery slammed his briefcase shut. "We leave for Florida first thing tomorrow."

Dear Reader,

It's often said that many women marry younger versions of their fathers. I was thirteen the first time I heard this statement, and must confess to a certain amount of teenage horror. However, as I progressed through those early years and into more serious dating, I found myself measuring my dates against my own father.

Dad was—and still is—a man who commanded both the respect and love of his wife and six children. He taught us by example, laughter and praise, not by lectures or threats.

Dad openly adored my mother, loved his children and stood firm when his mind was made up. His biggest contribution as a family man was teaching me about priorities.

Once on a trip to the grocery store for milk, I stopped at a stop sign, looked left and neglected to look right. I broadsided an empty school bus with our brand-new car. The bus escaped unharmed. Our car did not. I was horrified. I was only sixteen—a novice driver—but that was no excuse. I just *knew* my father was going to kill me.

But when Dad came to get me and I tearfully confessed my guilt, all he asked was, "Are you all right?" I nodded and he put his arm around me. "Then don't worry about it." Neither he nor anyone else was allowed to say another word about that awful time.

I gained a new insight into my father and men in general that day. And when I broke my leg and met a certain Navy corpsman who saw me at my very worst yet was still patient—even kind—I knew I'd met my own family man.

I think of that old saying about fathers and husbands when I see Roger calmly drag out the rug shampooer when our son dumps soda on the new carpet... When my husband sits and combs chewing gum out of our daughter's hair... Or when I'm hysterical over something I think *he* should be hysterical over, too—and he puts everything back in perspective. I believe a real family man knows what's truly important in the lives of those he loves. My father did. My husband does, too.

And so does my hero, Cass Montgomery. I hope you enjoy his story. And his family.

Sincerely,

Anne Marie Duquette

Anne Marie Duquette

Finding Father

Harlequin Books

TORONTO • NEW YORK • LONDON
AMSTERDAM • PARIS • SYDNEY • HAMBURG
STOCKHOLM • ATHENS • TOKYO • MILAN
MADRID • WARSAW • BUDAPEST • AUCKLAND

ISBN 0-373-70644-8

FINDING FATHER

ABOUT THE AUTHOR

Anne Marie Duquette has traveled extensively throughout the United States, first as an air force "brat" and then with her husband, a career naval officer. She has lived in both of the locations—Florida and Arizona—featured in this book. The family—Anne Marie, her husband, Roger, and their two children—has recently moved to California.

Anne Marie started writing as a young girl, with lengthy letters to relatives and friends describing her impressions of countless new duty locations. She has now published seven Harlequin Romance novels, an American Romance book and a romantic novella; she's also sold a script to the television program "Star Trek: The Next Generation."

This book is dedicated to my editor, who was there for
my first Harlequin romance novel and is here for
my—I can't believe it!—tenth. Thank you, Paula.
I couldn't have done it without your sharp pencil
and even sharper mind!

I want to mention that this, of course, is a work of
fiction. However, any resemblance between the
fictitious canine in this book and two cherished
real-life dogs named Peppermint Twister and
Baron is purely intentional. Both really are
"woman's best friend."

CHAPTER ONE

"ALL RISE!" the bailiff announced as the judge returned to the bench. "Civil Court of the City of Phoenix is now in session. The Honorable Georgina B. Davis presiding."

Her lawyer at her side, Mercedes Delacruz rose to her feet, as did her opponent on the other side of the court-room. She kept her gaze steady, defiantly refusing to back down from Cass Montgomery's intimidating glare.

"Be seated," the judge said with a bang of her gavel. "I've reviewed the testimony of both adults in this custody hearing." She steepled her fingers and studied the male plaintiff and female defendant.

"I'd like to go on record as saying I'm appalled at the way this case has been conducted. In all my years on the bench, I've never seen such flagrant disrespect for our judicial system. And over a *dog,* of all things!"

Mercedes watched with satisfaction as the judge then directed her remarks toward Cass Montgomery.

"I've seen many underhanded legal tricks from lawyers in my day, Mr. Montgomery, but yours definitely tops them all. The fact that you've chosen to represent yourself and therefore have no objective view in this matter makes it even more deplorable."

Mercedes saw Cass rise to his full height, which was considerable. She was a tall woman herself, yet he was easily a head taller. His blue eyes narrowed as he spoke.

"I refuse to pull any punches where either my daughter's happiness or my search-and-rescue work is concerned, Your

Honor. I want *full* custody of Twister, and I don't care how I get it!''

The man was a barracuda, Mercedes decided, a sleek barracuda disguised in a designer suit, expensive gold watch and thick chestnut hair that, at the moment, framed a dangerous expression.

Mercedes refused to flinch. Thanks to her position as an archaeologist at Phoenix's prestigious Native American Museum, her own lawyer was the best that money could buy. There was no way Cass was getting custody of her daughter's dog. No way at all!

"And you, Ms. Delacruz..."

Mercedes turned her attention away from the enemy and back to the judge.

"You're an upstanding member of this community, yet you've deliberately turned what should be a simple civil suit into a public brawl! Calling in the local media to interview your tearful daughter ranks right up there with Mr. Montgomery's underhanded courtroom tactics. Between reporters, TV cameras and photographers, you've turned these proceedings into a media circus. Bank robberies have received less publicity than this canine-custody hearing!"

Mercedes just barely managed to hide her triumphant smile. Calling in the media had been her daughter Nina's brilliant idea. Budding actress Nina was crazy about that dog—and unafraid of TV cameras. She'd given a sterling performance as the heartbroken child whose beloved dog, Baron—aka Twister—was being snatched from her arms. Nina's experience with the local amateur community theater had paid off. And because this was a slow news week, the media had grabbed the story and run with it.

Nina and Baron had made front-page news. But there was a price to be paid: their photographs were accompanied by painful companion pieces on Gilles St. Clair, Nina's father and Mercedes's husband. Gilles was a world-famous mountain climber whose books and TV documentaries on the Himalayas were considered required study for all new climbers.

But Gilles had disappeared somewhere in the Alaskan mountains. He and his six-member expedition had left for a routine climb in Alaska. Without warning, a savage blizzard had sprung up, and somehow the experienced Gilles had become separated from the group. After weeks of futile searching, he'd been presumed dead. That tragedy had occurred the November before last. It was now July, well over a year and a half later.

Despite the lack of a body, the other climbers and Mercedes held out no hope. Gilles St. Clair was never coming back. And now his wife and ten-year-old daughter were in the news again.

The pain caused by such lurid headlines over Nina's photo as "First Her Dad...Now Her Dog?" had caused Mercedes to question her own judgment in going public. She spent more than one sleepless night worrying about her daughter. And seeing that old newspaper photo of Gilles setting off for Alaska had taken a heavy emotional toll on both of them. But despite all that, Nina's strategy had worked. Everyone in Phoenix was rooting for them to win custody of Baron.

Mercedes's lawyer was impressed by how quickly public favor had sided with Arizona residents Mercedes and Nina. Cass Montgomery's refusal to have anything to do with the media only reinforced the pro-Delacruz feeling. Mercedes's lawyer had learned that he'd left his eleven-year-old daughter, April, back home in Florida, and even the media hadn't known of her existence. So he ended up looking like the villainous outsider to media and public alike.

The judge looked solemnly at both of them. "For the last time, won't the two of you consider a compromise, instead of continuing this suit for sole custody?"

Mercedes didn't wait for her lawyer to answer. Her "No, Your Honor," was spoken at the same moment as Cass's, "No, ma'am, I do not." But Cass added a few more words.

"Twister is a highly trained search-and-rescue dog. I want him back before this multiple ownership seriously damages his skills."

"We've had Baron three years, Your Honor!" Mercedes broke in. "Whatever rescue skills the dog might have had are probably gone. We had a professional dog handler testify to that. My daughter, Nina, is his primary handler now."

"I'm well aware of today's testimony, Ms. Delacruz," the judge said irritably.

"Your Honor," Mercedes's lawyer began, "Mr. Montgomery is a questionable pet owner at best. He left his dog to die in a strange city—"

Mercedes nodded vigorously. The man *wasn't* responsible enough to own a dog. After all, it was at the Phoenix airport during the Montgomerys' vacation that Baron had been lost by his former owners, then hit by a car and left for dead until Nina Delacruz had rescued him. And as far as Mercedes was concerned, possession was nine-tenths of the law.

"I did no such thing!" Cass interrupted furiously, but Mercedes's lawyer ignored him.

"—a dog who's now ten years old. I doubt that this aged animal could still perform the strenuous search-and-rescue activities Mr. Montgomery has outlined. Not only is this an erroneous assumption on the part of the plaintiff, it proves my client's point. Awarding Mr. Montgomery custody could seriously endanger the health of this animal. Ms. Delacruz alone has the dog's best interests at heart."

Cass gave Mercedes's female lawyer another of his black looks. "Your Honor, this is pure speculation. The dog is mine, and I have Twister's pedigree, tattoo registration and purchase papers to prove it."

Cass's words were gravestone-cold. Mercedes's were not.

"I'm not going home and telling my daughter some stranger stole her dog!" she declared passionately. "If I have to keep appealing this case until Baron dies of old age, I will! Do you hear me?"

The judge banged the gavel.

"One more outburst and I'll cite you both for contempt of court!"

"I apologize for my client's behavior, Your Honor," Mercedes's lawyer said when Mercedes refused to apologize. Cass Montgomery didn't bother with apologies, either.

The judge's expression was grim. "So neither of you will reconsider?"

Cass replied first. When he spoke, his voice revealed an underlying emotion that startled everyone in the courtroom.

"Your Honor, search-and-rescue work is my life," he said quietly, a contrast to the angry words he'd hurled just moments before. "My wife died eleven years ago because there weren't enough search-and-rescue dogs to go around. There still aren't." He paused, the silence heavy in the courtroom. "I don't want what happened to my wife to happen to anyone else. I don't want another daughter to be raised without her mother, like mine's being raised. But it *will* happen, because one more trained search-and-rescue dog is being taken out of circulation. Twister is that dog."

Mercedes froze. His wife was dead? He'd raised his daughter alone? And all because of a shortage of rescue dogs? Cass hadn't mentioned that tragic piece of history during the hearing, not even once! No wonder he was so adamant about regaining custody of Baron! Why hadn't he said anything about having a daughter?

The judge must have wondered the same thing. "Why isn't your child's name listed on the petition for custody, Mr. Montgomery?"

"I prefer to keep my personal life private, Your Honor. I had hoped that I could return Twister to my daughter without dragging her into court. We had enough publicity when her mother died."

Mercedes suddenly felt sorry for him. However, capitulation was out of the question. She had Nina's welfare to consider. "I'm sorry about Mr. Montgomery's tragic loss, Your Honor," she said, her gaze including him, as well as the judge.

Her lawyer took it from there. "We both are, Your Honor. But according to earlier testimony, Mr. Montgomery works with only one dog at a time. Since he replaced his missing dog with another soon after he lost Baron, his argument has no bearing on this custody hearing."

Mercedes nodded her agreement. Cass did not. His earlier calm disappeared, and the anger returned.

"My present dog is nowhere near as skilled as Twister. And even if she was, Twister wasn't just a working dog. He was—*is*—a member of the family! My daughter and I planned to keep him with us long after he retired."

"Baron *is* retired! With us!" Mercedes retorted.

"Enough!" The judge banged her gavel again. "This is your last chance to negotiate a reasonable and amicable settlement."

Mercedes shook her head at her lawyer's raised eyebrow.

Cass vetoed the idea, as well. "I don't see how that's possible, Your Honor. I live in Florida. Ms. Delacruz is here in Phoenix."

"Then you leave me no choice," the judge said impatiently. "Regarding the custody issue of the male Labrador retriever known both as Twister and Baron, I'm hereby ordering a continuance."

A continuance? Confused, Mercedes glanced first at the judge, then at her lawyer.

"No custody issue will be decided until the following conditions are met. Condition number one: the dog will travel to Mr. Montgomery's Florida residence."

"What?" Mercedes heart stopped with a painful crushing lurch. She'd failed Nina! Dear Lord, how would she ever tell her daughter the bad news?

"The dog and Ms. Delacruz will remain in Florida for two weeks at the Montgomery residence. Then she and the animal will return to Phoenix, where Mr. Montgomery will spend two weeks with the dog at Ms. Delacruz's residence. This is condition number two."

"But Your Honor!" Cass protested, even as Mercedes's own lawyer was adding her protests. Mercedes's mouth dropped open as the judge rapped her gavel again for order.

I have to move in with that man? And then let him move in with me? Never!

"During those visits both plaintiff and defendant will observe the animal's behavior. The animal will observe *your* behavior. In one month's time, the plaintiff and the defendant will return to this court with the animal in tow."

"She wants the dog in court?" Mercedes whispered to her lawyer.

The judge overheard the remark. "That's right, Ms. Delacruz. Since the two of you can't decide who gets this animal, I'm going to let the dog decide. You can stand on one side of the courtroom, and Mr. Montgomery can stand on the other. The dog goes in the middle. Whoever he chooses when you both call him gets permanent custody."

"What kind of a test is that? I haven't seen my dog for three years!" Cass burst out at the same time Mercedes protested, "I can't leave my daughter and my job to go clear across country to Florida! This is totally unfair!"

"It certainly is!" he snapped.

Mercedes looked at Cass, startled. Their gazes locked for a brief moment. Amazingly enough, this was the first thing they'd agreed on.

The judge leaned forward, her expression not at all pleasant. "So is this foolish use of taxpayers' money! My job requires that I preside over this ridiculous case, but I *don't* have to like it. I've ordered a continuance, and my order stands. This court will reconvene in thirty days." The judge stood and rapped her gavel one last time. "Adjourned!"

"All rise!" ordered the bailiff.

Obviously not an animal lover, Mercedes thought sourly as she watched the judge leave the room. But that wasn't the reason she felt sick to her stomach. The injured dog Nina had saved *still* wasn't theirs! Mercedes turned toward her lawyer. "What do we do now?"

The voice that answered was a deep male one. "I suggest, Ms. Delacruz, that you buy yourself and *my* dog an airline ticket." Cass Montgomery slammed his briefcase shut. "We leave for Florida first thing tomorrow."

CHAPTER TWO

"You said we'd never give Baron up! You *promised* the
lawyer would fix it so no one could take him!" Mercedes's
daughter flounced in her seat in the airplane's first-class
section, every expression and word screaming enraged disapproval.

"I'm sorry, sweetheart." Mercedes sighed. "I know this
isn't what we wanted."

Nina scowled. "It's not fair! And school just got out. I
want to spend my summer vacation *at home. With Baron.*"

"Please, Nina, lower your voice."

Her daughter huffed audibly, but did as she was told.
"First he tries to steal my dog, then I have to leave all my
friends! I don't know anyone in Florida! How come I have
to spend summer vacation *there?*"

"Because that's what the judge ordered. And it's not
forever, Nina. It's only two weeks." Mercedes reached out,
offering comfort, but Nina jerked away from her mother's
touch. Mercedes let her child's rejection pass without comment.

"Two weeks is forever!" Nina flounced again in her seat,
her long black hair, so like her mother's, whipping about her
shoulders.

"You could have stayed with your *abuela,*" Mercedes reminded her. "Nana's always happy to have you."

"Mo-*ther*, Nana lives way across town in a retirement
complex! I'd *still* never see my friends."

Mercedes studied her daughter. Nina had always been an outspoken emotional child. It was one of the things that made her such a talented amateur actress. But her openly expressive personality was a definite handicap in situations like this.

"Maybe you can make friends with Mr. Montgomery's daughter," Mercedes suggested. "She's just a year older than you."

That suggestion was immediately shot down. "She's the enemy!"

"No, Nina. She's a child who's just as upset about this as you are. Losing the family dog must have been very hard on April."

"That was three years ago. Baron is *my* dog now, not hers! And he wants *me,* not some strange girl who gave him a stupid name like Twister." Nina blinked rapidly, stubbornly keeping her tears at bay. "Baron's probably crying for me right now! What if he's cold? What if he's thirsty? What if someone's luggage falls on his cage and smashes him?"

The man directly across the aisle lifted his head from his paperwork and spoke. "I personally made sure that the cargo handlers took good care of him," Cass Montgomery said. "They let me check on Twister and promised to be extra careful when they loaded him."

Mercedes laid a calming hand on Nina's shoulder, even as she braced herself for the explosion she knew would come. *Five, four, three...*

"His name is Baron, and you stay away from him!" Nina spat. She gave Cass a black look.

"Nina, manners, please," Mercedes rebuked her daughter, while as Cass said quietly, "I wanted to see him, Nina. It's been a long time, and I love Twist—Baron, too."

"I'm not talking to you," was Nina's response. She defiantly switched to Spanish. It was her first language, the one she and her mother used at home. Arizona-born Mercedes had retained both her maiden name and her parents' culture. "He's a thief! And so's his daughter with the stupid name! She sounds like a calendar! *April*'s as goofy as *Twister!*"

"That's enough, Nina," Mercedes ordered, switching to Spanish, but at a much lower volume than her daughter. She didn't like Cass Montgomery's eavesdropping on their conversations any more than Nina did. "I know this is hard for you, but your behavior isn't helping."

Nina clenched her fists. "It's bad enough we have to go to Florida. But do we have to *sit* with him, too?"

Mercedes took a deep breath. Silently she agreed with Nina. They were the only three passengers in first class, yet Cass had deliberately sat next to them, instead of in one of the other empty seats.

Still, Nina *did* need to be corrected. Ever since Gilles's disappearance, Nina had turned into an angry child—and she'd stayed angry. Her behavior was growing more and more out of control—just like right now. Unfortunately Gilles had been the parent Nina really listened to. The outgoing emotional Gilles had understood his outgoing emotional daughter in a way the quieter Mercedes never could. Despite Gilles's frequent and lengthy absences, he'd commanded Nina's respect and obedience.

Mercedes knew Nina loved her. Yet even after a year and a half as a single parent, it was an uphill battle for Mercedes to keep her daughter in line. It was hard to be stern with an angry child who'd lost so much and might lose even more, but it had to be done.

"If you aren't happy with the seating arrangements, Nina, perhaps *you* should move elsewhere. At least until you calm down."

Nina's eyes flashed rebelliously, a look Mercedes knew meant trouble. She steeled her heart and resorted to the old parental standby—the threat. She hated doing it, but Nina was in no mood to listen to reason.

"The movie will start in a few minutes. If I hear one more outburst, one more insult concerning the Montgomerys, you can kiss those headphones goodbye!"

Instant silence. Nina, who swore she'd become a famous movie star some day, loved watching and reenacting scenes from the movies, and Mercedes knew the in-flight musical was a particular favorite. Nina immediately unfastened her seat belt, grabbed her headphones and rose. Her next words were deliberately spoken in English, and were loud enough for all to hear.

"When it's time for us to go home, Mother, buy coach."

She moved three rows ahead with as regal a passage as a ten-year-old amateur actress could produce. But her mother's aching heart wasn't fooled. Nina was close to tears.

Mercedes watched her daughter until she was seated, desperately wishing there was something she could do to erase Nina's pain. The movie started, and eventually Nina appeared to settle down. It wasn't until then that Mercedes closed her eyes and rubbed her temples, trying to forestall the beginnings of a headache.

"Is she okay?"

Mercedes looked up in surprise. "I beg your pardon?"

"Your daughter. Do you think she'll be okay?"

The dark concern in his eyes was a welcome contrast after Nina's anger, but Mercedes's answer was cautious. "It's hard to say. This isn't exactly an everyday situation for her."

"How about you?"

Her fingertips froze on her temples. "Me?"

"Yes?" There was more than just politeness in his request. "Can I get you something? A couple of aspirin?"

"Either that or a good strong drink." Mercedes let her hands fall back into her lap. "I suspect neither one would help. But thank you for asking."

"If you change your mind, let me know."

Mercedes was aware that Cass continued to watch her. It would be rude of her to close her eyes again just yet. She waited for him to go back to his briefcase and paperwork. No luck. The conversational ball was still in her court. She contemplated several openings, discarded them and asked, "And *your* daughter? How's she doing?"

Cass tilted his head ever so slightly. That assessing look was like the one he'd used in the courtroom when sizing up the opposition—her. His next words confirmed it.

"Is that just a polite request or are you really interested?"

"I'm really interested." Mercedes hesitated, then, like Nina, decided to speak her mind. "Look, Mr. Montgomery. You and I may not ever join the friends-for-life club, but I would prefer that any hostility stay under wraps around our daughters. If you agree . . ."

Cass nodded.

". . . then my learning about April might help me to better deal with this situation."

"I'd like that."

An actual smile crossed Cass's face. Mercedes was taken aback by the appealing change it made. She found herself almost—but not quite—smiling back.

"So, tell me about April," she urged.

"Tell you about April . . ." Cass echoed. "Well, she's easy enough to describe. From the little I've seen of your daughter, I'd have to say mine's the exact opposite."

"She's shy?"

"Not exactly, but she does tend to keep to herself. Or maybe she just finds it harder to confide in me now that she's getting older. I'm a single parent, too."

Mercedes saw Cass's smile fade and felt a sudden pang of sympathy. A parent's relationship could become difficult with *any* child, but especially a motherless young girl. At least Mercedes never worried that Nina wouldn't come to her with questions. Nina talked about anything and everything under the sun—anytime, anyplace. Even on a long flight like this.

"Being a single parent can be hard," Mercedes murmured.

"Yes. And it wasn't any easier when Twister disappeared. April hasn't been the same since."

"That..." She'd started to say, *That long?* but stopped herself. "That's really hard," she improvised.

"It was, until just a few months ago. Spotting the picture of you and Twister was a miracle."

Mercedes's lips thinned at the mention of that accursed photograph. Her job as an archaeologist required her to both collect and catalog early Arizona Indian artifacts. Working outside as much as she did, she often took Nina and Baron with her to the state's numerous archaeological sites. The museum's magazine regularly published articles and photographs documenting her work.

Mercedes had been in one of those photographs, along with Baron. There was no mistaking the black Lab's white chest marking in the shape of a diamond—perfectly distinct even in a photograph. It was unique to Baron.

Unfortunately for Nina, Wyoming-born Cass Montgomery had an avid interest in Southwestern art and history and subscribed to the magazine. The Montgomerys' miracle had become the Delacruzes' bad luck. Mercedes had been contacted by Cass a few days after the magazine had been mailed out. She'd refused to surrender the family dog, and the custody battle had begun.

"April actually cried when I showed her the magazine," Cass was saying. "I was pleased to find Twister again, but knowing April was so happy was the best part." The warmth in his eyes faded. "At least it was, until I told April she was getting Twister back for only two weeks."

Mercedes nodded sympathetically. "Nina was practically hysterical when she heard about the judge's decision."

"I'm afraid April's reaction was pretty much the same." Cass tapped his pen on the paperwork spread out on his seat tray. "She's not very happy. I've made arrangements to take an extended leave of absence from my legal practice. Maybe spending extra time with April will help her deal with the situation."

Mercedes took in a deep breath. "Mr. Montgomery, I'm sorry. I really am. But your daughter's had three years to adjust to your dog's absence. My daughter, on the other hand, would be severely traumatized if she had to give Baron up."

"You're forgetting something. Twister is specially trained for search-and-rescue. I want him back for work just as much as I want him back for April."

"That's not going to happen, Mr. Montgomery. *Baron*—" she emphasized the word "—would be dead if it wasn't for Nina. Nina was the one who spotted him bleeding in the airport parking lot three summers ago."

For the first time since the courtroom, Mercedes saw Cass's anger return.

"I told you what happened," he said tersely. "The cage door somehow sprung open in the baggage area. Twister escaped outside before the handlers noticed."

"The circumstances don't matter, Mr. Montgomery. *Nina* was the one who urged me to put him inside our car, instead of calling animal control. *Nina* nursed the dog back to health when he came home from the veterinarian's. *Nina* was the one who insisted on giving me her allowance week after week to help pay the vet bills."

"I did offer to reimburse you," Cass said stiffly. "Plus interest."

"I don't want your money!"

"No, you just want my family's dog."

"*My* family's dog!" Mercedes insisted, then flushed as the flight attendant glanced at them curiously.

"Let me tell you something, Mr. Montgomery. If it wasn't for us, your *former* dog—a dog not even wearing a collar—wouldn't even *be* here for us to argue over."

"I had a collar on him," he ground out. "Twister must have slipped it somewhere."

"So you claim." Mercedes didn't hide her skepticism. "The fact remains that Baron wasn't properly cared for. His cage wasn't securely fastened, he had no ID, and he was more dead than alive after that car hit him. The humane thing to do would have been to put him down. Both the vet and I agreed on that. Only Nina wouldn't allow it." Mercedes shook her head at the memory. "My daughter can be very stubborn when she wants."

"Like her mother—and the word, madam, is *unreasonable*."

Mercedes refused to be baited. "This whole custody thing has been very rough on Nina. And the dog isn't the only issue here, either."

"Please don't tell me there's more, Ms. Delacruz," Cass said irritably.

"Well, there is." Mercedes took a deep calming breath. "You may already know this, but Nina's father is Gilles St. Clair."

She saw Cass's startled reaction. "The Canadian mountain climber?"

"The one and only." She hesitated. "Did you read about our hearing in the newspaper? Or watch the TV coverage?"

"Not much. I was too busy preparing for court. But I thought Gilles St. Clair was—" Cass abruptly broke off. "Didn't he leave for Alaska the November before last?"

"Yes. My husband wanted to try out some new equipment on Mount McKinley before his trip to the South Pole."

"Antarctica? That was never in the papers."

"Gilles planned to scale some never-before-climbed peaks, set some new records and write about them in his next book. As I'm sure you know, he...he never came back."

There was a long pause from Cass. "The newspapers said Gilles St. Clair was presumed dead."

"No one actually saw my husband die, nor have they found his body. The official verdict is that he's missing," Mercedes corrected in a tight voice.

"Surely you can't believe he's still alive?" Cass was incredulous. "Not after all this time!"

"Of course not! I know he's gone. I wouldn't have arranged for a memorial service or put a marker for him in the family plot in Canada otherwise! But it doesn't matter what I think. What matters is what *Nina* thinks."

Mercedes watched the shock and realization spread across his face. "You don't mean..."

"That she still believes her father is alive? That he's trapped somewhere in Alaska, waiting for someone to rescue him and bring him home to us? That's exactly what I mean, Mr. Montgomery."

Mercedes thought back to Gilles's smiling face. Funny, how it was becoming more and more blurred in her mind as time passed. She brushed away that disquieting thought. "The last time we saw Gilles was the day we took him to the airport to catch his flight to Anchorage—the same airport where, a year and a half before that, we'd found Baron bleeding in the parking lot," she added bluntly. "Nina adores her father—we both do. Baron helped fill a very big gap in her life when Gilles disappeared."

"I'm sorry, Mrs. St. Clair. I didn't know," Cass said quietly. "It must have been rough on you both."

Mercedes took a shaky breath. How surprising. He actually sounded sympathetic. But she refused to be drawn in by the sudden softening of his expression.

"Thank you, Mr. Montgomery. You're very kind. However, I prefer Ms. Delacruz," she said. "I kept my maiden name. And even before we were married, Gilles was quite the celebrity, so Nina also uses Delacruz, instead of her legal Delacruz-St. Clair. It makes life easier for us both."

"I understand."

"Good. I hope you also understand that Nina's grasp on reality is...tenuous at the moment. Some of Gilles's climbing trips lasted three, four, even six months, Mr. Montgomery. Nina thinks this present stretch of time is just another one of her father's long absences. She's positive he's going to pop up out of the blue, and life will go on like before."

Mercedes saw the compassion in Cass's eyes as he said, "Of course that's not going to happen."

"No. But try to convince Nina of that. She's an amateur actress and she tends to live in a fantasy world anyway. I've had everyone talk to her—from friends and relatives to paid therapists. Nina refuses to face the truth."

Mercedes couldn't help glancing over to her daughter a few aisles up.

"She's lost enough already, Mr. Montgomery. I'm not going to add to that. So when these four weeks are over and we go back to the courtroom, be prepared for a fight. Gilles's books were all bestsellers, and his TV documentaries did very, very well. Not only that, I have a good job. Nina and I can afford any legal fees."

"As can I, Ms. Delacruz."

There was a long pause. Mercedes checked on her daughter again and steeled her heart. "Perhaps you can, Mr. Montgomery. But I'll see to it that this case never leaves Phoenix. Unless you're prepared to give up your law practice in Florida, pull your daughter out of her home and school, and permanently settle in Arizona for the numerous appeals I intend to file, you haven't got a prayer of winning unless Baron lives to be a hundred. And probably not even then.''

Cass's eyes sparked with anger. "That's quite a strategy. But I made April a promise, and I have no intention of backing down. Let me warn you, Ms. Delacruz—where my daughter is concerned, I, too, can go for the jugular.''

Mercedes refused to back down. "My daughter's welfare has to come first.''

"Oh, I understand.'' His gaze was level, his voice dangerously even. "Because I feel exactly the same way.''

Mercedes felt an eerie sense of foreboding at those words. That more than anything made her say, "Please, Mr. Montgomery. Let me take Baron home before April sees him. There's no need to stir up all this emotional trauma. You have another pet, so what's the point of all this?''

"The point, Ms. Delacruz, is this. Twister is the best search-and-rescue dog I've ever seen, and in the past eleven years I've seen a lot. I'd planned to breed him. I see no reason not to continue with that plan or keep working him in search-and-rescue. Dogs like Twister can mean the difference between life and death.''

"You should consider Baron's health. He's too old!''

"Maybe he is, maybe he isn't, but I'm not going to find out in Phoenix. I've made arrangements for a search-and-rescue refresher course for Twister in Florida—along with campsites for the four of us.''

"You didn't say anything about that in court!'' Mercedes protested.

"The judge said the dog was to live his normal routine with me. Search-and-rescue was normal for him.''

Mercedes bit back her angry words. It was bad enough that he'd dragged her and Nina away from their home. Now he was arranging their every waking minute, too?

"You could have checked with me first," was her terse reply.

"I'm checking now."

"And I'm not thrilled with the idea. I still say Baron's too old. And if you aren't concerned with *his* health, at least consider Nina's emotional well-being. It isn't good to separate a child from something she so desperately loves.

Mercedes was surprised to see a look of pain cross his face. Then he spoke again. "I'm doing the best I can for April. As for Twister, I'm sure he can handle the work."

"What about Nina?" Mercedes demanded, her voice growing shrill.

Cass hesitated. "Ms. Delacruz, sometimes sentiment has to be set aside for more important issues. There are countless missing victims who may never be found without Twister."

"Like Gilles?"

"I didn't say that. But since you brought it up... yes."

"Ah. I think I see now."

"See what?" he asked sharply.

Mercedes studied him, her expression thoughtful. "You're one of those crusader types, aren't you?"

Mercedes received no answer—only a stunned silence from Cass.

"You want to play superhero," Mercedes continued with sudden insight. "And Lord help those who stand in your way. Like Nina and me. As for poor old Baron..." She shook her head. "What are you going to do, Mr. Montgomery? Breed him and work him until he drops in his tracks?"

"I didn't say that, Ms. Delacruz."

"But I think it's what you intend to do."

He turned his head away from her and refused to answer. Mercedes wondered if it was anger or guilt keeping him silent. Anger at her—or guilt over his wife's death....

Deep inside, she felt an unexpected surge of disappointment. She couldn't help but admire Cass's dedication to his daughter, even in court she'd sympathized with his motives. But now—now she had to wonder. Cass Montgomery wanted to take an aging family pet and throw on the work harness again, even though the dog had been replaced, even though an innocent child's happiness was at stake.

That realization made her ruthlessly blunt.

"This question may be out of line, Mr. Montgomery, but I must confess I'm curious."

Mercedes watched him face her again, the expression on his face as icy as her words.

"Do you *really* think you can save the whole world?"

CHAPTER THREE

CASS WAS FURIOUS. So furious, in fact, that he'd stood, gathered his briefcase and paperwork, and moved to another seat without saying a single word.

Frankly he didn't trust himself to speak. Right now he felt an intense desire to throttle his courtroom opponent.

The woman was a shark, he decided. He should never have let those full feminine lips, those rich mocha-colored eyes and waves of glossy black hair get to him. Beneath the beauty of that delicately sculpted face lurked a predator.

It seemed that neither of the Delacruz females believed in civilized negotiations. No, full-fledged frontal attacks with all teeth bared was more their style.

Nina's blows he could withstand. After all, she was just a child. Cass was sympathetic to her anguish; because of his own daughter, he understood it all too well. Unfortunately Nina promised to make a bad situation worse. She'd actually called him a thief and then made fun of April's name. As if it wasn't a perfectly lovely name!

And while Cass was mature enough to understand the reasons for Nina's anger, he knew his daughter wasn't. As a lawyer in Florida with its large population of Cuban locals, he'd honed his Spanish—so he'd had no difficulty understanding Nina's rapid-fire tirade.

But Cass couldn't be angry with Nina any more than he could be angry with April. He understood the two girls' reactions when it came to Twister. As for the mother...

That was another matter. Right now, he was trying his best to remain calm. It wasn't easy. First, Mercedes Delacruz had outmaneuvered him in court using media coverage she claimed was her daughter's idea. Next, she'd actually feigned an interest in his daughter on the plane. She'd lulled him into a false sense of security, then gone in for the kill. Mercedes had done her best to draw blood with her accusations.

Foolish accusations, he fiercely told himself.

"Do you *really* think you can save the whole world?" she'd asked with that cool expression.

What did she know about his daughter, anyway? What did she know about *him?*

Not a damn thing. But he'd learned one valuable lesson about *her.* She was a dangerous adversary. And a good lawyer never underestimated his opponent—whether in the courtroom or outside it.

It wasn't until the in-flight movie ended that Cass regained his composure. By then Mercedes had moved next to Nina and stayed there. Without trying, Cass heard them speaking in Spanish. Nina's loud voice carried easily in the near-empty first-class section, but so did her mother's softer one.

It was uncharacteristic for Cass to eavesdrop, even morally, still as a lawyer, knew the truth of the old saying—the best offense was a good defense.

He pushed aside his briefcase to concentrate on the conversation three rows ahead. The Mercedes he heard was different from the one he'd listened to in that Arizona courtroom. Her love for her daughter rang clear and true. And despite the girl's anger, Nina's devotion to her mother was just as obvious. Both were surprisingly open.

Cass found himself envying that. Nina wasn't afraid to express her opinion or her emotions. The girl obviously didn't fear any parental censure. And Mercedes was a good listener. She didn't try to preach or moralize; she empathized and guided. He felt a sudden guilt as he thought of April. He couldn't remember the last time they'd really talked about anything, although Lord knew he'd tried.

He'd start a conversation and April would answer with a nod, a shake of the head or a few sparse words. In their worst moments, Cass would lecture and April would cry. But as for talking, really talking...

Honesty compelled him to admit that he and April shared nothing that resembled what Mercedes shared with Nina. And honesty forced him to acknowledge that he was jealous. Because by the end of that plane conversation, Cass knew mother and daughter had joined forces to face the bad times.

That was what families were *supposed* to do. That was what Cass wanted for his own family. But it hadn't happened. Not with Cass and his daughter now. Not with Cass and his parents in the past, after his wife's death. When it came to the Montgomerys, bad times always made things worse. Horribly worse. *Not this time,* he vowed. *I'm not going to let that happen to April and me this time.*

But even after the plane had landed and they'd collected Twister and everyone's luggage, even after he'd retrieved his car from the long-term parking lot at Jacksonville's airport, Cass was still worried about the present state of affairs.

He and Mercedes were upset, as was Nina. And he knew April would be hysterical if they didn't regain custody of the dog. Twister was the only contented one in the bunch. And although it had been three years, Twister *had* recognized him down in the Florida cargo area. The dog's frantic barking and tail-wagging inside his travel kennel had been proof of that. Cass had missed Twister more than he'd let on, even to April.

As a distraction if nothing else, he would have welcomed some civil conversation on the drive to his house. But Mercedes Delacruz and her daughter sat far away from him, in the back of the minivan. Their disapproval was almost palpable. To make matters worse, he still had April to deal with once they arrived home; unfortunately that would be difficult—a real guessing game—because she rarely gave much visible sign of her feelings. He found April increasingly hard to fathom.

And Mercedes Delacruz was a definite wild card. Damn the woman! Could someone who loved her own child so much truly wreak such havoc in April's life? Or in his?

Cass shivered with sudden foreboding, and he wasn't a man who frightened easily.

"Are you all right?"

Startled, Cass looked in the rearview mirror.

"If you're cold, why don't you turn off the air and roll down the windows? Nina and I don't mind the heat."

"Thanks. Maybe I will." Cass switched off the air-conditioning and reached for the master switch to open the electric windows. The glass panels hummed down, letting in the muggy air of a tropical summer.

"Ugh! What is that terrible stink?" Nina asked in Spanish.

Automatically Cass started to answer, then stopped himself. The time to confess his knowledge of Spanish was back on the plane. Saying anything now would just make the situation more awkward. The poor kid had enough on her mind. Cass kept quiet and let Mercedes answer Nina's question.

"I think that... unusual smell is swamp water and vegetation," she replied in English. And then Cass heard her whisper in Spanish, "Nina, this man is our host! I don't want to hear you saying his home stinks! And since he's our host, we should both use English in front of him and his daughter. Do you understand?"

"*Sí*, Mama. I mean, yes, Mother."

A quick glance in the mirror showed Nina with her hands over her face, her nose tightly pinched between thumb and forefinger. Despite his mood, the corners of Cass's mouth twitched.

"Is the smell bothering you?" he asked innocently.

Nina nodded.

"Florida has almost as much water as it does land, Nina. The smell is rotting vegetation and stagnant waters. But believe it or not, that's a good thing. Florida wetlands support a huge plant and wildlife population, many of the species endangered. So we don't want to get rid of all our swamps."

Nina choked as she tried to hold her breath, failed and was forced to breathe again. Even Mercedes's nose was twitching, Cass observed in his mirror, although her hands remained in her lap.

"Not even the ones near the airport?" Mercedes asked.

"Hey, the alligators have to live, too, you know," he quipped, then was immediately sorry as Nina gasped. Another quick check in the mirror showed Mercedes looking a little nervous herself.

"Don't you worry," he hastened to reassure them. "There are no swamps where April and I live. Even if there were, alligators rarely bother humans. That's just in old movies, Nina. As for the smell, your nose will adjust. In a few days, you won't even notice it."

Nina still held her nose. "Does it smell like this at Disney World?"

Cass's lips curved in a full-fledged grin this time. Maybe Mercedes's little sharkette had some plain ordinary child in her, after all. "No. The swamp smell isn't bad in urban areas, and Disney World is near the city of Orlando. Don't tell me you've never been there?"

"Nope." A pause, then, "I mean, no, sir."

Cass assumed Mercedes had given her daughter a warning look. Well, he wasn't interested in manners as much as he was in establishing some sort of rapport with the child.

"Nina, you and your mother can call me Cass. We're pretty informal here in Florida." He wondered if Mercedes would allow Nina and herself the intimacy, then found himself hoping she would. "As for Disney World," he continued, "it's a great place. It's like Disneyland, only bigger."

Nina sighed heavily. "I've never been there, either."

Cass noticed that the pinching fingers had dropped from her nose with the change of subject. Obviously Mickey Mouse was a good distraction. "I'll tell you what, Nina. April and I can take you to Disney World and prove that there's no smell. And as long as we're there, we could go on a few rides. My treat."

There was immediate silence from the back of the van. Cass glanced in the mirror again and watched Nina's emotions wage silent battle on her expressive face. He felt a sudden pang. If only April was as easy to read.

"They have kennels there," he added. "We could bring Twister—"

"Baron!"

Damn! He'd have to keep reminding himself to call Twister by his new name when April wasn't around.

"We could bring Baron with us to Disney World, instead of leaving him at home. That way you could check on him whenever you wanted."

More silence. Cass had to hand it to Nina Delacruz—the kid was stubborn. She wouldn't give an inch, refusing to even utter another word. The mother, however, did have something to say.

"Thank you for the offer, Mr. Montgomery." There was a definite chill in her words as her arm encircled her daughter's stiff shoulders. "However, Nina and I wouldn't want to... impose on you. Right now, the most important thing is Baron's welfare and the girls' happiness."

Cass's grin faded. "I was just trying to be hospitable," he said quietly.

"Don't insult my intelligence, Mr. Montgomery. I know *exactly* what you were trying to do. Please don't let it happen again."

Oh, great, Cass thought, realizing his error. *She thinks I'm trying to buy Nina's friendship. I'm not, I just wanted to see her—and you—smile....*

But he couldn't say that, not in front of Nina. So Cass finished the rest of the drive home wordlessly, the tension in the van hanging as heavily as the humid tropical air.

"Are we there yet?" Nina asked wearily some time later.

"Almost," Cass replied. "We get off at the next exit."

Cass's home was in Orange Park, a suburb of Jacksonville. It was basically a military town that provided services for the nearby Jacksonville Naval Air Station. Cass had chosen to move there for three reasons. The first two had to do with April. Public-school accreditation here was very high, and the crime rate very low. People left their cars and their homes unlocked during the day. Even the youngest child could walk or bike to school without fear. Everyone knew everyone else, and while small-town living was like living in the proverbial fishbowl at times, at least April could grow up safe and secure.

The third reason had to do with him. After his wife's death, Cass had decided to throw himself into rescue work. Orange Park was within an hour's drive of Gainesville— home to a branch of the American Rescue Dog Association and the perfect place for a new rescue volunteer to start.

ARDA had been the first place Cass called after settling in. He'd acquired a bright Labrador retriever puppy, named the tail-chasing black ball of fur Twister and soon became part of the huge national coalition of canine-human search-and-rescue teams.

The work had been good therapy for Cass, so much so that he'd continued with a new dog even after Twister's disappearance. That work, together with Florida's hot sun and lush tropical growth, warmed his frozen heart—frozen by the memory of an icy Wyoming blizzard and the day he'd lost his wife forever.

But the June sun wasn't helping the chilly atmosphere in the minivan right now. Cass was glad to get off the interstate, and he drove the few remaining miles home as quickly as he could.

Cass expected April to come dashing out of the house as soon as he pulled into the driveway. She did come outside, but without the excitement he would have considered natural. He lifted his hand in greeting, but as usual there was no answering wave or smile from his daughter. April stood quietly away from them, even after he'd parked the van and climbed out.

Cass wondered why she couldn't show enthusiasm for *something*. If not for his arrival, then at least for their long-lost pet. He found himself wishing his sullen daughter, dressed in her drab rescue uniform, had more of Nina's vibrant personality, then pushed aside that disloyal thought. He also pushed aside the hurt he felt at his daughter's rejection and concentrated on watching his live-in housekeeper hurry outside to unsuccessfully urge April toward him.

That burst of energy was no mean feat. Mrs. Borden, who also doubled as April's baby-sitter, had legs that were stiff with arthritis. Yet April sulkily remained near the bushes, refusing to greet either her father or their guests. Cass stole a glance at Mercedes, but her attention was on her own child.

Mercedes unbuckled her seat belt. "We're here, Nina. Now remember what I said about behaving," she added in soft Spanish.

"I know," Nina replied in English. She tossed her head, unbuckled her seat belt and opened the door, all in one graceful motion. "*I'll* take care of Baron."

Behind them the dog whined eagerly at the sound of his name. His tail thumped rhythmically against the sides of the traveling kennel as Nina dug through her carryall for his leash.

"Would you like any help?" Cass asked through the car's open window.

Nina scowled, but remembered her manners. "No, thank you. I can do it."

"That's my girl." Mercedes ruffled her daughter's hair, then grabbed her purse and slung the strap over one shoulder. Before she could reach the inside door handle, Cass opened the van's sliding panel from the outside.

"Thanks," Mercedes replied. She'd get the rest of the luggage after she'd seen to Nina and Baron's needs. If the way she felt was any indication, they both had to be thirsty, hungry and tired.

Cass held out his hand to assist her, and Mercedes hesitated. The plane ride from Phoenix to Florida had taken forever, followed by a forty-minute drive from the airport. Her back ached from the hours of sitting. But she was still angry enough over the stunt he'd pulled with Nina earlier not to want his assistance.

"No, thank you," she replied.

"I'm sorry about earlier," he said in an undertone. "I shouldn't have brought up Disney World without checking with you first. It was wrong of me, and I apologize."

Mercedes looked at him carefully. Not only had he read her mind—or at least her hostile expression—he even sounded sincere. But then, successful courtroom lawyers usually did. Whether he was sincere or not, Cass Montgomery was clearly determined. He continued to hold out his hand.

"No hard feelings?" he asked.

Mercedes decided it would be churlish to ignore either his hand or his apology. She'd give him the benefit of the doubt—for now.

"None at all, Mr. Montgomery," she said politely. She stepped outside, feeling his warmth against her palm. His strong grip was gentle, and his hand surprisingly callused. It appeared that, lawyer or not, Cass was no stranger to physical work.

Then, annoyed with herself for letting her hand linger in his, Mercedes pulled away. "You have a lovely home here, Mr. Montgomery." Her glance took in the thick plush grass that her Arizona yard would never see, then slid toward the woman who was approaching. She had salt-and-pepper hair, deep ebony skin and a toughness that belied her frail appearance.

Cass never had a chance to make proper introductions, for Mercedes was bombarded by a blitz of words.

"I'm Tamara Borden—that's *Mrs.* Borden to you. I don't hold with this *Ms.* stuff. I may be a widow, but I was proud to be a married woman. I know all about making homes for babies and grandbabies *and* April," she said, in case Mercedes didn't get the point.

Mercedes did.

"I'm a good Baptist, and I don't hold with cussing, carousing and taking the good Lord's name in vain under this roof. You'll eat what I cook and sleep where I tell you, because I'm seventy-two years old and this ain't no hotel. And

I don't hold with any back talk from children, either. So if you don't have any problems with those rules..."

Mercedes hid a smile as the woman planted her hands on two bony hips and gave her a fierce stare.

"I don't, Mrs. Borden."

The tiny powerhouse nodded with satisfaction. "Then, welcome to Florida, Miz Delacruz."

Mercedes couldn't tell if "Miz" meant Mrs. or Ms., or was just the woman's Southern accent. After all, the airplane's in-flight magazine had said Jacksonville was only a half-hour drive south of the Georgia border.

She decided to let matters rest as Mrs. Borden added, "Nice meeting you, Miz Delacruz. I'll go start dinner, Mr. Montgomery." With a nod of her grizzled head, the woman turned and headed back to the house.

Mercedes blinked and turned her attention back to Nina and Baron. Baron bounded away from the minivan, yanking his leash out of Nina's hand, and raced toward Mercedes to give her a slurpy kiss. Before she could grab the trailing leash, Baron trotted toward the nearest set of bushes and lifted his leg.

Cass caught her worried gaze and shrugged. After a long airplane ride, the dog's actions were to be expected. Mercedes watched Nina as she nonchalantly studied her fingernails, the dog, her toes, then the boy with the blond hair standing near the same set of bushes Baron was so interested in sniffing. Nina dismissed the child after a quick glance, preferring to keep her eyes on Baron.

Mercedes smiled at the boy, but there was no answering smile. *Too bad,* she thought. That petulant face would look much better with a smile. Inwardly Mercedes frowned at the boy's clothes. She'd never approved of miniature military fatigues on children and couldn't understand why parents encouraged them. The thick material of the international-orange jumpsuit and heavy black boots made the boy seem overdressed, especially for Florida. The army-green T-shirt and fatigue hat weren't very summerlike, either. Only his hair with its shaved sides seemed practical for the heat.

Mercedes wondered if he was just a curious neighbor boy or a good friend of April's. Cass approached the boy then, and she noticed that the child immediately backed away. Perhaps the boy wasn't as shy when April was around. She was about to inquire as to April's whereabouts when Baron finished his business with the bushes and started sniffing around the grass in earnest.

"Nina, curb the dog," Mercedes ordered.

Nina flushed and hurried to retrieve the dog's trailing leash. "I'm sorry, Mr. Montgomery. At home Baron goes where he wants, and Mom just has me clean up after him later."

"We do the same thing here," Cass replied easily. "Only, why don't you take Baron around back? There's a water bowl there and a big fenced yard. You can let him off the leash. I'm sure he needs to stretch his legs after being cooped up for so long."

Nina glanced at her mother for confirmation, and Mercedes in turn asked Cass, "But what about your other dog?"

"Some friends of mine, the Andersons, are keeping Buddy. I thought it best for the two weeks you were visiting. Twist—Baron will be quite safe in the backyard."

"Go ahead, Nina." Mercedes nodded her approval, also approving of Cass's attempt to be diplomatic regarding the dog's two names. "Take him around back. I'll bring his food in a minute."

"We already have a bowl filled for him," Cass said.

"But we brought his own bowl! I mean, thank you, Mr. Montgomery." Nina corrected herself with only a trace of petulance.

Good for you, Nina, Mercedes thought, giving her a warm smile. Cass did the same. *When he's away from the courtroom, he has a very nice smile,* she realized.

"There's no need to thank me, Nina. This was Twister's home for seven years. I want you to feel at home here, too."

Mercedes watched Nina's eyebrows rush together at the use of Baron's old name. So much for diplomacy, she thought, but Nina managed to keep her temper in check.

"I'm sure Baron and I will," Nina answered sweetly. Mercedes hid a smile. That was Gilles's daughter for you— she could never let anyone else have the last word.

"Come on, Baron." Nina tugged at the leash. "Let's go out back."

"Why don't you go with her?" Cass suggested to the boy.

He hadn't moved or said a word since they'd driven up, Mercedes noticed, but he hadn't taken his eyes off Baron the entire time. Well, that was nothing new. There wasn't a child back home who didn't love Baron. He was a sociable dog who welcomed attention from everyone, especially kids.

Mercedes took Cass's hint. "Nina, why don't you introduce Baron?"

Nina's polite facade started to slip. "Baron has to *go,*" Nina said stubbornly. "He doesn't want to play with strangers right now." Nina took a step closer to the other child. "See?"

It seemed true enough. The dog hadn't shown the slightest interest in the boy, not giving so much as a sedate wag of the tail. And the flight *had* been a long one. Mercedes changed her mind.

"Maybe Nina's right, Cass. Baron needs to be fed and exercised. Perhaps this young man here can come back tomorrow. April herself should go with Nina. Where is she?"

"*I'm* April!"

Mercedes and Nina froze as the words exploded from the other child's lips.

"You're..." Mercedes looked from the angry child to Cass and back again. She started to apologize, but April's attention was only on the dog.

"Twister! Don't you know me? It's April! Here, Twist! Come on, boy!"

Baron did just the opposite. With his massive black body, he protectively pushed Nina away from the pleading child. And when April advanced with outstretched arms, he bared his teeth and growled. The sound sent a shiver down Mercedes's spine. This was no playful pet anymore. This was a dangerous animal.

"Heel, Baron!" Nina ordered, but for once Baron refused to obey. In fact, the dog started to advance on the other child, but Mercedes immediately made a successful grab for Baron's leash. It took two corrective yanks before the growling stopped, and even then the hackles on Baron's neck stayed up.

"Nina, take this dog out back!" She was so disturbed she lapsed into Spanish. Baron had never acted that way around another child before. "Now!"

A wide-eyed Nina, all defiance gone, scurried to obey her mother, as April Montgomery ran into the house.

Cass sprinted after his sobbing daughter, his parting words ringing in Mercedes's ears.

"Lady, what the hell did you do to our dog?"

CHAPTER FOUR

POOR APRIL, Mercedes thought. Never in a million years would she have guessed that the miniature soldier out front was April! It wasn't just the clothes, either. April hadn't exhibited any of the affection or enthusiasm most children showed when a parent came home. And Cass had certainly been gone long enough to rate at least a hug and a kiss.

Now Mercedes was in the guest bedroom rummaging through Nina's suitcase. Nina would need fresh clothes to wear after her bath. Mercedes herself had already showered in the guest room's private bathroom and changed in preparation for dinner.

Judging by April's tearful reaction to Baron, dinner might be a long time in coming. Once Nina had dragged Baron to the backyard, Cass had hurried after April, Mercedes right behind him. But Cass had bluntly told her to stay put before disappearing up the stairs of the two-story home. Mercedes had hesitated, but Mrs. Borden had proved a formidable obstacle at the foot of the stairs.

Finally Mercedes had brought in their luggage and called Nina inside. By then it was safe to venture upstairs. As for the dog, she prudently left him out in the yard. So now she was waiting in her room, wishing she and April had started off on a more cheerful note.

Mercedes sighed. She pulled out a pair of denim shorts with pink lace trim for Nina, then found the matching pink T-shirt with little denim hearts on its pocket. She quickly unpacked the suitcases, slid the clothes into the empty drawers of the dresser and made a quick check on Nina.

"Aren't you done yet?" she asked, automatically switching to Spanish.

"I'm washing my hair, Mama."

"But Nina, you just washed it last night!"

"You washed yours again, so I washed mine. It smelled like cigarette smoke." Nina wrinkled her wet soapy nose in distaste. The airport's lobby had been full of tobacco enthusiasts. "Besides," she said with maddening logic, "I've already put in the shampoo."

"Well, hurry up," Mercedes urged. "We don't want to be late for dinner."

She laid two clean towels on the counter for Nina, then headed back to the bedroom area, surprising April Montgomery in the hallway.

"Hello, April. Please don't go," she immediately said as the child started to bolt.

April hesitated, one hand on the doorjamb, the other on the knob. She'd showered, too—the short blond of her geometric cut was still wet. The military fatigues were gone, replaced by a simple blue jumper. The outfit was well tailored and looked expensive, but it was extremely conservative and didn't flatter April's long delicate build. Mercedes suddenly wondered if the elderly Mrs. Borden did April's shopping.

"Come on in," Mercedes invited, sitting down on the bed. "I imagine your father sent you to see if we're ready?"

No answer from the motionless figure.

"Well, if he did, tell him Nina's stalling in the bathtub. I figure she'll need at least another twenty minutes before she's dressed and downstairs. I have a terrible time getting her out of the water. Her father once said she was part fish." Mercedes smiled. "You should see her in her grandmother's pool."

April tilted her head in a motion that Mercedes found charming, even elegant. When the girl finally spoke, it was in a quiet little voice. "My dad and I like to swim, but we go to the beach."

Mercedes nodded. "We have lots of sand in Arizona, but no beaches. I've visited a few beaches in Northern Canada, but it was too cold and rocky to swim."

Mercedes busied herself smoothing Nina's clothes in an attempt to seem less threatening. She was rewarded as April took a few more steps into the room. Despite those coltish legs and arms, a direct contrast to Nina's shorter more rounded body, April was very graceful.

"Does . . . did Nina's dad swim?" she asked shyly, not looking at Mercedes.

"Gilles? Not much. He learned, but he wasn't much for the water."

April approached another few steps, her hands clasped behind her back. She had beautiful blue eyes, Mercedes thought. They were exactly the same shade as her father's. They held the same wary expression, too.

"Dad said your husband was dead."

Mercedes took a deep breath—children could be so blunt—but she didn't dodge the question. "Gilles went missing November before last. He was mountain climbing at the time."

"You never found him? His . . . his body?"

"No, and it would be easier for Nina if we had. She keeps thinking her father might come home, but I know he won't."

Another pause that Mercedes was grateful for, considering the topic of conversation. She was used to Nina's immediately blurting out whatever was on her mind. April, it seemed, thought out her responses more carefully.

"I think swimming would be more fun than mountain climbing, don't you?" April eventually asked.

"Warmer, anyway," Mercedes replied. She watched as April's hand slowly moved toward the pink lace on the jean shorts. Tapered fingers traced the delicate hem just once, then withdrew.

"I swim a lot. That's why I cut my hair short." Despite April's quiet statement, Mercedes recognized the barest hint of defiance—and of hurt.

"I think it's lovely," Mercedes said with a smile. On closer viewing, she thought the style suited April. It emphasized her long neck and delicately molded head. "I don't know how I confused it with a boy's haircut. My eyes must have been on sabbatical."

Confused, April tilted her head again.

"Vacation," Mercedes said.

"Your eyes were on vacation?" There was no smile, but there *was* a suggestion of amusement on April's face.

"Yes—they weren't working. Listen, April, I didn't mean to upset you. I'm sorry about the mixup. And I'm very sorry the dog frightened you. My only excuse is that we were all tired from the long flight. I'm sure he'll behave from now on."

"Dad said if Twister's going to be vicious, he'll have to sleep outside while he's here," April said.

From the tone of her voice, Mercedes couldn't tell if April had accepted her apology or not. Or if she was upset about Baron's banishment.

"Mama, I need an extra towel!" Nina yelled out in Spanish, momentarily distracting her.

"I gave you two." Mercedes turned toward the bathroom to call back.

"Yeah, well, I dropped one in the tub before the water ran out."

"*Nina!*"

"It was an accident!"

Mercedes sighed. Nina's boundless energy and rapid movements frequently caused small crises. "I'll be there in a minute," she replied, then turned back to April. "April, I—"

But April was gone.

Nina wasn't ready until well after six. Montgomerys and Delacruzes alike practiced their best manners at the dinner table, but it didn't matter. Nina, of course, started things off on the wrong foot by offending Mrs. Borden, who approached her plate with the intention of serving her.

"I'll serve myself, please," Nina said, holding her hand over her empty plate, blocking that heaping ladle.

Mrs. Borden scowled. "I don't hold with wasting any food in this house. If you serve yourself, you eat what you take."

"I will." Nina was true to her word. She settled for a side dish of yellow beans, some salad and a slice of plain corn bread with jam, then proceeded to eat every morsel, accompanied by frequent gulps of milk.

"Is that all you want?" Cass asked curiously.

"Yes, sir," Nina replied, wiping her hands on a napkin.

"You need more than that!" Mrs. Borden insisted, bristling. In front of her sat the bowls of candied yams and cheesy broccoli. Nina had also bypassed the greasy chicken-fried steaks, mashed potatoes with pepper, meat-drippings gravy and the corn bread with butter oozing down the sides.

"No, thank you, Mrs. Borden," Nina replied, happily munching away at her salad.

"These are our guests," Cass gently rebuked his housekeeper.

Mrs. Borden then looked to Mercedes for assistance, but Mercedes's food selection was identical to Nina's. Mrs. Borden had enough cholesterol, calories and grease on the table to kill an elephant. It was a miracle both Cass and April were as thin as they were!

"It never hurts to try new things," Mercedes said weakly, adding a little more food to her plate in the interest of politeness. It was too late. Mrs. Borden pushed away from her chair in disgust.

"You all will just be getting this food again for lunch tomorrow—and the next day—until it's gone. There's plenty of starving children in this world who'd be glad to taste my cooking!"

Mrs. Borden left in a huff. The two girls left soon after, April to watch TV and a tired Nina to go upstairs for the night. Nina was so exhausted she only made a single protest when Mercedes reinforced Cass's refusal to allow her to bring Baron into the house.

Cass and Mercedes were left alone to stare at each other across unfinished plates of food.

"Well. So much for the welcome-home dinner," Cass remarked.

Mercedes wisely said nothing. She was busy picking the greasy batter off the steak with her fork, only to discover that the meat underneath was just as saturated with grease.

"For heaven's sake, you don't have to eat it," Cass said irritably. "It's quite obvious that you and your daughter don't like Southern cooking."

Mercedes set down her fork. "I didn't mean to offend your housekeeper. It's just that Nina and I are careful about proper nutrition. We were converted years ago."

"Converted?"

"By Gilles. My husband took good nutrition very seriously. He was strict about healthy eating."

"I imagine he had to be. He was one heck of a mountain climber."

"Too bad all that heathy food didn't keep him alive." Mercedes surprised both of them with her bitterness. "I'm sorry. I didn't mean for that to slip out." There was an awkward pause. "And I didn't mean to upset your house-keeper, either. If you want me to go apologize to her, I will."

"I'd drop it for now. Mrs. Borden can be pretty touchy."

"How long has she been with you?" Mercedes asked, grateful for the change of subject.

"Oh, since I moved here with April eleven years ago."

"And you still call her Mrs. Borden?"

"At her insistence. And I'm Mr. Montgomery. Mrs. Tamara Borden is a very formal woman—like you."

"I'm not *that* formal."

"Aren't you? Despite my request, you haven't used my first name yet." Cass ran one forefinger up and down the beveled edge of the heavy crystal saltshaker. "Tell me, Ms. Delacruz. Which offends the most? The meal, the situation in general or me?"

Mercedes heard no note of censure. But she did hear disappointment and that affected her decision. The enemy had extended a white flag, and she decided to honor the truce—for now.

"Chalk it up to jet lag and a guilty conscience," she said. "I've managed to offend everyone today except Baron. And if I don't check on him soon, I'll have to add him to the list." She stood up, pushed her chair back, then hesitated. "Would you like to come with me?"

"Out back?"

"No, I'd planned on taking Baron for a walk around the block. I know it's late, but the neighborhood looks pretty safe." Mercedes saw the question on his face. Something in his eyes—or was it her own loneliness?—made her add, "You're welcome to join us. I know it's been a long time since you've seen Baron."

She was rewarded with a warm smile. "I'd like that."

After telling Mrs. Borden and the girls of their plans, Cass followed Mercedes outside. A few minutes later, they were walking away from the house, and Baron happily padding between them.

"I think he missed you," Mercedes after a few minutes. "His tail wags every time he looks your way."

"And I missed him."

Cass's fingers brushed the dog's head. Mercedes was again surprised by his gentleness. She expected a man to caress a dog more exuberantly. She remembered Gilles's fond tugging of Baron's ears or tail, and how her husband would roll the dog on his back to energetically rumple the fur on Baron's belly.

Then she remembered April's graceful dancer's movements and suddenly she knew where the girl had inherited them. But where April's grace was delicate, Cass's was stronger, more masculine.

He'd probably make a terrific lover, Mercedes thought idly, then flushed at the turn of her thoughts. The muscular, fiercely athletic Gilles might not have been the perfect physical match for Mercedes, but their mutual affection and long months apart were great equalizers. Despite Gilles's wanderlust, his lengthy mountain-climbing expeditions and infrequent stays at home, he'd always been most considerate of her needs while in her bed.

Strange how she never thought of it as *their* bed. Stranger still to be thinking of such things at all. She thought she'd finally become used to sleeping alone, but judging by the sudden hot longing in her veins, her body obviously felt otherwise.

"Are you hot?" Cass asked curiously. "We can go back if you want. It can stay in the eighties all night this time of year."

"No, I'm used to the heat," Mercedes managed evenly.

"Are you sure?"

"Yes. Phoenix is a good ten to twenty degrees hotter than Florida in the summer," she replied. And then, to get those piercing eyes off her, Mercedes held the leash toward him. "Would you like to take Baron for a while?"

"It's okay," Cass replied, but there was enough yearning in his voice to make her insist.

"Here, take him. We can hardly expect our daughters to share him if we don't set a good example ourselves. And please, feel free to call him Twister around me if you want."

The dog looked up expectantly.

"Are you sure?" he asked. "About the name, that is?"

"Of course. I'm not Nina. I won't throw a fit. In fact, I rarely even lose my temper."

"You and April..." Cass said half to himself.

"Pardon?"

"April," he repeated. "I worry about her. She never loses her temper, either. I can see adults having that kind of control of their emotions, but April's just a kid. It worries me."

Mercedes looked at him with new sympathy. "Not much you can do except keep an eye on her," she said.

"I don't know if that's enough."

"Maybe not," she agreed. "But at least April doesn't live in a fantasy world where the dead are still alive." And then, not wanting him to think she was making light of his concern or making a bid for pity, she said again, "Here. Take the leash."

He did, and as the leash was passed, Baron immediately switched over to the proper "heel" position, on Cass's left side. That placed Cass in the middle, with Mercedes on his right.

They walked in silence, the lush green vegetation of the neighborhood properties shadowing the sidewalk. The trunks of the palm trees were barely visible among the leafage of the many ponderosa pines and oak and magnolia trees. Mercedes's head turned constantly as she took it all in. There was never so much green back home, nor such diverse shades of it. Even the blooms of lowly weeds were brilliant tropical hues, contrasting with Arizona's more subdued desert colors.

As the sun dipped lower in the sky, Mercedes noticed that even the sunsets were different.

"Nice sunset tonight," Cass remarked.

Mercedes started. This wasn't the first time his thoughts had been on track with hers. "More than just nice," she said after a moment. "I'm used to brilliant shades of orange. But this..." She gestured toward the horizon, amazed at the rose, pink and purple streaks.

"The humidity refracts more colors than desert air does," Cass explained.

"It's so beautiful! You're very lucky."

"I think so. April and I always used to watch the sunsets together. But she's outgrown that now." His words were matter-of-fact, but there was a wistful quality in his voice.

"You're never too old to appreciate beauty. Or to enjoy the company of someone you love—even if that someone is just a boring parent. Maybe you should tell April that."

Cass actually stopped at her words. "You're right," he said. "I've always believed that family's important, but I never applied it to little things."

"Sometimes those little things—like watching a sunset with your child—are the most precious of all."

Baron looked expectantly from Mercedes to Cass and back again, as if impatient at the delay. They resumed walking.

"So what's on the schedule for tomorrow?" Mercedes asked.

"I'm sure you and Nina will want to sleep. But I intend to get up early to pack for the four of us."

"Pack?"

He nodded. "I want us to head out tomorrow afternoon for the week-long search-and-rescue refresher course."

Now it was Mercedes's turn to stop in her tracks. "I told you Nina and I weren't interested in going camping. And I don't remember agreeing to it."

"April and I were already signed up. The Andersons will meet us in Gainesville with Buddy. This will be an excellent chance for the two animals to meet. And for the girls to spend more time together."

Mercedes felt her good mood evaporating. "The girls have been through enough stress already! Why add to it? You should consider canceling."

"I don't think so," was the maddening response.

Mercedes had just claimed that she rarely lost her temper, but her reaction certainly compromised that statement. She had to compose herself before she could speak.

"I had to waste two weeks of my vacation to come here, two weeks during which my daughter and I usually enjoy ourselves. Nina isn't big on camping and neither am I. I'm forced to do enough of that in my work. I'd rather take Nina sightseeing or to Disney World, places we can both enjoy."

"I can see your point," Cass said reasonably. "Feel free to enjoy your vacation however you wish—as long as you leave Twister with me."

"Forget it! Baron goes where we go!"

"Then unless you want me to contact the Phoenix courts, I suggest you be ready to leave when I say."

Mercedes didn't bother to hide her anger this time. "That won't be necessary. I'll be ready on time. But realize this, Mr. Montgomery..."

His eyebrows rushed together at the formality.

"I have *no* intention of participating in any rescue course. Nor will I allow Nina to participate. And if you think you can force this dog to do anything strenuous without my permission, you're sadly mistaken."

At that, Mercedes pivoted and made her way back to the house. Behind her in the growing darkness she heard Baron whining. Then she heard the sound of her name. Mercedes ignored both. *How could I have been so stupid?* she berated herself. A few tropical flowers and palm trees, a salt-laden balmy breeze, and she was all set to trust the man. So much for her instincts, she thought dismally.

This was business—strictly legal, court-ordered business. As long as she remembered that, she should be okay.

Then why did she feel so disappointed? she asked herself as she entered the dark guest room where Nina lay. The glowing numbers on the alarm clock said it was after eight. That was ten o'clock Phoenix time. *Close enough to bed for me,* Mercedes thought. She changed into a short summer nightgown and climbed into the double bed with her daughter.

She felt physically exhausted and emotionally drained. And lonely...

"Mama?" came Nina's sleepy voice. "Is that you?"

"Yes, it's me, sweetie. Go back to sleep."

"I can't." Nina snuggled close to Mercedes, who responded by wrapping her arms around her child and kissing her cheek. "I keep waking up."

"Why?"

"I'm used to sleeping with Baron. I can't hear him breathing, and it wakes me up."

Mercedes sighed. "I'm sorry, baby. But Mr. Montgomery won't let him in the house."

"He's afraid he'll bite April," Nina said smugly. "But I can control him. So Mr. Montgomery should let him in."

"Well, Nina, he won't. It's his house, so there's nothing we can do." Mercedes smoothed back her daughter's long hair.

"He might howl. He'll be lonely!"

"We all get lonely at times, Nina. We just have to live with it."

There was silence in the dark room; only the hum of the air conditioner was audible. Then, "Do you ever get lonely sleeping alone, Mama?"

"Sometimes." Mercedes kissed the top of her daughter's head. "But it's nothing for you to worry about."

"After vacation, Baron could sleep in your room, instead of just mine. We could take turns," Nina offered generously. "But only until Papa comes home."

"Oh, Nina...your father isn't coming back. I've told you that."

"Sure, he is. And when he does, I get Baron back in my room."

Mercedes closed her eyes and willed away her tears. "We'll talk about it later. For now, just go to sleep. We have a big day ahead of us tomorrow."

"You always say that," Nina murmured sleepily.

Mercedes tenderly stroked her daughter's brow. "It's a mom thing. I have to say it every night or I lose my 'mom' license."

Nina giggled. "Liar. You just made that up."

"Nina!" Mercedes exclaimed in mock horror. "Calling your own mother a liar!"

Nina giggled again. "You tell stories all the time. Just like about Papa."

The happiness in the room dimmed. Mercedes said what had to be said. "The 'mom' license I made up. I would never lie about your father."

Silence. Mercedes sighed. Now wasn't the time to argue, not if she wanted either of them to get any sleep.

"Close your eyes, baby. Sweet dreams."

"*Buenas noches*, Mama."

"*Buenas noches*, Nina."

And Mercedes lay awake until the deep rhythmic sound of her daughter's breathing told her Nina was finally asleep. But sleep wasn't as easy for Mercedes. She was used to nights with her windows open, not an air conditioner. She was used to her daughter safely in her own bed, Baron at her feet. She was used to Gilles at her side, her head on his shoulder.

Only now she was trapped in a strange room in a strange house with her dog whimpering outside, her husband gone, and her confused daughter huddled close for comfort. And tomorrow they were off to search for pretend victims in the swamps. So far, it was proving to be one hell of a vacation.

Mercedes sighed once more, then mentally scolded herself. She had to be strong for Nina's sake. And Baron's. And yes, even April's. As for Cass Montgomery, well, he didn't need her help. And since he didn't care about anything except his own interests, he was on his own as far as Mercedes was concerned.

At least that was what she thought until a couple of hours later. She was still awake when she heard a light knock at her door. She refused to answer, not ready for another argument. That didn't stop her visitor. A minute later the hall light shone into the room as the door opened. Mercedes sat up in bed at the sound of toenails clicking on the hardwood floor.

"Baron?" she called. She heard his tail thump and a cheerful whine, then a moan of contentment as Baron sank to the floor and sprawled on the braided rug. Looking up, she saw Cass's form outlined against the hall light.

"Twister was making a racket. I hope you don't mind taking him, but I can't allow him to disturb the neighbors."

That sounded about as close to an apology as she was going to get. Mercedes chose her next words carefully.

"Of course you can't. I'll make sure he's quiet."

"The neighbors would appreciate that."

"I'm happy to help."

In the awkward silence that followed, Mercedes pulled the sheet up over the bodice of her nightgown.

"Well, I'll let you get back to sleep," he finally said. "Good night, Ms. Delacruz."

"Good night . . . Cass."

CHAPTER FIVE

"ARE WE THERE YET?" Nina sighed.

Cass gritted his teeth. The hour's drive to Gainesville was barely under way, yet this must have been the tenth time Mercedes's daughter had asked. It was obvious the child was uncomfortable. In his rearview mirror, he'd seen her squirming in the back seat of the minivan.

April sat next to her in silence. Behind the girls, Baron was whimpering nonstop. Obviously the dog now associated the travel cage with long airplane rides. Between the whining girl and the whining dog, Cass was beginning to get a headache. He didn't know which was more irritating—the whining or Mercedes's inaction. She hadn't tried to quiet either of them.

"Are we there yet?" Nina repeated with added volume.

Mercedes, sitting in the front passenger seat, glanced at Cass. "How much longer?"

"A good forty-five minutes."

Mercedes turned around, a worried expression on her face. "Nina, are you doing okay?"

"I think so," Nina replied.

For the next few minutes even the dog ceased whimpering, and there was blessed silence. Cass had just begun to relax and was enjoying the drive for the first time when Nina spoke up in her loudest voice yet.

"Pull over!"

Cass blinked. "What?"

Even April got into the act. "You're not his boss," she said to Nina disdainfully.

"Mama, please! My stomach hurts!" Cass heard Nina cry in Spanish. The note of panic had him looking for a spot even before Mercedes grabbed his arm and urged, "Please, Cass, she gets carsick!"

"You'd better not get sick in our van," April warned, wrinkling her nose in disgust.

"I want out, Mama!" Nina begged. "Please, let me out!"

"In just a second. Try to hold on, Nina!" Mercedes ordered, unfastening her seat belt. Cass was already on the side of the road and slowing down as she added, "Don't touch the door handle. Wait until we stop!"

By now Nina was frantic. Cass parked the van, but Mercedes was sweeping Nina outside even before he'd set the brake. Nina shook off her mother and ran to a small clearing. There she stood heaving, her arms wrapped around her middle.

"Deep slow breaths, Nina," Mercedes was saying as Cass hurried over, April trailing behind.

"This is too gross," April said. Cass shook his head at her and asked, "Why didn't you tell me she has motion sickness?"

Mercedes shrugged. "She usually doesn't. I thought she'd outgrown it."

Cass looked from mother to daughter. Something in Nina's behavior caught his eye. As a lawyer, he'd trained himself to observe the tiniest signs, and he didn't like what his instincts were telling him. Her breakfast hadn't left her stomach. Somehow Nina looked far too healthy for a carsick child.

"She doesn't look too bad now," he said cautiously.

Mercedes ignored him, her hand on her daughter's shoulder, all her attention on her child.

April observed Nina with that characteristic tilt of her head. "Does this happen *all* the time?" she asked. "If it does, we're going to be late."

"Try to be a little more understanding, April," Cass rebuked her. He saw his daughter flush, and he also saw the tiny glint of triumph in Nina's eyes.

Mercedes was right. Nina *was* one hot little actress. Too bad it had to be at his and April's expense. Cass's forehead creased with annoyance. Nina saw him watching her and ducked her head, continuing to take deep gulping breaths.

"When was the last time she was actually carsick?" Cass asked Mercedes, his gaze still on Nina.

"Not for some time. As long as she doesn't read in the car, she's usually fine."

"Well, she wasn't reading today."

Mercedes didn't catch the suspicion in his voice. "Maybe it's the change in vehicles."

"She didn't have any problem coming home from the airport in this van."

"I know that! Does it really matter? She obviously doesn't feel well." Mercedes rested her hand against Nina's forehead. "Nina, honey, how are you now?"

"Terrible. I want to lie down. I wish we were home," Nina moaned with the appropriate pathos.

"Oh, Nina, I'm sorry." Mercedes turned toward him, her eyes pleading. His anger flared, then faded as he saw the worry on her lovely face. He felt a strange sensation in the pit of his stomach. Cass sighed, knowing he was about to do something totally illogical.

"Nina, would you like me to take you home?"

Nina nodded, but Mercedes hesitated. "Cass, I don't want to separate her from Baron. And you said—"

"I'll take the dog home with us," Cass snapped, more irritated at himself than her. Judging by the uncertainty in

Mercedes's eyes, last night's conversation had come back to haunt him. "We'll all go home."

"Dad?" April was clearly confused.

"We can't go camping if Nina's sick."

April's eyes opened wide at that. But to Cass's surprise, she didn't protest. In fact, she said, "Maybe we should roll the windows down for Nina. Fresh air might help."

Now what was going on? All of a sudden it was three against one for the expedition.

Nina continued to pretend she was sick. "Can I nap with my window down at home, too?" she asked weakly.

Now Cass was positive she was faking it, but he didn't let on. "If that's what you need. Come on, April, let's get back in the car. Mercedes, when Nina feels up to it, we'll leave for home again."

"Can I sit in front?" April asked as they walked away.

"Not unless Mercedes wants to sit in the back."

"But I don't want to sit next to Nina! What if she gets sick on the way back?"

"Don't worry, April. I doubt we'll have that problem," Cass said dryly.

"But—"

"Just get in the van, please."

Cass opened the door for his daughter, then looked over his shoulder. He caught Nina's satisfied smile; a smile that disappeared as soon as she noticed him. For just a moment, Cass was caught by the child's loveliness. *Lord, but she's going to be a beauty when she grows up. Just like her mother.* Too bad her mother didn't take a stronger hand with her. The girl needed it. That smile coupled with Nina's temperament spelled big trouble in the years ahead. He could just imagine her as a teenager, and shuddered at the thought.

If she were my daughter... Cass guiltily checked that thought. He had enough worries with April, let alone someone else's child. Still, perhaps he could drop a few tactful words to Mercedes later. Sometimes an objective view helped.

A few minutes later Nina was in the back seat, only this time Mercedes was by her side, with April in front as she'd wished. Cass made the drive home with the windows down and no more feigned attacks of car sickness. Nina didn't once ask, "Are we there yet?" Baron had stopped his whining completely, while the taciturn April managed to look a little less sullen than usual.

As he pulled into his driveway, parked the minivan and shut off the ignition, Cass wondered if the remains of this day could be salvaged. He had to force himself to act as if he was taking all of this in his stride while he and April unloaded the van's camping gear into the garage. Mercedes saw to her luggage and Nina's. Mother, daughter and dog then headed for their upstairs bedroom.

"April, can you finish up here?" Cass asked. "There's only one more box to put away."

"Where are you going?"

"Inside to use the phone. I need to call and cancel our registration. I know you're upset, but—"

"That's okay. I don't mind."

"You don't? But..." Now Cass was confused. He'd expected more of a fight from April. "I thought you were looking forward to the rescue course."

April shrugged. "This was supposed to be a refresher class for Twister. If he won't go without Nina, we might as well stay home."

"Maybe you and I can work Twister ourselves."

April shrugged again. "If that's what you want."

"April, I'm trying to find out what *you* want!"

"No, you're not." She tilted her head and studied him. "You only care about what Nina's *mom* wants. That's why we came home."

"April!" Cass didn't know what shocked him most—eleven-year-old April's accusation or the truth behind it.

"You just didn't want to upset Mercedes. Nina didn't throw up once. She wasn't *that* sick."

"So you noticed it, too?" Cass said, glad to skirt the issue of Mercedes and his sudden weakness where she was concerned.

"I don't like Nina," April announced. "We don't need her here."

"As long as she owns Twister, we do. And I expect you to behave while she's a guest in our home. Understand?"

April didn't answer. She hurried back to the minivan and started to unload the last box of camping gear.

"Don't walk away when I'm talking to you, young lady. April, come back here!"

She didn't. Cass almost went after her, then walked into the house, instead. Nothing he said to April made any difference—and hadn't, not since Twister's disappearance three years ago. April hadn't been the same since.

At first Cass had suffered with her over the loss of Twister. But when April didn't bounce back after a few months, even after he'd purchased Buddy, he became worried. He'd made a special effort to spend more time with her. When she refused to open up to him, he made arrangements for her to talk to her school counselor and their church minister, who happened to be a woman. But as time went by and April still seemed depressed, Cass signed her up for family counseling at the community mental-health center. April had refused to participate in any counseling sessions there, too.

It drove Cass crazy with worry. With a lack of real information, he and all the experts had been forced to guess at April's problem. All the terrible causes that triggered such behavior in a child, such as trauma, molestation or abuse, didn't apply in April's case. She'd been a baby when her mother had died, and so had been relatively unaffected by the loss. Cass and Mrs. Borden were loving and trustworthy primary care-givers. April was never allowed to stay with anyone else, so physical and emotional abuse were definitely ruled out. Both Cass and those he'd consulted were left guessing as to the cause of April's depression.

Cass had been told that April was a sensitive child; she was probably still grieving for her dog and taking longer to get over it than most children. But deep inside, Cass had never really believed that story. And now his hunch had been confirmed. A very-much-alive Twister was suddenly back, and April was still acting strange. She was so detached and unemotional at times, so withdrawn and uncommunicative, that it broke Cass's heart.

Maybe he ought to look into having a psychiatrist examine his daughter, he thought reluctantly. April's mood swings were getting harder and harder to understand. He didn't think her problems were chemical; his father's instinct told him they were emotional. But at this stage of the game, he was feeling desperate. April was so unhappy.

He knew it wasn't normal. As a single parent determined to foster a family atmosphere for his daughter, he'd been to all of April's Girl Scout, school and church functions. He'd met her few friends—thank goodness she at least had those—and they all acted like ordinary children. April didn't seem to fit.

Lord knew he hadn't been able to make head nor tail of April's problems so far. Yes, a psychiatrist might help. He'd look into it just as soon as the Delacruz females left.

In more ways than one, both Mercedes and Nina were proving to be a distraction he hadn't counted on. Here he was trying to concentrate on his daughter and getting her dog back, yet Mercedes had somehow awakened feelings he'd pretty much repressed since his wife's death. Ordinarily he could keep his hormones under control. He'd never been the type of man to be ruled by simple biology.

But his hormones damn well refused to ignore Mercedes. And her personality was tugging at his soul, too. Her obvious love for Nina and her efforts to establish some sort of relationship with April had made him go soft. Look at the way he'd given in to Nina's phony sick act. This wouldn't do. With April's problems and Twister's future up for grabs, the last thing Cass needed was a complication like Mercedes. Or her daughter.

Yet he found himself worrying about Nina, too. The poor kid actually believed her father was still alive and refused to be convinced otherwise. No wonder Nina was so angry. No wonder she was such a handful for her mother.

So much for child therapists, Cass thought morosely. All the money he and Mercedes had paid out obviously hadn't helped a bit. The girls' problems had been dumped right back into their parents' laps. And damned if he had a clue how to solve them. He might as well have spent his money on a crystal ball.

Those thoughts did nothing to improve his mood. Nor did the conversation he overheard between the two girls as he sat at the kitchen table a few minutes later, the phone book at hand.

"Where's your mother?" It was April, her words wafting in from the front entrance.

"Out back with *my* dog," Nina replied with pointed emphasis.

"You're supposed to be lying down," April said.

"Make me," Nina replied.

"Maybe I should tell your mother you're a faker. You weren't really sick."

"Go right ahead," Nina flung back. "She'll never believe you, you liar."

"You're the liar!" April's accusation carried loud and clear.

Cass hesitated over the phone book. Was it time to referee, or should he let the girls work things out themselves? At least the usually stoic April was talking to someone, even if it was in anger.

"Oh, yeah? Well, guess what? My dog likes me! Baron *hates* you, so there!"

"That's not true!"

"Is so, you dog thief!" Nina declared.

"You're the thief!"

Cass rose and pushed back his chair. Definitely time to referee. He heard more insults exchanged, then the sound of one girl bursting into tears and the other running up the stairs. He hurried into the foyer, wondering how to effect damage control. Maybe he'd walk Nina outside to her mother first, then go upstairs to talk to April.

"Nina, why don't we—"

Cass broke off abruptly. It wasn't Nina Delacruz sitting on the foyer floor with wet cheeks. It was April.

"THIS VISIT isn't working," Mercedes said to Cass an hour or so later. "It's not working at all."

"Tell me something I don't know," Cass replied tersely. Mercedes was preparing lunch, and Cass was setting the table. The two of them were alone in the kitchen. Baron was napping out back under Nina's watchful eye, while April was upstairs in her room. At least that way the girls could maintain a temporary truce. "Our daughters are ready to murder each other, the dog is either growling or whining, and my housekeeper has abandoned ship."

"I hope that wasn't on my account," Mercedes said from the counter. She sliced some turkey breast for sandwiches. "The housekeeper, that is."

"Partly. I'd told her that since we were going camping for two weeks, she could take a vacation herself. She'd already made plans. I couldn't ask her to change them."

"Of course not."

"But that's beside the point."

"Oh?" Mercedes finished with the turkey and began to slice some tomatoes to go with it.

"This is going to be one miserable visit if we don't all pull together."

"Pull together?" Mercedes actually had the nerve to smile.

"What?" Cass asked suspiciously.

"You sound like a football coach before the big game. Clichéd pep talks won't get you far with Nina. Or with me."

"I wasn't being clichéd, and a little discipline might help improve Nina's behavior."

Mercedes flushed. "You're probably right. Nina isn't much for regimentation. And I have been somewhat more lenient with her since Gilles died. But usually the more flexible I am, the happier she is," she said defensively. "And the more open she is to conforming. I thought you realized that."

Cass shook his head in confusion. As a lawyer, he was used to the twists and turns the human mind could take, but Mercedes's train of thought was hard to follow. Especially when she was bending over the refrigerator door, her linen shorts outlining a nicely rounded behind.

"What do you mean?" he asked, forcing his eyes away.

"You were very patient and understanding with Nina earlier today. You didn't order her back to the car—you let her choose her own time. That's just the kind of handling Nina responds to. So you see, recommending that I discipline her doesn't exactly match your actions."

She bent even lower and started rummaging through the shelves. Cass tried to concentrate on setting the table and failed miserably.

"Don't you have any fat-free mayonnaise?" Mercedes asked. "Or maybe a substitute?"

"No. Mrs. Borden says real cooks use the real thing."

"I wonder how she reached seventy-two, eating the way she does." She straightened. "Nina will just have to settle for mustard."

"And you've just proved my point," Cass said in his best lawyerlike manner. "There are lots of limits in this life. Children should know what they are."

"Of course they should." Mercedes grabbed the mustard, along with a head of lettuce, and closed the refrigerator.

"That should include not letting your daughter get away with pretending to be sick. You cater to Nina far too much."

Mercedes slowly rose. "You think Nina faked her car sickness?"

"Yes."

Mercedes bit her lip. There was a long silence, and Cass almost, *almost*, regretted his words.

"Maybe you're right. Maybe she did fool me. I won't let this matter drop if she did. But you know something, Cass? I don't sweat the big things. I'd rather have a happy little hellion than a perfectly behaved girl on the outside who's simply miserable inside."

"April isn't like that!"

"I didn't use April's name, Cass. You did." Mercedes tactfully returned her attention to assembling the sandwiches.

There was another uncomfortable silence.

"Maybe April *is* miserable," honesty forced Cass to say minutes later. "She doesn't smile or laugh anymore. I don't know what's wrong with her. The counselors don't know what's wrong with her. She's just this quiet, stoic little girl who rarely talks, let alone laughs. Today was the first time in ages I've seen April cry."

Mercedes set the plate of sandwiches on the table. "Well, you can thank Nina for that. She'll be riling April up whether April wants it or not."

"We can't be playing referee all the time!" Just the thought caused Cass's fingers to tighten around the forks and knives in his hand.

"I don't intend to play referee at all," Mercedes said firmly. "Let the girls work out their differences alone."

"But...Nina's a year younger and a good foot shorter than April."

Mercedes smiled. "Nina can hold her own. She's one tough little scrapper, thanks to her cousins back home. She's taken on kids twice her size. But I'm not talking about roughhousing here. I'm talking about pecking order."

"Pecking order?"

"Sure. Just like with dogs. Both girls are trying to establish dominance. This is your territory, and April rules supreme. But Nina definitely has the advantage when it comes to Baron. Things were fairly well balanced until you canceled the camping trip for April. That's definitely a point in Nina's favor."

"Point?"

"Of course." Her eyes caught his with sudden understanding. "You must have been an only child."

"I was."

"Ah. That explains it. I have two sisters, and believe me, children do keep score." Cass watched Mercedes get the milk and soda out of the refrigerator. "And since you sided with Nina and canceled the trip, April now has to fight to regain the ground she lost—whether she wanted to go to the camp or not. Hence the argument in the hall a while ago. Which, by the way, was only round one. I'm sure we'll be witness to rounds two, three and four. Just sit back and things will eventually calm down."

"It's not that simple," he insisted.

"Of course it is." She poured milk for the children and soda for the adults. "Let the girls get used to each other. As long as they're not actually fighting, I have no intention of interfering. And if you're smart, you'll do the same. Believe me, it's a no-win situation for an adult."

Cass sat down in the chair. He *was* an only child, raising an only child, and lately he didn't seem to be doing a very good job of it. Perhaps Mercedes was on to something. All that screaming and posturing between the two girls sounded terrible to his ears, but perhaps it might benefit April. He'd tried everything else to bring her out of her shell... and failed.

The Delacruz family, too, consisted of a single parent and a daughter. Yet to Cass, they seemed much more of a family than he and April were. Cass wanted that atmosphere of domestic love in his own home.

"I suppose I could try it your way for a couple of days."

Mercedes smiled widely. "Congratulations. You've just saved yourself from going gray overnight."

Cass blinked. Her smile transformed her in a way that rang warning bells in his head—the same bells that rang in his head when he found himself sympathizing with the opposition in court. He deliberately strengthened his defenses. "Where our daughters are concerned perhaps," he said finally. "That doesn't solve our original problem. What about the dog?"

All the light her smile had generated faded away. "I see you have your priorities straight as usual."

"Mercedes, he tried to attack my daughter! Why do you think I kept him in his cage in the van? I think April's physical safety is just as much an issue here as Nina's emotional well-being."

There was silence in the kitchen.

"You're right, of course," Mercedes said. "And I haven't forgotten about that. But I've been watching Baron closely, and there haven't been any repeat episodes. The dog was just tired. I don't think there's a problem here, and I didn't think you did, either. You did let him back in the house after we first arrived," she reminded him.

"True. But that doesn't explain why Twister hasn't warmed up to April. Don't you find it odd that he's completely ignoring her?"

"To be honest, Cass, no." There was censure in her voice. "I'm more concerned with Nina than why Baron hasn't wagged his tail over a child he hasn't seen for three years."

She had to pass him on her way to the kitchen door, and Cass reached for her arm to stop her.

"Don't preach to me about priorities, Ms. Delacruz. I started search-and-rescue work soon after Marian died. Eleven years ago a rescue dog found my wife in twenty minutes. Only she'd died of exposure two hours earlier, *three* hours after I'd called for help."

He heard Mercedes's soft gasp, a barely audible intake of air.

"Do you know what the dog handler said to me afterward?"

Mercedes shook her head.

"She said, 'I'm sorry, Mr. Montgomery. There just aren't enough of us to go around.'"

Mercedes's eyes were wide as she watched him relive that wintry day of horror.

"You think Twister's too old for search-and-rescue? Fine. Maybe he is. You think April can do without Twister? Maybe you're right there, too. But let me tell you something. I raised a motherless infant alone. Twister was the one who played with April when the paid help wouldn't. Twister kept me company all those lonely nights when April was asleep in her crib. And Twister helped chase away the nightmares each and every time we saved someone else. So you see, your claim on him is nothing compared to mine."

He released her arm, and Mercedes took a deep breath.

"Is it?" she asked quietly. "That animal comforted Nina the same way he comforted you. Only the way I see it, Nina's claim is much more recent and certainly more urgent."

"You haven't heard a word I've said, have you?"

"I have," Mercedes calmly replied. "Nina's just a child. You're not. It's quite obvious you can carry on without Baron. You replaced him quite easily. So don't throw your own personal crusade and your hypothetical victims in my face. Or expect me to ignore Nina because of your own tragedy. As for the dog, Baron deserves his retirement and healthy doses of love and attention. Nina and I can do that for him."

"And April and I can't?"

He watched the uncertainty flit across her face. He knew that expression—he'd see it in the courtroom often enough. It was the look of a person who hadn't decided whether or not to tell the truth. But this time, he sensed, he *would* hear the truth.

"Cass, I doubt you and April know how to love each other properly, let alone a dog. I don't see you two hug. I don't see you kiss. I've yet to hear you laugh together. In case you haven't realized it, April isn't the only Montgomery around here who never smiles."

That isn't true! he wanted to say. But the words wouldn't come. He was still reeling; still searching for an answer when Mercedes said quietly, "I'll go get the girls."

And left the room.

CHAPTER SIX

"THANKS FOR FIXING LUNCH, Mama," Nina said happily.

"You're welcome, Nina." Mercedes was sitting on the back-porch step, watching her daughter throw a tennis ball for Baron.

"I was starving." Nina retrieved a slightly damp tennis ball from Baron's mouth and threw it again. He bounded after it. "Are you going to cook all the time now?"

"I certainly intend to help out. Nina, let the dog rest a minute and come sit next to me." Mercedes waited for the cursory protest and wasn't disappointed.

"But we were having fun!" Nina complained, although she did as she was told. Baron, tennis ball still in his mouth, plopped down at their feet.

Mercedes gently tucked a few strands of hair behind Nina's ear. "We have to talk."

Nina was immediately on the defensive. "I haven't been mean to April!"

"This isn't about April, Nina. This is about us."

"Oh." Nina stroked Baron's head. "What?"

"Remember how upset you were when our vacation plans were ruined?"

Nina nodded.

"We've done the same thing to April and her father."

"They ruined ours!"

"No, Nina. The judge did that. The Montgomerys weren't to blame."

"I'm not taking Baron to that rescue camp!" Nina's arms immediately encircled the dog's neck tightly. Instead of drawing away, Baron dropped the ball and licked Nina's face. "I don't want him to learn search-and-rescue again! April will want to keep him!"

"Is that why you pretended to be carsick when you really weren't?"

Nina ducked her head. Her guilty flush gave Mercedes her answer.

"Nina, let go of the dog and listen to me." Mercedes waited patiently until her daughter complied. "First, pretending to be sick when you aren't is lying. And deliberately ruining April's vacation isn't right, either. She and her father had planned this trip for quite some time."

"But Mama—"

"Don't interrupt. The judge said we had to let Baron live his old life. Search-and-rescue work is part of it."

"You said Baron was too old for that!"

"Yes, I did, and I'm against Baron's becoming a working dog again. But I do know that Cass—"

"Who?"

"Mr. Montgomery—wants to breed Baron. Good working dogs need good memories. We could let Cass and April see if Baron still has that memory—if he still remembers his old job."

"Why?"

"Because if he does, he would probably pass that trait on to his puppies. And also because the judge ordered it, Nina. Remember what you learned about good citizenship in school? We'd be breaking the law if we didn't do what the judge ordered."

"She'd never know," Nina stubbornly replied.

"*We* would know, Nina."

Nina was still mutinous. "I'll bet April and her father won't listen to the judge when they're at *our* house."

"Ah, but that's the beauty of it," Mercedes cajoled. "Think of this as one big game. The judge is the referee, we're one team, and the Montgomerys are the other. Whoever plays the game best wins the prize. And if the other side cheats, they automatically lose the prize."

Nina blinked. "And Baron's the prize?"

"Exactly. So *we* want to follow the rules, and we'll hope that they don't. That's our legal system in action."

Nina wasn't convinced. "That's not how our teacher explained it."

"Trust me, that's how it works—especially in this case. Now, if we don't let April and her father take their vacation with Baron, we've cheated."

"But Mr. Montgomery said we didn't have to go camping."

"Only because you pretended to be sick in their van. The judge might call foul."

"Like when we're playing kickball?"

"That's right. So if we want to keep Baron, we have to play by the rules."

Nina thought about that. "I still don't want Baron to go to that camp."

"Neither do I. But we'll go, anyway." Mercedes gave Nina a wise smile. "You and I know Baron's too old for all that work. The sooner we make the Montgomerys realize it, the better our chance of keeping him."

Nina's eyes opened wide with sudden comprehension. "Do you really think so?"

"Yes, Nina, I do. After all, they already have Buddy. And if Baron's no good for rescues, maybe we can convince the judge they don't really need him anymore. And you know what *that* means."

Nina threw her arms around Mercedes for a tight hug. Mercedes held her close, then gently drew away.

"Now why don't you take your dog inside? The two of you need to cool down."

"*Sí*, Mama." Nina whistled for Baron, who immediately grabbed the tennis ball and jumped to attention. "Come on, boy. Heel."

Mercedes sighed with relief. That was one dam temporarily plugged—at least until Nina's next emotional crisis. She watched them leave, youthful childish exuberance followed by not-so-youthful canine exuberance. Her expression grew pensive as she remembered how, in the past, that same procession had sometimes included Gilles. Not often, mind you, but sometimes. Nina had always enjoyed having her father home. Mercedes tried to picture Gilles with Nina and Baron now, but all she could conjure up was Cass.

Cass Montgomery. He was in her thoughts more and more. Mercedes shook her head. Too bad Gilles hadn't been as much of a family man as Cass. Cass talked about attending April's school and church activities with a familiarity and an interest Gilles St. Clair had never shown. Cass's concern for his daughter was paramount in his mind, but all Gilles ever talked about to his family was his next book, his next climb, his next documentary—and his next flight out.

How had Cass ever managed to take care of April for eleven years without help from anyone but an employee? Mercedes had only been doing it for twenty months and had the assistance and support of her family, but she was still exhausted—physically and emotionally exhausted.

She straightened her shoulders. Well, that was her problem. In the meantime, she had other business to deal with, such as informing Cass of their change of plans. She was about to go in, then saw Cass step onto the porch.

"I saw Nina and Baron come inside. Is everything okay?" he asked.

"Aside from being a little overheated, they're both fine."

"I meant with you." To her surprise, Cass sat down next to her on the steps, his bare feet joining hers in the lush green grass. Mercedes absently studied her shoes. Thanks to the cactus, scorpions and sizzling hot pavement back home, she rarely went barefoot outside.

"You didn't come in with them."

"No...I wasn't ready yet. I wanted a little fresh air, and it's so beautiful out here."

"The heat isn't bothering you?"

Mercedes smiled. "I love the sun."

Cass nodded. His eyes swept the tropical blooms along the backyard fence, the humid summer breeze carrying their rich scents toward the house. He absently fingered the grass and was content to say nothing.

Mercedes enjoyed the peaceful silence. Gilles had always been talking—about his profession, his plans, his triumphs. Mercedes had loved that part of him, but he hadn't had an off switch. He'd operated at full bore every waking moment, as did his daughter. The rare times he was home were pure chaos.

Cass's low-key personality was a surprisingly pleasant change. So pleasant, in fact, she felt comfortable enough to speak her mind. "I was thinking..." she began.

Cass looked up expectantly.

"I don't want you to cancel the camping trip."

"Why not?"

"Because you were right. Nina *was* pretending to be sick. I can't let her get away with that."

Cass turned his face away from the flowers until his gaze met hers. "Is that the only reason?" he asked quietly.

"The judge did order it."

"So...you want to keep your record clean for the courts."

"That's part of it."

"Part of it?" He paused, then added, "I'd like to hear the rest."

"Fine." Mercedes drew a deep breath. "You canceled your plans—plans that you had every legal right to hold us to—because of Nina. That means a lot to me. I know this trip was important to you, so if you and April still want to attend the camp, Nina and I will be good sports about it."

"Thank you. But . . . we can't."

"There's a problem?"

"Yes. The course was overbooked. They told me over the phone that our slot would be filled immediately if I canceled."

"Oh. Cass, I'm really sorry."

He studied her for a long moment. "You mean that, don't you?"

"Well, of course I do! Just because I don't want to give up our dog doesn't mean I'm totally coldhearted where your child is concerned!" Mercedes rose to her feet under the watchful gaze of Cass, who remained seated.

"I didn't mean to make you lose your temper, Mercedes."

"I haven't lost my temper." She reached for the hose on the pretext of filling the dog's water bowl. "I told you, I *never* lose my temper."

For a few moments there was only the sound of water splashing against the sides of the metal dog dish. When Mercedes dared to look his way, she saw that Cass could barely contain his grin.

"Nina's lucky to have such a patient mother," he managed to say with a straight face, although his eyes were twinkling.

"I ought to turn this on you," she retorted, but there was no real sting behind her words.

"It's so hot I wouldn't mind, but that would hardly set a good example for the girls."

"No, I guess it wouldn't." Mercedes remained where she was and turned off the water. Cass continued to watch her.

"About your offer," he finally said, "we could still go camping. I don't need a formal course for Twister's refresher training. A more comfortable setting might be easier all around. I own a beach cabin. What do you think about going there?"

Mercedes considered his idea as she neatly recoiled the hose. "That might work out better. Nina isn't interested in search-and-rescue exercises for Baron, let alone for a whole pack of dogs. And she's never been swimming in the ocean. It might be a good distraction."

"Good. Then why don't we leave this afternoon after lunch?"

"That's fine with me."

Cass rose to his feet, his body just inches from hers. "About your name..."

"Delacruz?"

"No, your first name. It means 'mercy,' doesn't it?"

Cass tilted his head, and again Mercedes was struck by the resemblance between father and daughter. Except that the daughter's enchanting air held nothing of the father's potent—and provocative—charisma. That was what made her answer with a lightheartedness she was far from feeling.

"It means a very expensive automobile."

Cass continued to wait, his attention never wavering. "Give me the real answer, Mercedes. My Spanish is adequate, but nowhere near as fluent as yours."

"You speak Spanish? But you never said a thing about that on the plane!" Her eyes narrowed. "Or in the van."

He ignored her reprimand. "I'm saying something now. Am I right about your name?"

Mercedes relented. "Close enough. It means to favor or to dispense mercy."

"Mercedes...." Cass spoke the word slowly. " It's a beautiful name. It suits you."

Mercedes almost felt the caress in his words. "I had nothing to do with it," she said, striving for an air of nonchalance. "You'll have to thank my parents."

"Perhaps I will. Introduce me to them when I'm in Phoenix."

"I don't think so, Cass. Bringing a man home to Hispanic parents means much more than it does in your culture."

"I'm fully aware of that. But I'd like to meet them, anyway."

She noticed that her hands still grasped the coiled length of hose. She carefully laid it down in the grass. When she stood up, he was right in front of her, his mouth only inches from hers.

He couldn't be serious! Her expression must have revealed her thoughts.

"I'm serious, Mercedes."

"About what?" she asked.

"About...investigating possibilities."

The sun-warmed bricks of his house were already at her back. There was no place to retreat even if she could—or had the inclination—to do so. His kiss was unexpected, taking her totally off guard. His lips descended swiftly, but the boldness of his assault was tempered by gentleness as his mouth moved with exquisite tenderness across hers. It would require no effort at all for her to end the intimacy.

Then why did it take her so long to do it?

Mercedes's cheeks were flushed when she finally turned her head away. One of his hands was against the bricks, bracing his weight. The other rested lightly on her shoulder.

"Now what?" she asked breathlessly, amazed to find she could even speak.

Cass gently toyed with a glossy strand of her hair. "You can either go inside, or..."

"Or?"

"Let me kiss you again."

Her mouth parted at his suggestion, and his own started to descend again. But this time Mercedes turned her head and refused to let him repeat the experience.

"I don't think another kiss is proper, considering we're both strangers—and I have something that you want."

Cass actually had the audacity to smile, even as desire flickered in his eyes. He didn't bother to hide either reaction.

"I meant the dog," she quickly clarified.

"Mercedes, you're too intelligent a woman to be bribed by a few kisses. I certainly wouldn't insult you by trying."

"I'm glad. Especially since I'm still a..."

"A what?"

She dropped her gaze, unable to meet his eyes. "A grieving widow."

"Funny. You don't kiss like a grieving widow." Cass's gaze became hard, the sultry softness of earlier gone.

She turned her own gaze away. "It's too soon for this. I'm sorry, Cass."

After a moment, he slowly released her. But, Mercedes noticed with a detached part of her brain, he didn't apologize. Unlike her, he wasn't sorry. Not one bit. Her reactions were a confused tumble of regret, guilt and neglected wants. But laced through them all was a strange sweetness, which she hugged to herself.

She should have come right out and said it. *I don't want to marry again—ever.* She'd loved her husband and he'd loved her, but marriage to Gilles St. Clair had been too much work. He'd never been home to help with Nina. Her Arizona relatives had filled the gap his frequent absences had created. And she couldn't really even blame Gilles for her dissatisfaction. She'd known who and what he was long before she married him, for Gilles had been an honest man.

He'd told her before the wedding that he didn't intend to give up his career for her.

Mercedes had been certain she could cope with that kind of life-style. In her younger days she'd even held out a secret hope that Nina's birth would change things. She'd been wrong on both counts.

And now a man who believed in dropping everything for rescues—everything—was kissing her. He might be a more dedicated father than Gilles, but this all-consuming commitment to a cause, a belief, was something they had in common. Dog or no dog, there was no way she was getting involved with another single-minded man. A man with something to prove.

"I'm sorry," she said again.

"Nothing to apologize for, Mercedes. A tropical sea breeze, a single man and a very beautiful woman..." His relaxed manner eased her embarrassment. "It's a potent combination."

"So... we're going to blame it on Mother Nature?"

"As good a scapegoat as any." He reached for her hand and carefully led her away from the brick wall. "Why don't you check on the girls and let them know about our change of plans?"

She nodded.

"With any luck, they haven't unpacked yet. I'll be in as soon as I fix this." He gestured toward the now-tangled hose at her feet.

Mercedes gave him one last look and hurried through the back-porch sliding door.

Cass watched her go. He set aside the magic of the moment for just a minute to let his lawyer's mind kick into gear. Mercedes Delacruz was hiding something. Every courtroom instinct he'd honed over the years told him that. Cass backtracked and reviewed their encounter.

She'd felt so good in his arms, so responsive to his touch. His own urges had surprised him, but he'd acted on those very natural impulses. She'd felt the same thing, he was sure of it. He was positive Mercedes was as attracted to him as he was to her. A response like that couldn't be faked. But for some unknown reason, she'd pulled away. The explanation she gave for her withdrawal *should* have seemed logical, considering Gilles St. Clair's fate. But her widowed state had nothing to do with that look of panic on her face. She'd only used it as an excuse to get away from him. No, she'd panicked for another reason.

Mercedes Delacruz had lied, pure and simple.

He'd stake his career on it—and his career had been built on being able to separate truth from falsehood. Mercedes Delacruz had given him one kiss, an undignified retreat and a lie. But what was she lying about? And why?

The lie challenged the lawyer in him. That beautiful face intrigued the man in him. And the woman herself jump-started feelings he thought he'd never have again. Maybe it was the way she hugged her daughter. Maybe it was the way she smiled at his. Maybe it was the way the house had felt since Mrs. Borden had left and she'd moved in. He wasn't sure.

But one thing was certain. Somewhere along the way, Cass's desire for Mercedes's dog had subtly changed to include Mercedes herself.

And for the life of him, he couldn't tell if that was good or not....

"YOU LOOK FUNNY. Are you okay?"

Mercedes was surprised. April, not Nina, sat cross-legged on her bed.

"Pretty much. It's awfully hot outside." *And then some.* Mercedes stepped into her bedroom, noting that Nina was nowhere in sight. She wondered where she was.

"Nina's in the TV room with Twister," April said.

Mercedes froze, then sat down in the room's comfortable rocking chair. "You know, your father does that," she commented.

"What?"

"Answers my questions before I ask them."

April tilted her head. "People can talk without words. Just like dogs. If you watch, you can tell what they're thinking."

Considering the father's potent attraction and the way her pulses were racing, it certainly wouldn't do to let April know what she was thinking now, Mercedes thought. Thank goodness there was no way April could tell that Cass had just kissed her. And Mercedes had no intention of revealing it—especially since she wasn't even sure why she'd let him.

"Did your father teach you about body language?"

"Yes. You have to be careful to keep a secret around him."

"Speaking from experience?" she asked casually.

To her amazement, April swayed and went deathly pale. Mercedes was instantly on her feet, afraid the child would pass out. She reached for the girl's shoulders to steady her.

"April, what's wrong?"

"I don't want to talk about Twister," April said hoarsely. "Please don't tell on me!"

"Sweetheart, I wasn't talking about Twister." Confused, Mercedes continued to hold her, trying to undo whatever damage she'd just done. "I was talking about keeping secrets like surprise birthday parties. Or Christmas presents."

"Oh." Slowly the color came back into April's face. Only then did Mercedes hurry into the bathroom to get her a drink of water.

"Take a sip of this," Mercedes ordered. April complied. "Better?"

A slight nod.

"I think I should go get your dad."

"No!"

Now Mercedes was really baffled. "Fine. But I'm going to sit next to you until I'm sure you're all right, okay?"

April's only answer was a shudder. Mercedes wrapped an arm around the girl's thin shoulders. After a moment, April sank to her chest. Mercedes gathered her close and rocked her.

"Would you like to tell me what's wrong?" she asked softly after a while.

The response was a muffled, "There's nothing wrong."

Mercedes smoothed the short blond hair. "It has to be something, April. What can I do to help?"

April lifted her head, her dry eyes solemn. "What do you do when Nina's in trouble?"

"Well, I see if she wants to talk to me. If she doesn't, I have her write down what's wrong. Then I ask her to think of a way to fix things and write that down, too. Sometimes Nina can come up with a solution herself."

"What if she can't?"

"Then I try for find a solution for her."

April bit her lower lip for a moment. "What if you can't?"

Mercedes was shocked by the urgency in April's voice. "Well, that does happen. Not all problems can be fixed." For a fleeting moment, Mercedes thought of Gilles. "But sometimes it helps to educate yourself about what's going on in your life. And then you're better equipped to deal with it."

"It sounds like homework."

Mercedes smiled. "Nina says that, too."

"I don't want to be like *her*." In a sudden move April pushed away from Mercedes, slid off the bed and wandered about the room. Mercedes diplomatically kept silent.

"Do you like dogs?" April asked after a few moments.

"I love dogs."

"Do you like rescue dogs?"

Mercedes frowned. That was a strange question. "I like Baron, so I guess my answer is yes. Why do you ask?"

"Because rescue dogs have to find all kinds of people. Dead people, too."

Now she understood. Mercedes immediately thought of April's mother and realized that the subject of Twister was what had upset April in the first place. "Does that bother you?"

April fingered the trinkets on the dresser, her back to Mercedes. "Dad says the dead can't hurt you."

Mercedes tried to see April's face in the mirror, but the girl herself was blocking the reflection. Yet something in April's pose, something in the droop of her head, prompted Mercedes to ask, "Are you afraid of finding a dead person, April?"

"I...I shouldn't be. They never use dead bodies at the rescue camp. And Dad never lets me go on body searches."

Mercedes shivered at the matter-of-fact way those grim words fell from April's lips.

"I mostly help out with training the puppies."

"I'm glad to hear that. Of course your father wouldn't want you to do anything that frightened you."

It wasn't really a question. Mercedes might not care for Cass's legal tactics, but as a father, she couldn't fault him. April might have problems, but at least Cass was trying. At least he was around for his child. *Unlike Gilles.* Mercedes pushed aside that thought and concentrated on April.

The girl picked up the comb, running one fingernail over its teeth. They tinkled like a plastic harp.

"Once in a while I go on the practice live searches," April said. "It's better to find a live person than a dead one."

April hadn't responded to Mercedes's suggestion that rescue work frightened her. She tried a more direct approach. "Do you like rescue work?"

"Dad likes it." April paused, the comb still in her hand. "He wants me to like it, too."

The words weren't an answer, but the look on April's face was.

"Perhaps you should tell him you don't like it, April."

April replaced the comb on the dresser. "You don't know anything," she said so softly Mercedes had to strain to hear the words.

But it was the weary desolate look of pain on the child's face that kept Mercedes silent. And April had obviously decided she'd said enough. Cass's daughter spun with ballerina grace and ran from the room.

Mercedes heard her descend the stairs, then heard Nina and Baron coming up. Baron entered the bedroom first. He hurried to lay his head on her lap, happily wagging his tail in greeting. But when his enthusiasm wasn't returned, he turned back toward Nina and licked her face.

Mercedes could only look at her giggling daughter and wonder, *Nina, just what did you get me into?*

CHAPTER SEVEN

"WHEN YOU SAID you were taking us camping, I never imagined anything like this!" Mercedes took a deep breath, basking in the sunshine of the Florida morning. Yesterday they had reloaded the minivan and driven south late into the night. The primitive cabin she'd expected had turned out to be a lovely three-bedroom cottage with complete utilities, set slightly back in the cooling shade of lush protective trees.

She'd heard the ocean, so she'd known they were within walking distance of the beach. But the lateness of the hour, plus getting two tired children into their shared bedroom, had prevented her from seeing much. Mercedes had risen early, intending to follow the cottage path down to the beach, but Cass had risen even earlier.

"I'm glad you like it," he said. He was on the front porch, a cup of coffee in his hand. Like her, he was dressed in shorts and a T-shirt, his feet bare.

"Like it? I love it! And it's even more beautiful in the daylight. Oh, look! What are those?" She pointed at the white birds carefully picking their way through the marshy waters off to the right. "The white ones with the long legs?"

"Snowy egrets," Cass said.

"And the birds heading toward the ocean?" Mercedes gestured overhead.

"Brown pelicans."

"Pelicans? But where are their big pouches?"

"The lower half of the beak is expandable. When they aren't feeding, the beak remains streamlined for flying."

Mercedes took a few steps after them as they flew away, then stopped, feeling foolish. She could hardly chase after them, she thought reluctantly, but she wished she could have had a longer look.

"Haven't you ever seen a pelican feed?" Cass asked, obviously noticing her disappointment.

"I've never seen a pelican, period."

"It's quite a sight. They dive into the water with their beaks wide open—almost like net fishing, only much quicker. If you want to watch, we can hike down to the beach right now," Cass suggested.

"Now?"

"Sure. It's just beyond that marshy area past the edge of the trees. You won't even need shoes. It's about a five-minute walk."

Her pulse quickened with excitement, then slowed again. "But what about the girls?"

"They'll be perfectly safe. This is a private beach—residents only. April and I know all the neighbors. They're good people."

Mercedes was tempted, but still hesitated. "I really should wait for Nina."

"If she wakes up—which I doubt—Baron will be there. And you'll be able to see the cabin from the beach," Cass assured her. "Trust me, I wouldn't leave April here if I didn't know it was safe."

That decided her. "All right. Lead the way."

The walk *was* a short one, and the cabin remained in view at all times. She turned around more than once to make sure of that. But as Cass didn't seem worried, she finally relaxed and made her way toward the sound of the waves.

"Just over this rise and we're there," Cass announced.

Mercedes's face flushed with eagerness. She hurried forward, then stumbled as her feet slid on a small mound of warm shifting sand. Cass caught her hand in his to steady her.

"Hey, careful!" he laughed.

Her eyes sparkled with eagerness as she let him tow her forward. "I—"

She froze at the sight. Before her, miles and miles of frothing waves curled and collapsed on sparkling sand. The rising eastern sun shone through the backs of the waves, coloring the blue water with silver highlights and leaving diamondlike glitters on the wet sand. Her free hand flew to her lips, the other tightening around his.

"It's so... so *blue,*" she said, surprised, turning toward Cass. She caught a strange look on his face and colored with embarrassment.

"I must seem like such a tourist. It's just that the beaches I've seen aren't— Well, of course the ocean would look different here—so far south," she stammered.

Cass merely smiled. "Come on," he said. "Let's get your feet wet."

Hand in hand, they walked to the water's edge. Except for the occasional jogger, they had the beach to themselves. Mercedes found herself staring at the waves. Their rhythm was so even and unbroken they had an almost hypnotic effect.

Cass had to tug hard on her hand to get her attention. He pointed in the direction of three brown pelicans. "Look! They're fishing!"

Mercedes focused on the trio. They didn't remain in formation for long. Each flew over a different section of water.

"Look!" Cass exclaimed. "He's going in for a fish."

Sure enough, one of the pelicans dived into the water and emerged successful.

Mercedes watched as the pelican flew into the distance. "Oh, I wish Nina could have seen this!"

A pause. Then Cass said, "I'm sure she'll have plenty of opportunities.

The clipped note in Cass's voice temporarily overrode Mercedes's fascination with the ocean. "Is something wrong?" she asked.

"Your mind is always on your daughter. Don't you ever see yourself in any role besides mother?"

"And just what...?" As his thumb caressed the top of her hand, which he still held, realization dawned. "No, Cass. I'm not ready for *that* role," she said, pulling away.

Cass held her hand for just a second more, then released it.

"You're a beautiful, intelligent, vibrant woman. Why not?"

"Why not?" she echoed incredulously. "Because of Gilles!"

"You may be a widow, Mercedes, but you don't feel bereaved," he said quietly. "I've been that route. I'd know suffering if I saw it."

Mercedes was stunned into silence. The breeze picked up, whipping her long hair about her face. She ignored it, ignored everything except the truth in his words, a powerful truth that even the roar of the ocean couldn't block out.

"The way I see it, there are one of two explanations. Either you didn't love your husband—"

"That isn't true!"

He tilted his head and studied her. "Or he didn't love you."

She opened her mouth to protest, but the words wouldn't come. *Had* Gilles loved her? Or had he only loved how easy she made his life? After all, he had a home, a wife and daughter—without most of the responsibilities. True, he deposited money in their account regularly. And he made a special effort to satisfy Mercedes in bed the rare times he was home. But as for anything else, well, the press had spent more time with Gilles than Mercedes and Nina had.

"Which is it, Mercedes?"

Mercedes managed to make her reply sound calm. "Don't play twenty questions with me, Cass. I'm not one of your criminals to cross-examine. My private life with Gilles is none of your business. Frankly I don't see why you're so curious."

"I'm trying to understand why Nina thinks her father is still alive. The way he dropped in and out of your lives..." Cass shook his head. "I could never leave April for such long periods of time. Never."

"That's what Gilles wanted," Mercedes said stiffly, angry that Cass had said aloud what she'd silently thought for years. "What he needed. To be able to concentrate on his climbs and nothing else."

"But to endure such long separations? I've read a couple of his books, Mercedes. He was gone weeks, sometimes a whole winter at a time." Cass ran his fingers through his hair. "Just to leave you two alone like that..." He shook his head in amazement. "Didn't he ever invite you along?"

"I told you—Gilles didn't want any distractions," Mercedes said tersely. "And then when Nina was born, well... The Himalayas are no place for an infant or for a young child. Gilles preferred to see us at his convenience, not ours."

Cass's eyes were troubled. "I know it's not my place to say, Mercedes, but that's not normal! No wonder Nina's having trouble adjusting to Gilles's death!"

"You're right. It's not your place to say." Mercedes hoped that would be the end of it. She was taken aback by his next words.

"I could help you."

"Help? With what?"

"With Nina. I know how searches are done, and I know how meticulous the rescuers are. If your husband *was* alive, he would have been found."

"Don't you think I know that?"

"Yes, but Nina doesn't! I could talk to her for you. Maybe hearing the facts from someone who's been involved with rescue work would make a difference."

Mercedes went cold inside. "Oh, no you don't. I don't want you anywhere *near* Nina when it comes to Gilles. You've done enough damage already trying to take Baron away!"

She began to move away, wanting to end the conversation, but Cass took her arm firmly and held her fast.

"This isn't about Baron, Mercedes. This is about Nina. She's living with a delusion that isn't healthy. It isn't fair to let her continue with it."

"Don't talk to me about delusions or being fair! Considering the shape April's in, you're in no position to judge."

"April?" Cass recoiled in surprise, and Mercedes took advantage of that to yank her arm free.

"What are you talking about?" he demanded.

"She *hates* search-and-rescue work!"

"And just how would you know that?"

"I've talked to her! Or rather, she's talked to me."

"To *you?*" he asked painfully.

Mercedes nodded. There was a pause while Cass assimilated the news and strove for calm. He finally said, "Go on," his voice low and a bit hoarse.

She took a deep breath. "April pretends to be the proverbial chip off the old block when you're around. But it's just an act. She only does it to please you."

"She told you that?"

"Not in so many words, no. But I can tell you this—she's afraid."

"April? Afraid? I find that hard to believe."

More than anything it was his scoffing tone that made her blunt.

"Cass, she's terrified. Terrified that some day, on some real rescue, she'll end up finding a corpse. I can't believe you'd actually drag her into situations where that's possible. For heaven's sake, Cass, she's just a child!"

"I've never dragged April into anything," he said furiously. "She helps me train the puppies, nothing more. I don't take her on searches."

"No, but you expect her to come in the future, don't you?"

"Yes, I *will* expect her to help out during life's misfortunes! She may only be working with the puppies right now, but it's still rescue work."

"Misfortunes? *Misfortunes?* My God, Cass, is *that* how you label corpses for eleven-year-old girls?"

His anger was so great, Mercedes actually shrank away from him, as though from a physical threat. But his next words hit harder than any physical blow ever could.

"At least I've taught my daughter to acknowledge the harsh realities of life," he ground out. "Which is a hell of a lot more than I can say for you!"

Mercedes gasped at his accusation. It was so hurtful she actually felt faint. She closed her eyes and wished she was anyplace but there.

Her wish wasn't granted. When she opened her eyes again, she was still standing on the beach. With Cass.

"I'm sorry," he said abruptly in a voice she barely recognized.

She just stared at him. She couldn't speak at first, even if she'd known what to say. Her throat was tight, and her eyes burned with unshed tears. An iciness seemed to invade her heart, to spread through her whole body. Even the tropical warmth of the sand and sea had disappeared.

"Save the apology," she finally managed. "You meant every word."

"Mercedes . . ." He reached for her.

"Don't! Just...don't." She backed away. "You couldn't possibly understand. It's so easy for you."

Cass shook his head in confusion. "Easy?" he echoed.

"Yes! You have a grave and a headstone to show April! You have *proof,* Cass. They found your spouse. But they never found mine."

And then the tears did come. Mercedes turned toward the cabin and Nina, the one treasure she still had left. Despite his calls to come back, she left Cass exactly as Gilles had left her.

Alone.

THE BEACH WAS FILLED with happy families. Children frolicked in the sand, while smiling parents stretched out lazily on beach chairs, watching over them. Only Cass wasn't smiling.

It had been three days since he'd taken Mercedes to watch the pelicans, three days since he'd upset her. He'd done his best to make amends, but nothing—neither his words nor his actions—had helped. A fair distance away from him Mercedes sat quiet and unsmiling, her eyes on Nina or April or the blue horizon beyond, but never on him.

Cass hated seeing Mercedes so withdrawn and hated himself even more for being the cause. He'd been so stupid! His loss wasn't fresh like hers was. And he should never have accused Mercedes of failing with Nina.

It wasn't her fault, either, that the child maintained her delusion. Time after time he'd seen families hold out hope for the victim long after there could be no hope. Mercedes had accepted her husband's death. And as far as he could tell, she hadn't lied to Nina about Gilles's fate. No, it was Nina herself who refused to be convinced. But Cass had practically accused Mercedes of being an unfit mother, and the result had been an atmosphere of gloom and tension at the cabin.

To make matters worse, April's passivity had turned into downright hostility.

"You didn't have to make her mad!" she'd spat at him. "Now she'll never like me!"

Cass was staggered by the attack. "April, I didn't mean to upset Nina's mother. But our...disagreement had nothing to do with you."

"You ruined *everything!* You *always* ruin everything!"

"April, please...let's talk about this."

But April had run away from him to retreat into an angry silence that both hurt and confused him. He loved his daughter so much—she was the center of his world—but she seemed to be drawing farther and farther away from him.

Only Nina Delacruz and Baron seemed happy. Cass looked down at the shoreline where Nina happily splashed and squealed every time a wave crashed. She'd race up the beach to outrun the wave, then boldly follow the water back until the next curling wave chased her away again. Baron pranced like a puppy around her, the pair drawing smiles from other parents on the beach.

Cass found that Nina's enjoyment of life contrasted starkly with April's depression. And knowing Nina's happiness was fueled by fantasies only made things worse. Nina had chosen to avoid the harsh realities of life, while April had let them—whatever they were—overwhelm her. One situation was as tragic as the other, but right now, Cass would have given anything to see April smile the way Nina did.

He watched his daughter. Her bathing suit was bone-dry. She hadn't bothered to go into the water at all. She doodled in the sand a good distance away from him but near

Mercedes. He sighed. His daughter was much closer to Nina's mother than to her own father.

Could Mercedes be right? Cass wondered. *Does April really hate what I do? And hate me because of it?* That thought created such a feeling of sickness that his hand dropped to his stomach in an attempt to ease the pain. *Is that what's tearing this family apart?*

"Miz Arizona's cookin' giving you heartburn?" came a familiar voice.

Cass looked up, startled. "Mrs. Borden!"

"That's right." She plunked the beach chair she carried next to Cass, and sat down. "We working folks like the ocean, too, you know. My daughter, Lanie, drove me down to get some fresh air. She's taking me out to lunch."

"How nice." Cass glanced around, intending a polite greeting to Lanie. "I don't see her."

"That's because I sent her to get the car. I'm an old woman. I don't feel like walking back. Besides, I started wondering . . ."

"What?"

"What you're doing here, instead of at the rescue camp."

"I didn't go."

Mrs. Borden snorted. "I can see that. I may be old, but I'm not blind." Her gaze traveled up the beach. "I can also see you've lost your touch with the ladies. If Miz Arizona and those girls were any farther away, I'd need my glasses to find 'em."

Cass didn't argue, and Mrs. Borden gave him another sharp look.

"For a lawyer, you're awful quiet, Mr. Montgomery."

"For an employee, you're awful outspoken, Mrs. Borden."

"You never minded that in all the years I've been working for you. So I'm going to have my say, and you're going to listen."

Cass sighed and resigned himself to the inevitable.

"Things haven't been right in your house for a long time, Mr. Montgomery. Your *daughter* hasn't been right for a long time, and nobody's made any sense out of it. Not me, not you, not her teacher or pastor or that fancy hospital therapist."

"I'm well aware of that," Cass sighed.

"That girl needs someone to talk to. Looks like she's found her."

Mrs. Borden gestured toward April. Sure enough, she and Mercedes were talking. Or rather, April was talking and Mercedes was listening.

Cass turned away from the sight, envy in his heart. His expression didn't go unnoticed.

"Now I know it must hurt to have your baby attach herself to a total stranger. I know, because it hurts me, too. I've been with April most of her life. But she didn't want me to be her mama any more than she wants you to be her daddy now."

"Don't say that," Cass ordered.

"I gotta say it, Mr. Montgomery, because that girl needs help. I'm seventy-two years old. I can't take care of you and April like I used to. It's time for me to quit, and it's time for you to find someone to replace me. Like Miz Arizona."

"Right. As if life can be so easily arranged." Cass stood up, but Mrs. Borden put her hand on his arm.

"Don't you walk out on an old lady. I'm no fancy lawyer, but I've been on this earth twice as long as you and I've learned a few things in my day. You sit down and listen."

It was the kindness, rather than the words themselves, that swayed him. Cass reluctantly sat down again. "Go on."

Mrs. Borden gazed out over the ocean, her eyes old and wise...and sad. "The human heart's a funny thing, Mr. Montgomery. It has a will of its own. Now, for some strange reason only the good Lord can fathom, April's heart has gone sour. And when a heart goes sour, the mind and body soon follow."

Cass felt the sick feeling in his stomach spread to his chest. "I don't know what else to do! I've tried everything to make April happy."

The elderly woman patted his hand. "I know that. You're a good man, Mr. Montgomery."

"Tell that to April," Cass said bitterly.

"Wouldn't do any good." Mrs. Borden straightened the skirt of her dress. "April's heart doesn't want you or me. But don't you give up hope, because for some reason, April's heart has attached itself to that woman." She gestured with her free hand to Mercedes. "Just like your heart's attached to April. Or the way Twister's heart has attached itself to Nina."

Cass shook his head, confused. "What are you trying to tell me?"

"Mr. Montgomery, you can't reason with hearts. You have to do what they tell you. Your heart says you can't let April suffer. But April's heart says she wants someone else. So don't you separate April from Miz Arizona."

"How in the world am I supposed to manage that?" Cass exclaimed. "Ask Mercedes to move to Florida? Or pay her to keep my daughter? Just what do you expect me to do?"

"You'll have to ask heaven to answer that question, Mr. Montgomery, because I surely can't," Mrs. Borden solemnly replied. "But if you want your old April back, if you don't want that child's heart to sour and die, you'll latch on to that woman and hold tight."

"Excuse the cliché, Mrs. Borden, but that's easier said than done."

Mrs. Borden refused to back down. "April's heart thinks Miz Arizona can help her. That's half the battle. Miz Arizona looks like a smart lady. She might just do the trick."

Mrs. Borden sniffed, her hand still patting his. "Even if she can't appreciate good cookin' like mine."

Cass felt a little of the old woman's hope grow in him. He gave her a quick smile of gratitude. "I wouldn't worry about your cooking, Mrs. Borden. Mercedes and Nina are from the Southwest. I'll bet all those chili peppers and spicy foods have burned out their taste buds. They probably can't taste a thing."

Mrs. Borden looked up, surprised. "I never thought of that. But it does make sense . . ."

"Of course it does! Why else would anyone in their right mind turn down the best chicken-fried steaks this side of the Mason-Dixon line?"

She glared at him fiercely. "And the other side, too!"

Both of them pretended to maintain their dignity, but finally Cass smiled, and Mrs. Borden did the same. "I'm going to miss you when you leave, Mrs. Borden."

"Why? Aren't you going to come visit me?" she said with mock disdain. "Aren't you going to invite me to your home? Or doesn't the help get to mix with the family? I'm more family than help, you know. And just 'cause I'm quitting doesn't mean I'm lyin' down in my coffin. I'll have you know . . ."

Cass rolled his eyes, but for the first time in three days, determination had replaced some of the desolation in his soul.

"APRIL, WHAT DO YOU think they're talking about?" Mercedes asked. "The two of them keep looking at us."

April looked up from the sand castle she'd started to build. "Mrs. Borden's probably complaining about me to Dad again. She always does." With a quick angry motion, April flattened the castle with her hand.

"No, that's not it." Mercedes thought fast. "I know— Mrs. Borden probably thinks my bathing suit's too skimpy.

Either that, or she's jealous and wants one for herself."
Mercedes snapped both straps of her black bikini top for
emphasis.

"No way!"

"What, you don't think so?"

"Mrs. Borden won't even wear slacks, never mind a bikini!"

Mercedes made a show of studying the older woman.
"You never know. Maybe you should buy her one and surprise her."

"Buy her some pants?"

"No, a bikini."

April actually laughed. Mercedes brightened at that, then
gasped when April boldly splashed her with water from
what was left of the castle moat.

"I'm going to get you for that!" Mercedes threatened
playfully, and then April was up and running, Mercedes
right behind. She chased April into the surf and scooped up
handfuls of seawater to splash her, ignoring the girl's protests.

Nina immediately joined them and started splashing
Mercedes. Suddenly the water fight erupted into a full-
fledged free-for-all. There were no sides, no allies, no
enemies, just two children and a woman, their laughter
blending with the excited barking of the dog.

Mercedes was breathless, her hair and suit full of sand,
when she finally edged away from the water. She picked up
her towel, but Nina sprinted up and grabbed it from her
grasp.

"Nina!"

Nina stuck out her tongue and pranced just out of reach,
waving the towel, deliberately taunting her mother.

"Nina Delacruz-St. Clair, give me my towel!"

Too late. Nina grabbed the towel and ran with it to the
water. In seconds it was drenched, Nina laughing devilishly

and marching around with her soggy trophy. April followed suit by grabbing Nina's towel and soaking it.

"You'll be sorry!" Nina yelled in outrage. She chased after April, trying to get her towel back. But April was taller and faster, and easily kept Nina at bay. There was only one thing to do. Nina stopped chasing April and grabbed her dry towel. With a heave, Nina tossed it into the foaming surf.

April gasped, but Nina crowed with delight. "If I can't have a dry towel, neither can you!"

April immediately carried out her revenge. She retrieved her wet towel, then dropped both it and Mercedes's over Nina's head. Nina spluttered and tried to fight her way free of the clinging sodden material. She overbalanced and landed on her bottom with a soft plop.

April laughed so hard she collapsed onto the sand herself. Then Mercedes started laughing again. Even stubborn Nina couldn't suppress her giggles, although she covered her mouth with her hand. Mercedes hugged the moment close, wishing the pure joy could last forever....

Mercedes recovered first. Reluctantly she exchanged her playmate role for a more maternal one. She went over to pick up the two sand-covered girls and three soggy towels. "All right, you two, I think we've had enough horseplay for one afternoon. Both of you get into the water and rinse off. Take those towels. Now march!" She led them back into the shallows, her arms slung around their sandy shoulders.

"And when you're done, rinse off that poor dog. Look at him! He's more sand than fur. He'll have cactus growing out of his coat at this rate!"

Both girls giggled at that. Mercedes tried to keep a stern face as she watched them follow her instructions, but she didn't succeed—and didn't mind. Some of the awful tightness in her chest was gone. Since Gilles's death, things had gone from bad to worse. Her own loneliness, Nina's delusions, the custody suit over Baron and then Cass's accusations had all taken their toll. But today, Mercedes felt as if she'd regained a little of the person she used to be.

She waited for the girls, who, while still not friends, at least didn't deny they'd had fun together. Then Mercedes led them back up the beach the same way she led them down, her arm around their shoulders.

Suddenly she saw Cass. He was staring at the three of them. The expression—the longing—on his face tore at her heart. There was so much need, so much hunger there, that she guiltily dropped her arm from April's shoulders. And then, so as not to offend, dropped her arm from Nina's shoulders, too.

"Nina, you go back to the cabin and shower. I think you've had enough sun for today."

"Aw, Mom!" Nina moaned, but it was only a token protest. Mercedes impulsively gave her daughter a kiss on the cheek, then watched as Nina headed for their cabin, wet dog and towel trailing behind her. She turned toward April, giving her a friendly touch on the back.

"April, why don't you check with your father and see what he wants you to do?"

"He'll want me to clean up, too," April said, following Nina and the dog. When Mercedes had seen them enter the cabin, she went to retrieve her own things.

Cass already had. In fact, he was right behind her.

"Oh. Thanks," she said awkwardly. "I told Nina to go shower," she added quickly. "April went with her. I did ask April to check with you first, but—"

"It's all right, Mercedes," he said evenly. "I know you weren't overstepping your bounds with her."

Mercedes breathed a sigh of relief. They'd had enough conflict already without piling on more.

"I can carry that if you want," she said, gesturing at her beach bag.

"No, that's okay."

The terrible loneliness she thought she'd seen on his face earlier was gone, but the lack of animation in his expression still worried her. It reminded her of April. For the first time, she understood clearly how he felt, what he feared. Cass was afraid of losing his daughter.

After three days, her anger had finally melted away. "Are you sure, Cass?" she asked, simply for the sake of something to say. Polite trivia allowed her to maintain their fragile contact.

"Do I look like a ninety-eight-pound weakling?" he asked with a bit of his old spirit.

"Well, no, but—"

"I'm fine, Mercedes. Unfortunately our daughters aren't. But then, you know that," he said bluntly.

Mercedes nodded.

"Why don't you run ahead and check on the girls? I'll shower down here at the public facilities. When we're cleaned up, I'll take you all out to dinner."

"Thank you, Cass." The expression on his face sent a chill down her back, a chill that had nothing to do with her wet suit and hair. "And after that?" she had to ask.

"After that, we need to talk. I have a ... proposition for you."

CHAPTER EIGHT

"ABOUT THAT PROPOSITION . . ." Mercedes began.

It was late. After a full day in the sun followed by a big meal, both girls had quickly fallen asleep. Even Baron had headed for the foot of Nina's bed, a loud yawn announcing his retirement for the night.

Cass and Mercedes were alone outside enjoying the cool breeze. Mercedes had taken one of the porch chairs, while Cass was perched on the sturdy wooden porch railing.

"In a bit," Cass said. "Right now I just want to relax."

She crossed her bare legs beneath her. "Fine with me."

For a while there was nothing but the sounds of nature. The surf could be heard faintly in the distance, while the noisy calls of a tropical wetland's numerous insects, amphibians and predatory birds filled the night air.

"I'm glad you and the girls enjoyed yourselves today," Cass said after a moment.

"Nina's really taken to the ocean. She'll have a lot of good memories to share with her cousins in Phoenix."

"And you, Mercedes?"

Mercedes bypassed the implied question for the safer one. "I like it here, too, but I miss the sky at home." She tipped her head back, looking in vain for her favorite stars. The moisture-laden air of the tropics and its cloudy summer skies rested like a heavy canopy over her. It wasn't at all like the clear turquoise blue of the desert that stretched forever high.

"In Phoenix I can see all the stars. Gilles taught me and Nina the constellations. But here, even the moon is hard to see."

When she lowered her gaze, she noticed that Cass was still watching her.

"My clients do that," he said.

"What? Stargaze?"

"No. Deliberately misunderstand me."

Mercedes shrugged, not happy at being caught evading, but still determined to avoid Cass's original question. "Nina's the talker in the family. She can take some Florida memories home for her relatives."

"So *you* won't be taking back any good ones."

Mercedes was glad the dark hid her sudden irritation. "You're playing lawyer again. Please stop. Besides, I'm too sensible to live on memories."

"And yet just a minute ago you were remembering your husband teaching you the constellations."

Mercedes had no answer for that. But she did feel sadness at his observation—sadness for the good times that might never come again.

"Tell me about Gilles."

Mercedes's head jerked up. What had brought *that* on? But the same dark that hid her expression from him also hid his. She could only make out the blurred planes of his face and couldn't tell if he was looking off into the distance or right at her.

"How did you and Gilles meet?"

That question was easy to answer. "We ran into each other—literally."

"A car accident?"

"Oh, nothing as dramatic as that. Gilles was in Phoenix promoting his second book. He'd been put up at some fancy hotel somewhere. Only—Gilles being Gilles—he hated their food."

"You mentioned that he was quite strict when it came to nutrition."

"So much so that he'd taken a cab to the supermarket where I happened to be grocery shopping. His cab was waiting, plus he had to get to a book signing, so he was in a rush. I'd promised to pick up my roommate from her dentist's appointment, and I was running late. Gilles came racing out of the produce aisle just as I zipped out of the dairy aisle. And *bang*. A major collision."

"Any casualties?"

"Just the eggs." Mercedes smiled at the memory. "What a mess! And you should have seen the grocery carts. They were locked together in some bizarre metal coupling."

Her choice of words reminded her of how long it had been since a man had held her close and coupled with her. Except that the biological craving she was suddenly experiencing had nothing to do with the past, nor was Gilles the man her body desired.

Disturbed, she rushed back into her story with new vigor. "Then we both lost our tempers."

"I thought you never lost your temper."

"Not now—but I did then. Gilles was cursing me in French, and I was holding my own with insults in Spanish. Of course the manager tried to straighten things out, but he only spoke English. And his diplomatic skills weren't the best, either."

"Then what?"

"Gilles turned on him. My husband could swear like a trooper, and he left nothing to the imagination. When he finally ran out of air, I applauded." She smiled. "I was much more impulsive then. Besides, when it came to insults, Gilles was an artist. You had to appreciate his technique, which is exactly what I told him. In French—which I'd studied in school. Gilles actually blushed, then apologized."

"I imagine he was quite embarrassed."

Mercedes smiled again. "He said he'd never have said those things if he'd known I spoke his native tongue. Which, considering the many generations of the manager's ancestors Gilles insulted in his tirade, was certainly understandable."

Mercedes heard Cass's soft chuckle. "What happened next?" he asked.

"I took my roommate to the dentist, and Gilles went off to his book signing, but not before insisting he take me out to dinner by way of apology. Two weeks later I told my girlfriend to find herself another roommate because I was getting married."

"Only two weeks?"

"That's exactly what my parents said. They were terribly worried. In fact, my grandmother cried for a week, but I was twenty-five at the time, so they couldn't stop me."

"And your mind was made up."

Mercedes nodded. "Gilles was off to another climb at the end of the month, and I was already working at the museum. I wanted to be married before he left."

"You didn't want to go with him?"

"I didn't want to become a mountain climber any more than Gilles wanted to work in a museum—but I would like to have gone along a few times," she said wistfully.

"Gilles didn't let you?"

"No. He said we each had our own lives to lead. We should concentrate on enjoying the times when our paths did cross. So we got married—and I stayed behind."

"Did your family ever come around?"

"Eventually. But I was positive we were right for each other the first day we met." She paused.

"If you don't mind the question—were you?"

His persistence seemed strange, but it was obvious that Cass wasn't about to drop the subject. Mercedes decided honesty was her only option.

"No," she sighed. "I should have listened to my parents and not rushed into things. It's not that my marriage was bad, you understand."

"It wasn't good, either?"

"I'd say it just wasn't. Period. He was never home. The mountains were Gilles's life. They meant more to him than I did. I always came second. I thought I'd accepted that, but I hadn't, not deep down. And when Nina was born and Gilles kept leaving her, too, I had to face the truth."

Cass silently waited for her to go on.

"Gilles wasn't the right person for me—I see that now. If it wasn't for Nina, I'd almost wish we'd never met. He wasn't much of a family man for either of us."

"I'm sorry, Mercedes," Cass said quietly. He continued to watch her from the porch railing.

"Don't be. Gilles was always honest with me, both before and after the wedding. I was the one who went into the marriage with false expectations. Too bad it took me so many years to realize it. And I did have Nina. She's the one thing Gilles gave me that I don't regret. So I guess I can't complain."

"And Nina has fond memories of her father," Cass reminded her.

"Yes," she agreed. "Nina adored Gilles. He was a loving father—when he was home." A pause, and then Mercedes asked, "How old was April when her mother died?"

"Only two months. So she of course has no memories of her mother at all. And I find that the few I *do* have of Marian get foggier and foggier with time. I've tried to write them down so April will have them for herself and her children some day, but it's not the same. And I'm no writer like your husband was." Mercedes saw Cass shrug.

"Still, it's something she'll treasure when she gets older," Mercedes said, touched by his thoughtfulness. Not many men would have attempted such a project.

"I hope so. April meant the world to Marian. She was so happy our first child was a daughter."

"Gilles wanted a boy," Mercedes blurted. "He'd even bought a football and blue baby blanket, the whole bit. Of course he was pleased to have a healthy girl, but..."

She left the sentence unfinished. Funny how that memory still had the power to wound after ten years.

"I guess every man hopes his firstborn will be a boy," she finally said.

"Not me. I wouldn't trade April for anything."

Mercedes smiled, his words easing some of her pain. "And I wouldn't trade Nina, either. My family loves her to death."

"I'm glad."

Something in his voice made her curious. "What about Marian's family? Don't you and April see them much?"

"No. I left home—Wyoming—right after Marian's funeral."

"But, Cass, why?"

"Because everyone made it impossible for me to stay. Marian and I were the traditional high school sweethearts—we went to college together, too. That first crush turned into a first love that never died. But when Marian herself died..." Cass shook his head. "My in-laws were very bitter. They never really forgave me for her death."

"How can that be?"

He shrugged. "They'd asked us, as well as my parents, over for Christmas. It was April's first Christmas, she was the first grandchild on both sides of the family, and they wanted to celebrate in style. Unfortunately all four of the grandparents were hounding April and Marian to death. April wasn't nursing well, and Marian was dead on her feet.''

"I can sympathize. I remember how everyone descended on us when Nina was born. It can be stressful.''

Cass nodded. "The doctor was worried and so was I. So I decided we'd spend Christmas at my vacation cabin in the mountains—just the three of us. A freak blizzard hit, Marian was caught in it and . . .'' Cass took a deep shuddering breath. "Marian's parents and I were never close after that.''

"Cass, how terrible." Her heart went out to him. After losing his wife, he'd lost his wife's family, too. "But that was a long time ago. Have you tried to patch things up since then?''

"More than once. But they've been very cold to my overtures. Strange, when you think that April is all they have left of Marian.''

"But Cass, they're *family*." Mercedes couldn't help her dismay. She thought of her own loving family. Yes, they were always noisy, often nosy, occasionally even obnoxious, but they were there for her, through the good times and bad. She couldn't have remained sane during her marriage to Gilles or after his death without their support.

"They're very bitter. My in-laws held me responsible for her death then, and they do now," he said evenly, but Mercedes could hear the sorrow in his words. "I send them a Christmas card with April's picture every year. In return, they send April a check to cover gifts for the holidays and her birthday. That's as far as it goes.''

"Well, at least you tried," Mercedes sympathized. "How about your own parents? Have you and April kept in touch with them?''

"I've tried, but strangely enough, it's even harder with them than it is with Marian's parents.''

"Surely your own parents don't blame—" Mercedes broke off suddenly. But Cass answered what would have been her next question.

"Blame me for Marian's death, too? No. But they tried to take April away from me."

"My God, Cass, why?" Just the thought of someone trying to take Nina from her filled Mercedes with horror. She shivered at the very idea. Cass, however, merely shrugged.

"My parents insisted April would be better off with them than me. I packed my bags and left town with April over their protests. Everyone swore they were just trying to help, but I refused to give up my daughter."

"Of course not! How could they even think such a thing?"

There was a long pause before Cass answered. When he did, Mercedes winced at the harsh painful edge in his voice.

"They said they could do a better job raising April than I could. Which, considering how she's turned out, might have been the truth." Mercedes felt, rather than saw, his bitter smile. "We'll never know. The custody case didn't make it to court. I saw to that."

The dangerous look on Cass's face unnerved her. But more than anything, it evoked compassion in Mercedes's heart. "I'm sorry your wife's death cost you both so dearly."

"I've tried to mend the fences with my parents, too, but it's hard. I'm afraid to leave April with them for fear of what they'll say—or do. My parents claim I really haven't forgiven them."

"Have you?"

"Yes," Cass said, his sincerity ringing true, "I have. But most cases of child abduction are by relatives, and grand-parents have been known to be offenders, as well. If they went so far as to file a custody suit against me, I can't help but wonder..." He left the thought unspoken. "April's everything to me. I refuse to leave her in the hands of four confused adults. She's my daughter, and I'll raise her. When she's older, if she wants to contact them, she can. I've left the doors open. I can't do any more than that."

"I think you've been extremely generous, Cass, considering the past."

"Maybe. I don't dwell on it. What I'd like to talk about is the present," he said bluntly. He rose and gestured toward the chair beside hers. "May I?"

She nodded, then took a deep calming breath as he joined her. "I'm listening."

Cass hesitated, and for a moment Mercedes actually wondered if he was nervous. But his next words were in that lawyer's voice she'd grown to recognize—his business voice.

"About that proposition I mentioned. It concerns April and Twister. Or rather, Nina and Baron."

"Oh, Cass, are we back to fighting about the dog again?" Mercedes moaned.

"Not exactly. I'm willing to give Twister back to you— *permanently*."

"Permanently? Nina would be thrilled! But..." Mercedes quickly reined in her enthusiasm. "I don't understand. Earlier you said you wanted Baron for yourself."

"I did. I still do. But to be honest, custody cases leave a sour taste in my mouth. And fond as I am of Twister, I'd rather have April happy and laughing than have him back." He turned toward her, his eyes luminous in the dark. "Do you know how long it's been since my daughter has laughed?"

Mercedes shook her head.

"Too long. Far too long. April's opened up more with you today than she has in years. I want to see that continue. And I'm willing to pay for it."

"Pay?"

"Yes. You can have Twister back if you find out what's wrong with April, what's happened to make her so... different. I want my old April back, and I want you to find her."

"Cass, I'd do anything to help, you know that. But how can I make any promises? I'm not her mother. I barely even know her! And if she's as disturbed as you say she is, well, maybe you should find a child psychologist."

"I have, more than one," Cass answered grimly. "Unfortunately April won't talk to them any more than she will to me. But I have a hunch she'll talk to you."

Mercedes bit her lip. "I don't know, Cass. I don't feel comfortable repeating anything April says. Children have rights..."

"So do parents. I can't help April if I don't know what the hell's wrong with her! And I don't believe that a sudden morbidity about rescue work is *all* that's going on here. There's something else, something she's not telling me. Physically, the doctors say she's fine. She hasn't been threatened, molested or battered. But emotionally, she's suffering. I can't help her, but I think you can. So does Mrs. Borden. And so does April, or she wouldn't be clinging to you like a lost soul."

Cass left his chair to stand by the porch railing again. "It's not as if she wants the dog back, you know." The words seemed to be torn out of him.

"Forget the dog for a minute. Just what do you expect me to do for your daughter?"

"Talk to her. Try to get closer to her. We have three more weeks together. That should be long enough."

"But what if it's not? Cass, I'm no miracle worker! If I was, Nina wouldn't be having these fantasies about her father still being alive."

"Nina will have more than just fantasies if I win custody of Twister. She'll have another loved one missing from her life."

Mercedes froze. *He's back again, that cold-blooded legal barracuda I saw in court.* But she could give as good as she got. Gilles had learned that the first day he met her. It was time Cass Montgomery learned the same.

"Let me see if I have this right. If I agree to spy on your daughter, you'll agree to stop threatening mine. Correct?"

Cass thrust out his chin. She could see he didn't like the sharp edge to her words.

"No, Mercedes. You agree to get April to confide in you about whatever's troubling her. When she does, you come to me with details. In return, Twister goes home with Nina to continue buffering the loss of her father. You and Nina get what you want. I get what I want."

Mercedes wasn't about to let that statement pass. "And what does *April* get when Nina, Baron and I go home?" she demanded.

"She gets a loving father to trust in. A father who understands her."

"The same father who wants a stranger to spy on her," Mercedes said coldly.

"*Help* her."

"Intrude on her privacy."

"Call it whatever you want! I won't argue semantics with you, Mercedes. I assume you don't approve of this plan?"

"No, I don't." She intentionally delivered her next words in a mild reasonable tone. "If you give me Baron and you don't allow April to trust me—because I have to report to you—that leaves her with no one to turn to *but* you. You'll have manipulated April into a situation where she has no options whatsoever!"

Mercedes ignored Cass's sharp indrawn breath.

"Manipulated?"

"Yes. Quite effective, Counselor. Cold-hearted, perhaps, but effective. Only, your plan has one flaw you seem
to have overlooked."

"And that is?"

"April might just decide against confiding in *anyone*.
And where will that leave you, Mr. Montgomery? Worse
yet, where will that leave April?"

"My daughter needs help, and I've exhausted all the
conventional methods."

"That doesn't make this right! I'll be April's friend, but
I won't do it on your terms. Anything she tells me in confidence stays that way, unless she says otherwise."

Even in the dark, Mercedes could see that his fingers were
clenched. But he stood his ground.

"I'd suggest you rethink your position, Ms. Delacruz. Do
you really want me to tell Nina that I offered to give you
Twister, and you turned me down?"

Mercedes gasped, and Cass followed up on the advantage. "What will Nina say when she hears you refused the
offer because you were more worried about *my* daughter
than *yours?*"

"You wouldn't!" Mercedes whispered, even as her heart
screamed, *Look at him! He would.*

Cass was fighting tooth and nail for his daughter.
Mercedes knew he'd ignore every principle of right and
wrong he'd ever learned to keep his child safe. And that she
understood, because she'd do the same thing herself.

Mercedes bowed her head. In that gesture was both
acknowledgment and defeat. Cass didn't miss its meaning.

"I see we understand each other."

Mercedes silently cursed the photographer who'd followed her and Baron out into the desert and plastered their
photograph in the museum magazine for all the world to see.

"Who knows?" Cass suddenly asked. "This just might
work."

"You'd better hope so. Because if either Nina or April suffers because of it—" Mercedes eyes became as hard as his "—you'll deal with *me*."

She went in then, leaving him alone in the dark.

"I'M BORED," Nina announced loudly.

Cass looked up from her fishing rod, whose line he was trying to entangle, and glance at his watch. Mercedes and April had been gone half an hour now. It was almost a week since he'd set down his conditions for Mercedes; in that week she'd spent more time with April than ever. Right now, they were out shopping, since Mercedes insisted April needed more appropriate clothing for a girl her age. The two had left Nina behind.

Nina was not happy about it. Not at all.

"I don't know if leaving Nina with me is such a good idea," Cass had said earlier back at the cabin. "Maybe you should take her along."

"Nina goes clothes shopping with her aunts. She doesn't like to go with me. She says I'm no fun."

"And you think she's going to have more fun with me?" Cass asked sarcastically.

"No, but we all have our crosses to bear," Mercedes replied with a chilly glance. "Besides, they need a break from each other. A few days on the beach together doesn't exactly make Nina and April bosom pals. They've been bickering all week. If this keeps up I'll have to take Nina out of April's bedroom and put her in mine."

Mercedes gestured toward the front window. Both girls wore sulky expressions and were seated on opposite ends of the porch.

"What reason did you give Nina for leaving her behind?"

"I didn't. I pulled parental rank. April won't talk when Nina's around, which defeats the whole purpose of me spying on her."

Cass flinched at the word. "It's not—"

"You'll have to take Nina for the afternoon unless you expect me to tell her about your little plan. Do you?"

He frowned.

"I didn't think so." Mercedes reached for her purse, then held out her hand. "Your car keys and credit card, please. Did you authorize my using it today?"

Cass nodded. He'd phoned the card company's service center earlier.

"Good. I'll see you both later."

So Mercedes and April had left, and he'd taken Nina and the dog to the beach.

Nina kicked at the sand, causing Baron to jump. "I'm very, *very* bored."

Cass looked up from her fishing line again, the line he suspected Nina had deliberately snarled.

"I thought you wanted to learn how to surf fish."

"I changed my mind. Unnecessary killing destroys the marine ecosystem and dehumanizes those entrusted with the earth's care."

Cass mentally counted to ten. He wondered how long she'd worked on *that* little speech. She'd probably begun rehearsing the minute April and Mercedes had climbed into his car and left for the nearest mall.

"That's a lot of big words for a little girl," Cass said evenly.

"Not really. It just seems that way because April talks like a two-year-old. You should teach her more vo-ca-bu-lary."

Cass's hands clenched the rod. *Damn!* That little brat had carefully set her trap and he'd fallen right into it! Cass counted to twenty this time, fully aware of Nina's bright eyes watching for his reaction. Well, she was going to be disappointed. He wasn't a trial lawyer for nothing.

"That wasn't a nice thing to say about April," Cass observed calmly. "In fact, it was very rude."

Nina shrugged, one bronze shoulder lifting in another move that looked carefully rehearsed—and was quite effective. "Killing fish isn't nice, either," she replied.

Cass's mouth tightened. He had to admit, the kid was good. Phoenix must have one fantastic community theater.

"That makes neither of us...nice," he replied. "It seems we have something in common."

Those words prompted an instant retort. "I'm *not* like you, you thief," Nina snapped in rapid-fire Spanish.

His lawyerly composure flew right out the window. "Maybe you're right!" His heated reply was purposely delivered in Spanish. "At least I have manners, which is a lot more than I can say for you."

Nina blinked, then her chin dropped and her lips curled into a silent "Oh!"

"What's the matter? Cat got your tongue?" he asked, translating the old English idiom into the appropriate Spanish.

"Shut up!" This time Nina's reply was in English.

"Not yet. I think it's time you and I had a little talk. Number one, I'm tired of your insults, in English *and* in Spanish. They're going to stop, or you'll find yourself sleeping on the sand, instead of in my cabin!"

Nina glared at the threat, but was silent as he continued.

"Number two. Your little actress routine is getting old. You were faking car sickness when I drove to the rescue camp, and you're faking boredom now. That's also going to stop."

"You're not my mother. I don't have to listen to you!" Nina flung out. She moved up on the dry sand away from him to resettle on her beach towel, Baron at her side.

"Number three. I've decided that maybe Twister belongs with you more than with April. If you don't want me to change my mind, I expect a radical change in your behavior."

Nina froze. She opened her mouth, then closed it again, confusion flitting across her face. Cass decided to give her a few minutes to calm down, and he continued to work on the snarl.

"Your line's free," he told her a short time later. "You want me to cast it for you?"

"You're lying about Baron," Nina said quietly. "You're just telling me that to shut me up. Just like Mom lies and says Dad's never coming home."

Cass's breath caught in his throat. He anchored the rod by jamming the pole butt into the sand and made his way to Nina. She averted her face as he sat down next to her. He decided to tackle the easier subject first.

"Nina, I'm not lying about Baron. He's obviously happier with you. For whatever reason, April doesn't seem to want him anymore. And I'm not trying to shut you up. If you want to talk, then talk. Say whatever you want," he urged gently. "And if you want to cry, that's okay, too."

"You can't make me cry," she insisted, although her voice trembled. "I won't cry when you tell Mom on me. And I won't even cry if you take Baron back, either. So there!"

"Nina, Baron's going home with you, and I'm not going to tell your mother anything," he said quietly. "This is between the two of us, I promise."

Nina lifted her head to finally meet his gaze, and Cass felt a twinge of guilt at not allowing his own daughter the privacy he had just granted Nina.

"You don't want April to have Baron?"

Cass shook his head. "It's been almost two weeks, and Baron won't have anything to do with April. I've already told your mother that you'll be taking him home."

"I don't believe you." Nina was clearly still suspicious.

"Well, it's true."

Nina's eyes narrowed as she studied him. "You aren't going to tell Mom we had a fight and that I yelled at you? Even though I started it?"

"You started it?"

"Yeah." She played with Baron's ears. "I like your ocean. It isn't cold. I wasn't really bored. I was lying."

Cass was startled by her honesty. It spoke well of the child—and the child's mother.

"Well, I jumped right in with both feet when it came to yelling," Cass replied. "And I wasn't completely honest myself. I should have told you that I speak Spanish."

"Not good Spanish. Your accent stinks."

Cass smiled ruefully. "Well, you understood me. That's what counts, at least with my clients."

Nina continued to stroke Baron, her fingers toying with the thick black coat. "Except for the ocean, this vacation stinks, too. You'll change your mind about Baron. And Mom probably won't even take me to Disney World, I've been so bad. *Great* summer."

"I'm sorry about that, Nina. There's nothing more disappointing than a bad vacation." Cass settled down more comfortably in the sand and crossed his ankles. "Maybe your next one will be better."

Nina gazed at him openly, her face as expressive as her mother's. Cass found himself wishing April's would reveal even a fraction as much. At least with the Delacruz women, you knew where you stood.

"What was your worst vacation?" Nina asked. "The one where you lost Baron and we found him?"

"No, although that was pretty bad." His gaze grew distant. "The worst one was Christmas vacation twelve years ago. April's mother died then. I haven't really been keen on

Christmas since. But I try to do right by April every December."

"Oh." Cass watched as Nina started playing with Baron's ears again. "Dad and I like Christmas. We get to pick out our tree together."

"Are you a good tree-picker-outer?"

"I am. Mom isn't." Nina frowned. "She likes small trees."

"Why?"

"Because in the desert, Christmas trees cost tons and tons of money. Mom says we're paying for the delivery, not the actual tree. So she picks small ones. But if I go with Dad, I can pick any one I want. Even the biggest one on the lot. We had a huge tree Christmas before last." The glow in Nina's eyes faded. "Then Dad left, so we had last Christmas without him. He didn't come home for Easter vacation. And now he's missing summer vacation, too."

She kept her head down, her eyes still on the dog. A pause. Then she whispered, "Mr. Montgomery?"

Cass froze, knowing what was coming, *hating* what was coming, and dreading it even more. "Hmm?"

"Do you think my daddy's dead?"

Oh, God, what to say? Mercedes had forbidden him to discuss the subject. But Nina herself had precipitated the conversation.

Cass closed his eyes. When he opened then, Nina was still waiting. He placed his hands on Nina's shoulders as he searched desperately for the right words. He swallowed, wishing there was some way of avoiding what had to be said. But the trust in her eyes wouldn't let him lie. "I'm positive he is, Nina. I think if he were alive, he would have come home to you long before now."

Cass expected hot tears, even hysterics. What he heard, instead, was the calm voice of logic.

"Dad's expeditions always take a long time. Sometimes a whole winter."

"But this long, Nina?" Cass asked gently.

"Maybe he's just hurt. Maybe he sprained an ankle. He'll be home when it gets better. He had supplies in his backpack."

"He couldn't have had enough."

Nina scowled. "You don't know that."

Cass released one of Nina's shoulders to smooth back her hair. "I do, Nina. I work on rescues, remember? And the longer any rescue takes, the less the chances for survival, especially in a harsh terrain like Alaska. As for those supplies in your father's backpack..." Cass shook his head. "He didn't have enough to last twenty whole months. That's how long he's been missing."

Nina bit her bottom lip. "He could have caught fish. Like we're doing now." She drew her knees to her chest and wrapped her arms tightly around her legs. "I don't care what you say. He's coming back. And when he does, we'll have the best vacation ever."

Cass saw the anguish on her face. It was so intense, so painful to see, that he was tempted to turn away. But he didn't. He gathered the trembling little girl close and rocked her back and forth. "I wish it was true, baby. I really wish it was true."

And still there were no tears on Nina's pale cheeks. "My daddy's alive," she insisted. Cass thought back to the awful hours when he was praying for Marian to come back. He drew Nina closer, remembering his own heart's devastation. An old verse he'd once read in school popped into his head: "Hearts can weep, even when eyes cannot."

He knew. Dear Lord, how he knew.

So did Nina.

CHAPTER NINE

DESPITE CASS'S best efforts to comfort her, it was a long time before Nina stopped shaking.

"How are you, sweetheart?" he asked quietly.

"I want my mama." She raised her head from his chest, but made no move to leave the shelter of his arms.

"I wish she was here, too. Is there anything I can do for you until she gets back?"

Nina shook her head.

"There must be something," he coaxed. "It's awfully hot out. Are you thirsty?"

"A little. My throat hurts."

Cass wasn't surprised. It hurt more to hold grief back than to cry and let it out. He'd learned that much himself. "Shall we go get a drink?"

She thought about that. "Can I have a milk shake?"

"Yep." Cass stood up and set the child on her feet, keeping one of her hands firmly grasped in his. "You want a hamburger and fries, too?"

"No. Talking about my dad makes me want to throw up."

Cass took a deep breath. His own stomach felt like it had been shredded by sharks. "Okay, then, milk shakes for two, hold the burgers. Chocolate or vanilla?"

"I want strawberry."

"This snack shack doesn't have strawberry. We'd have to go way down the beach, and I don't think you're up for that. Your mom has my car, remember?"

"I don't care. I want strawberry," Nina said with her old stubbornness.

"Have to be difficult, don't you, kid?"

Nina gave him the barest trace of a smile, and some of the tightness in Cass's chest abated. On an impulse he bent over and gave her a hug.

"Hey!" Nina protested, and Cass, ever mindful of the warnings he'd given April regarding strange men, immediately released her.

"What was that for?" Nina asked.

"For not being mad at me."

"Mad at you?"

"Because of what I said about your father."

"That would be stupid," Nina said. "Everyone makes mistakes." She retrieved her towel from the beach and slung it around her shoulders. "Besides, then you wouldn't buy me my milk shake."

Cass managed a smile as he retrieved his own towel and beach sandals. "You're a very intelligent young lady, Nina Delacruz. Have you ever thought of becoming a lawyer?"

"Nope. I'm going to be an actress. Or a famous mountain climber like my dad." Some of the animation disappeared from her face, and Cass reached for her hand again.

"You'd better settle for being a famous hiker, first," he said. "Come on. We've got a long walk if you still want strawberry."

"I THINK that's about it, April," Mercedes said. "You should have enough clothes here to take you till the start of school." She handed the cashier Cass's charge card.

April watched as the clothes were rung up. When the total appeared in green digital numbers, April blinked. "Wow."

Even Mercedes winced at the total, but there was no way around it. However well-intentioned Mrs. Borden had been, she knew nothing about dressing little girls in clothes that suited today's tastes. Even April's stark white underpants and T-shirts had been prudish, both purchased two sizes too large so April could grow into them. In fact, she was surprised that April even wore the uncomfortable baggy things. Nina would have refused. Mercedes had replaced them with youth-size camisoles and matching panties in delicate floral patterns.

"Dad's going to have a cow," April predicted.

"He can have a whole herd if he wants," Mercedes replied. "Being economical is an admirable trait, and I'm sure Mrs. Borden meant well, but your father makes a good living. He can afford to buy you nice clothing in the correct sizes."

"What if he doesn't like my new stuff?"

"You leave your father to me." Mercedes gathered up four of the clothing bags, leaving the remaining two for April. They set out for the exit and the parking lot. "When we get home, I want you to bag up all your old underwear and play clothes. We're getting rid of them."

April gasped. "All of them?"

"That's right. Does your church have a drop-off box?"

"Yes."

"Good. We can leave them there."

"Mrs. Borden will be mad," April warned, even as she contentedly fingered the edge of the new outfit Mercedes had insisted she wear home, complete with fresh underwear beneath. "She's still mad that you hate her cooking."

"Mrs. Borden's temper doesn't worry me. I've lived with Nina's for too long, and believe me, when she roars, the earth trembles. Now, where are the..." Mercedes struggled to find the car keys without dropping any of the purchases. "Ah, here they are."

Mercedes unlocked the car door. She and April dumped their bags in the back seat, then waited for the hot air in the overheated interior to escape from the open doors before getting in.

"If it wasn't so late, I'd get you some shoes, too." Mercedes frowned as she looked at April's feet. "Those sneakers of yours are just about worn-out."

"These are my beach sneakers. I have some good ones at home. And dress shoes, too."

"Who bought you those?"

"Dad did. I get to pick out my own shoes. They'll match my new stuff."

"Then you should be all set. We've bought you underwear, socks, tights, play clothes and good clothes..." Mercedes studied April with satisfaction. The new outfit was quite an improvement. Now if the child would only grow out the shaved sides of her hair... "Okay, the car's as cool as it's going to get," Mercedes announced. "Hop in, kiddo."

A few minutes later they were driving away from the mall, the air conditioner humming faintly. Mercedes noticed April stealing glances at herself in the side passenger mirror. Mercedes had been pleased to find that the girl had a sensible turn when it came to fashion. April leaned toward a classic understated style, as opposed to Nina, who preferred more flamboyant clothing.

"So, April, do you like your new look?" Mercedes asked.

April nodded happily, then her smile faded.

"What? Did we forget something?"

"School clothes."

"Those will have to wait for a couple of months."

"How come?" April asked.

"Because you're a borderline size right now. You might need the next size up come September, depending on how fast you grow."

"I don't want to go with Mrs. Borden again. Can't we go back and get them now?"

"No, you really need to wait until the end of summer."

April sighed, some of her animation slipping away.

"Maybe someone else can take you shopping. A friend, perhaps? A relative or neighbor?"

"There's no one."

April's plight tore at Mercedes's heart. It made her reply somewhat brisk. "Then have your father take you. You can pick out what you want and model it for him. He seems to have sensible taste in clothes, and so do you. It shouldn't be a problem."

April shook her head.

"What, you don't think that's a good idea?" Mercedes asked, taking a quick peek at April.

"No."

"Why not?"

"Dad doesn't like me," April said softly.

Mercedes braked for a red light. "April, that's not true."

"I'm not good at search-and-rescue work. I can't even train the puppies right."

"That has nothing to do with your father's feelings for you," Mercedes said firmly.

April was unconvinced. "Dad only pays attention to me when I'm working with the dogs. That's all he cares about. His stupid dogs."

"You're wrong. Your father cares about others, which is why he does search-and-rescue work. He doesn't want other children to grow up without a mother like you did."

"He'd rather look for strangers than be with me! I hate it!"

The anger and pain in April's voice took Mercedes by surprise. It wasn't until the light turned green that she spoke again. "Then I suggest you tell him."

"Dad knows," April mumbled. "He just doesn't care."

Mercedes reached out her right hand and touched April's arm. "He *doesn't* know, April! And he *does* care! But your father can't read your mind. He can't correct the problem if he doesn't know one exists."

April pulled her arm away and stared out the window. Mercedes struggled for the right words.

"Listen carefully to me, April. You have to start being responsible for your own emotional well-being in life. Do you know what that means?"

No answer.

"Emotional well-being means being at peace with yourself. When you're just a baby, your parents take care of you. But the older you get, the less your parents can do. If you're unhappy, it's up to you to do something about it."

April whirled around in her seat. "I did! After Twister disappeared, I told Dad we didn't need another dog! But he went right out and bought Buddy."

"So you *did* talk to your father."

"He didn't listen. He *never* listens."

"That was three years ago, wasn't it?"

April nodded miserably.

"So tell me, sweetheart. What have you done *since* then?"

April opened her mouth, then froze, her lips still parted.

"Don't you think it's time to try again?"

April turned her head back toward the side window, but Mercedes knew she'd made her point. She didn't belabor it. She and April both remained silent the rest of the way home.

Cass was waiting on the front porch as Mercedes drove up the sandy road to the cabin. He rose from his chair and hurried out to greet them, Baron close on his heels, tail wagging.

"Where's Nina?" Mercedes immediately asked as he opened her door.

"Asleep. We walked a good three miles up the beach and back. She was pretty tired."

"Three miles?" Mercedes echoed.

"Yeah. She wanted a strawberry shake, and our snack shack didn't have strawberry. She insisted on walking."

Mercedes nodded. "That sounds like Nina, all right. Well, April and I must have walked at least that far ourselves. So, what do you think?" Mercedes gestured toward April, who already had one shopping bag in hand. "Spin around, sweetie. Show your father your new clothes."

April did, her inherent gracefulness present despite her reluctance.

"Why, April, you're even more gorgeous than usual!" Cass couldn't believe the difference the clothes made in her appearance.

"You're just saying that," April mumbled.

"No, I really mean it. You look great. Here, let me take that for you."

"I can do it." April deliberately avoided his outstretched hand and hurried into the cabin.

The smile on Cass's face faded. There was an awkward silence, then Mercedes passed him one of her bags. "April's had a long afternoon. She could probably do with a rest."

Sure enough, April did lie down a short time later, the heat and the shopping excursion obviously taking their toll. Cass turned the ceiling fans on high and opened all the windows, then followed Mercedes out onto the porch.

She was sitting on the steps, her shoes off and her bare feet resting on the sand, Baron close beside her. "I wanted to talk to you about Nina," Cass began. Mercedes deserved to know about Nina's tearful conversation on the beach.

"I don't want to hear about it just now. April and I had a lovely time out, but it was exhausting."

Cass hesitated. "I think we should talk about Nina now."

"Tomorrow."

Secretly relieved, Cass gave in. "So, it was a trying afternoon?"

"It could have been worse. It could have been *my* money I was spending."

"Do I want to know the grand total?"

Her lips twisted upward in a slight smile. "Do yourself a favor, Cass. You don't. Your daughter has refined—and expensive—tastes."

"Marian loved to shop for clothes. She used to wear me out." Cass paused, then turned to Mercedes. "You know, I haven't thought about that in years. But the older April gets, the more I find myself thinking about Marian."

"What was she like?"

"Marian? She was smart. Funny. Full of life. And so very young." Cass traced a pattern in the sand with his forefinger. "Marian still remains the same age in my mind—while I keep getting older. When I look at our wedding picture, I have to make an effort to remember when I was young...what we were like together."

"I know the feeling, and it hasn't even been two years yet..." Mercedes looked off into the distance. The sounds from the marsh were subdued in the heaviness of the tropical afternoon.

"Maybe it's time to stop trying to remember," Cass suggested.

Mercedes sighed. "Maybe you're right."

He pulled her close, hoping she wouldn't pull away.

She didn't.

Her kiss was sweet and sad, hesitant and tender, resisting yet giving all at the same time. It was like Mercedes herself, a complex mixture of all the things he saw in her, all the things he wanted from her...

Until she pushed him away.

"Cass, we can't. Nina believes her father's alive, and this will confuse her even more."

"Nina's not here right now." Cass kissed her again.

INSIDE THE CABIN, April watched the two adults. Her teeth worried her bottom lip as she prayed for Mercedes to push her father away. The kiss ended. Her nose pressed against the window screen, she watched her father try to kiss her again, and this time Mercedes *did* push him away. After a moment, she saw Cass leave, striding down the path to the beach.

April breathed a sigh of relief and lay back down on the bed. If Mercedes didn't like her father, then there was hope. For the first time in a long while, April dared to dream that someone—Mercedes—could help her, could advise her and comfort her. Miraculously the thought of what she'd done three years ago—the terrible lie she'd told her father—had lost a little of its sting. Although it still sickened her stomach and ruined her sleep, it had retreated a bit in another adult's presence—Mercedes presence.

If only Nina's mother could make that awful sickness go away. Maybe she could if April dared to tell her that she'd tried to get rid of her very own dog and nearly killed him in the process.

April squeezed her eyes tight and started to pray. But then she stopped abruptly. God wouldn't listen to someone who'd turned a beloved pet loose in a strange airport. God wouldn't forgive her for Twister's injuries, even though April had only wanted Twister to find a new home, not get hurt. And God surely wouldn't forgive her for taking Twister away from her father's rescue work, taking him away from all those missing people Twister and her father could have found. Buddy wasn't as good a rescue dog as Twister. Everyone knew that.

April bit her lip again, hard. No, God hated cowards who hurt good dogs. God hated little girls who were too afraid to tell the truth. God, like her father, would never understand April's fear of search-and-rescue work. But for some reason, April was sure Mercedes would.

Not that April was going to tell her right now—or tell anyone else, for that matter. But it didn't mean the truth about that day at the airport wouldn't come out sometime. And if it did, April was positive her father would never forgive her. He'd never understand.

But Mercedes might, especially if April made an extra effort to be nice to Twister. Maybe she could make it up to him. She'd feel better. Twister would feel better. And maybe Mercedes would like her more—if Nina didn't get in the way.

April looked over at Nina's sleeping form. Nina was a spoiled brat. She really didn't like her. But perhaps she should start being nicer to the younger child. If Cass ever found out what she'd done and decided he didn't want her anymore, April would need someplace to go. Mercedes's house would be better than some foster home or the grandparents she'd never met.

Making friends with Nina wouldn't be easy. April was shrewd enough to know that since Nina wouldn't share her dog, she certainly wouldn't want to share her mother, either. But that could change. April could convince Nina that she wanted to be her friend. So what if it was a lie? Nina would never know. April was a good liar. After all, she'd had three long years of practice.

MERCEDES HEARD footsteps behind her. The light graceful tread wasn't Nina's.

"Hello, April. Have a nice rest?"

"No. It's too hot to sleep. I don't see how Nina can."

"Nina could sleep through an earthquake, a tornado and a hurricane combined. She always could."

April sat down on the steps, taking the spot Cass had vacated. Baron immediately rose and headed back into the house. April pretended not to notice Mercedes's look of pity. "Where's Dad?" she asked.

"He went for a walk."

"Oh."

"Is Phoenix a nice place to live?"

"I think you'll like it. Of course, since my family and I live there, I'm prejudiced. But the desert is fascinating if you can get beyond the traditional images of sand, cactus and snakes."

"Is your family nice, too?" she asked.

Mercedes gave April a sharp assessing look. "Why? Are you worried they won't welcome you during your visit?"

That was exactly what she'd been wondering. Nina's mom wasn't as easy to fool as her father was. April bit her lip.

"Because if you are, don't be. You're a very likable person, April. Everyone will enjoy your stay. I know I will."

April felt a lump in her throat as Mercedes slung an arm around her shoulder.

"Even though we weren't really invited?" she said quietly. "Even though the judge is making you?"

"That won't mean a thing to my family. Or to me."

"What's it like to have relatives? Relatives you actually know?"

"Well, that all depends. Every family's different, but my family and I enjoy living close to each other. We enjoy celebrating birthdays and holidays together, and Nina always has people she can count on. She's especially close to my two sisters."

"What about your husband's family? Do you see them a lot, too?"

"Gilles's family is from Quebec. We go there as often as I can manage with my work schedule. In the meantime, we keep in touch by phone and letters."

"I wish we did." April's face was downcast. "Dad's parents live in Wyoming. So do Mom's. I never get to see them at all."

There was a long silence. Mercedes looked so uncomfortable April wondered miserably if she'd said something wrong. After a moment she managed to sneak a look at Mercedes. Mercedes didn't seem angry, however, only sad. April relaxed a little.

"Having grandparents can be nice," Mercedes said. "Nina's spoil her rotten."

"She was born that way," April blurted, then covered her mouth with her hand.

"Well, she's an only child," Mercedes said, ignoring April's rudeness. "And Gilles spoiled her, too. Sometimes children need to have those good times to remember when bad times come."

"Like now."

There was a pause, then, "Are we talking about Nina's bad times, April, or yours?"

"Nina's," April stammered. "I'm not worried about anything bad."

"You act like you are, April," Mercedes replied. "Is there something else besides hating rescue work that you haven't told me?"

April thought fast. She didn't want to talk about herself anymore. She wasn't ready to tell anyone, even Mercedes, what she'd done to Twister. A quick change of subject was in order, one that would throw Mercedes off the track.

"I saw Dad kissing you. Do you like him better than me? Do you want to marry him?"

Mercedes's head sharply swiveled her way. "So *that's* what's bothering you."

April was pleased to have changed the subject so effectively. "Well, do you?" she demanded. "Like him better?" She held her breath as she waited for the answer. Adults always ganged up together. They always sided against kids. If Mercedes paired up with her father, then April wouldn't be able to trust her anymore.

"April, kissing does not necessarily mean marriage. And besides, there's Gilles."

"But he's—" April hesitated "—missing."

"He's dead, April. You can say it. And until I can get Nina to accept that, close friendship between me and your dad isn't... proper. Anyway, I'm no more ready for a new husband than Nina's ready for a new father."

April almost clapped her hands with glee. She wasn't interested in Nina's strange ideas. If Nina wanted to believe her father was alive, who was she was to argue? Mercedes was the important thing. "But you can still be friends with *me,* can't you?" she asked eagerly.

"Of course I can."

April's breath caught with relief.

"Sweetheart, are you all right?"

Drawing on the control that the years of lying had taught her, April made her face go blank. "I'm fine," she said.

Mercedes scrutinized her closely, but April didn't care. Her father was gone, Nina was out of sight, the search-and-rescue training camp was faraway, and no one had a clue about what she'd done to Twister three years ago. April slid closer to Mercedes on the step and savored the peaceful moment. She was safe, safe, safe.

CHAPTER TEN

A STORM WAS BREWING. It matched Cass's mood perfectly.

Moisture beaded on his forehead and bare shoulders while the air grew even heavier with humidity. Above, threatening black storm clouds rolled in from the Gulf. Locals and visitors alike were packing up their things and heading for their cars.

Cass had the beach to himself.

His bare feet splashed through the water as he continued his lonely run along the shore. A few locals yelled at him to go home before the storm hit, but Cass ignored them.

The events of the day had left him shaken. First Nina had asked if he thought her father was dead, then she'd refused to believe that he was. Cass had tried to tell Mercedes about the conversation, but somehow he'd ended up kissing her, instead. Their first kiss had left him reeling with its intensity; their second had shocked him with its abrupt end. Mercedes had rejected him—not because she didn't respond to him, but because she felt she had enough on her hands with Nina.

That was certainly an understatement. The child still believed her father was alive! He'd seen this before, especially with the families of drowning victims. Many times, bodies were never recovered. Without that stark proof, loved ones often refused to give up hope, no matter how bleak the chances of survival.

That misguided hope could drag on for years. One had only to look at the families of Vietnam MIAs. Decades later, some of those people still believed that one day, they'd be reunited with their missing husbands, sons or brothers. Would that be the case with Nina? Would she insist on spending years waiting for a man who would never come home?

Cass swore out loud and increased his speed. Gilles St. Clair was dead. Cass knew that. He'd worked search-and-rescue too long to believe otherwise. Even if he hadn't, logic insisted that being lost in the harsh Alaskan terrain for twenty months was a death sentence. But Nina stubbornly held out hope.

And if the situation wasn't tragic enough, Mercedes had put her own life on hold by worrying herself sick over her daughter. Nina was on her mind every waking minute.

Cass felt the tragedy of it all the way to his soul, because he felt this one more personally than any other since Marian's death. He and April had both opened up to another human being for the first time in years. Yet Mercedes couldn't handle the problems in her own life. How could she ever make room for April if she was forever focused on Nina?

Cass could only pray that Nina would soon see the light. Because if she didn't, his poor withdrawn little April would have no one. Nor would he—for April had absented herself from Cass's life as much as Gilles had absented himself from Nina's.

Through no fault of his own, he'd lost his wife, his parents and his wife's parents. Hell, he'd even lost his damn dog. April was all he had left in this world. If anything ever happened to her...

Cass shivered. The chill of the approaching storm had grown sharper. He picked up his pace, and the gusty wind seemed to do the same. Lightning flashed in the distance. The horizon grew darker, turning the ocean a murky gray as whitecaps frothed in the heaving waves.

"Cass! Cass Montgomery!"

The call was faint, so faint Cass almost didn't hear it. But at the second cry, he looked over his shoulder. It was Fred Schulberg, an elderly retiree who owned the beach cabin nearest his own. Reluctantly Cass pivoted and jogged toward his neighbor. His impatience at being interrupted changed to concern at the panicked look on the older man's face. "Fred? What's wrong?"

"It's my grandson. He's missing!"

"Missing?" Cass felt the familiar sick feeling in the pit of his stomach. "You mean Jake?"

"Yes! I put him down for his nap. I must have fallen asleep, because when I woke up, he was gone!"

"How?"

"The front door was open. He must have just wandered off!"

Cass gently grasped the old man's shoulders. "Are you sure he didn't go somewhere with his parents?"

"They took my wife to the mall hours ago!" Fred wrung his hands. "Cass, you have to help me!"

"You know I will. But first take a deep breath," Cass urged. "I can barely understand you."

When Fred did, Cass went on, "Now talk slowly. Do you have any idea where Jake went?"

Fred shook his head.

"Where did you look?"

"Everywhere. *Everywhere!* Then I saw you, and... and..."

"Okay. Did you call the police?"

"No. I— My God, Cass, you don't think he was kidnapped?" The old man's voice trembled on the last word.

"I doubt it. This is a private area. Everyone knows everyone else. But we do need to call the police. We might need an ambulance."

"But—"

"Fred, can Jake swim?"

The old man's face went even whiter. "No. He's only three years old!" he whispered, his knees buckling. Cass grabbed him to keep him on his feet.

"I can't help Jake if you pass out."

The old man rallied.

"Okay, Fred. Here's what I want you to do. Head back to your cabin and call the police. Then call our neighbors to start searching. When you're done with that, find me something of Jake's. A stuffed animal or a blanket would be good. Or some of his clothing. Only make sure they've been worn recently. I don't want anything that's freshly laundered," Cass cautioned. "Repeat all this back to me."

Fred did, and Cass nodded approvingly. "Good man. Okay, I'll meet you at your cabin in five minutes. Wait for me there."

"But I need to look for Jake!"

"No! *I'll* look for Jake. You stay home, make the calls and wait for the police." Cass started to move off.

"But . . . where are you going?"

"To get my dog!"

Mercedes and the girls were all in the cabin living area when Cass burst into the room. She took one look at his expression and immediately rose to her feet. "Cass? What's wrong?"

"I need Twister."

From his position at Mercedes's feet, the dog perked his ears at the sound of his old name. Nina and April ignored the jigsaw puzzle beneath their fingertips.

"Twister?" Mercedes echoed.

"My neighbor's three-year-old grandson is missing. I need the dog to find him."

April gasped, but Mercedes said calmly, "Of course, Cass. Take him."

"I'll go get his leash," Nina said. Mercedes was proud to see that Nina recognized the gravity of the situation.

"Get me a shirt, my shoes and a pair of socks," Cass tersely ordered his daughter.

April, also recognizing that a crisis was at hand, hurried to obey. Cass grabbed a pair of jeans from the laundry basket and pulled them over his swim trunks, then reached for his shirt as April emerged from his bedroom.

"Thanks, sweetheart."

April nodded, then sat down, drawing close to Mercedes's side, her face white.

"Is there anything I can do to help?" Mercedes asked when Nina returned and snapped the leash on to Baron's collar.

"Just answer the phone."

"Are you sure? Don't you want me to help look?"

"You don't know the area, and there's a big storm coming in. I'd rather you stayed here with the girls." Cass finished tying his sneakers and rose.

"Isn't April going?" Nina asked.

Mercedes felt April tremble at Nina's question. Mercedes placed an arm around the girl's waist and ignored Nina's startled look at the sign of reassurance and affection. "She's staying here, Nina. Children are only allowed to help train rescue dogs, remember? They don't go on real rescues. Now, give Mr. Montgomery the leash."

Nina obeyed. "Heel, Twister," Cass ordered.

The dog looked up from the floor and steadfastly refused to move. Cass tugged gently on the lead.

"Come on, Twister! Let's go!"

Still no response.

"Try calling him Baron," Mercedes suggested.

"Heel, Baron! Come on, boy." Cass gave the leash a short corrective jerk. The hair on the back of the Lab's neck rose, even as a low warning growl rumbled in his throat.

Everyone in the room froze. Mercedes was the first to regain her composure. "No, Baron!" she ordered.

The dog stopped growling, but the hair on his neck still bristled. Mercedes slowly stood up and took the leash from Cass's hand. His gaze moved from Mercedes to Baron. There was a long silence in the room.

"He really is your dog now, isn't he?" he finally said.

"We told you that all along," Nina announced. "You should have listened!"

"Nina, *silencio!*"

Both Nina and April started at the harshness of Mercedes's command. Mercedes ignored them. "Cass, is there a friend's number April has for emergencies?"

"Mrs. Borden's daughter and husband don't live far from here."

"Are they home?"

"If they aren't, Mrs. Borden will be. April knows the number."

Mercedes nodded. "Nina, please lock the door after we leave. April, you close all the windows. It's going to storm, and I want you girls to stay inside."

"But Mom! Where are *you* going?"

"Someone has to work the dog." Mercedes grabbed her jacket, then met Cass's eyes. "Let's go."

The wind had picked up even more by the time Cass and Mercedes reached Fred's beach cabin. Police cruisers and an ambulance were already parked on the wet sand. Mercedes stood some distance off, Baron quietly at her side, despite the commotion.

The parents had arrived home, and Fred was practically hysterical. He was being comforted by an older woman Mercedes assumed was his wife. Jake's father seemed to be in shock. His mother was left to deal with the police and the emergency medical team.

Mercedes's heart went out to them all. She remembered the first moment she'd been told Gilles was missing. Remembered the way she wanted to scream, and hadn't. Remembered the way Nina *had* screamed and those long hours on the flight to Alaska, then those even longer days when they waited and waited, until finally... "We're calling off the search, Mrs. St. Clair. I'm sorry, but there's no hope for him. No hope at all."

For a moment, the memories were overwhelming. Mercedes closed her eyes, her fingers resting gently on Baron's head. When she opened them again, Cass was standing before her.

"You're not okay with this, are you." It was a statement, not a question.

"What choice do I have?"

"There's always a choice, Mercedes. I've called in some friends of mine. They'll get here with their dogs as soon as they possibly can, hopefully within the hour. So if you want to go back to the cabin, you go. There's not a person here who wouldn't understand."

Mercedes took in the mother's white face as she quietly consulted with the police. The boy's father had collapsed in a porch chair, his face buried in his hands. Mercedes turned away. That horrible heartbreaking night in the Alaskan hotel, long after Nina had cried herself to sleep, Mercedes had buried her own face in her own hands that very same way.

She couldn't back out now. Mercedes took in a deep breath and pushed the past to the back of her mind. "You tell me what to do. I'll give Baron the commands."

Cass stared at her for a second, then took her face between his hands for a quick hard kiss. Before she could react, he grabbed her arm and guided her toward Jake's mother. The other woman held a pair of child's pajamas.

"These are Jake's favorites, Cass," she said without preamble. "He hides them, you know."

"Hides them?" Mercedes echoed.

The woman's gaze focused on Mercedes. "Yes. He's crazy about the dinosaur print. I have a devil of a time getting them into the laundry," she said with a tremulous smile that dissolved into tears. "Here."

She shoved them at Mercedes, then hurried back to her husband. Mercedes could see the woman's shoulders shaking. She started to go after her, but Cass reached for Mercedes's arm.

"There are others to help her," he said. "Right now, you and I need to concern ourselves with her son."

"I . . . Of course."

"Take the clothing and hold it under Baron's nose," Cass told her. "Then use the command, 'Scent.'"

Mercedes knelt down in the sand. "Scent, Baron."

Baron turned his head away and yawned.

"Baron, scent!" Mercedes ordered more forcefully. She rubbed the pajamas over his nose, unconsciously slipping into Spanish. "Come on, pup. Take a good whiff. You don't want to leave this little boy out in the rain, do you? Be a good dog for Mercedes. We have to hurry so we can go home. The girls are waiting for us. *Nina's* waiting for us."

At the mention of Nina's name, Baron suddenly stood up. His tail rose high in the air, and he began to quiver with excitement. Mercedes shoved the pajamas in his face once more.

"No Nina yet, Baron. Scent!" she repeated, this time in English. "Have you got it?"

"Just look at him! He's got it, all right," Cass said. "Come on, Twister. Seek!"

The dog didn't move. But he did prance in place, his ears lifted high, his nose frantically sniffing the air.

"Aren't we supposed to take off his leash?" Mercedes asked, pulling the clothing away from the dog.

"No. If he gets caught up in the search, he'll leave us both behind. Come on, Twister. Seek!"

The dog ignored Cass, his attention focused on Mercedes and this time she gave the order. "Seek, Baron! Seek!"

The dog pivoted so rapidly on the sand she barely had time to catch her balance and clamp her fingers tightly on the leash. Cass caught her arm to steady her, then they were both off at a fast pace, leaving the pajamas behind on the ground.

Jake had obviously taken a straight track, for Baron's trajectory ran directly toward the marsh. Mercedes heard Cass's muttered curse, and she heard the police and neighbors fanning out behind them. Cass continued to keep pace as Baron dragged Mercedes toward the muddy backwater behind the shoreline. Soon they were slogging through ankle-high mud made even muddier by the light rain.

Once they reached the deeper marsh waters and the sharp cutting marsh grasses, Baron slowed his pace. Mercedes slowed hers, as well. She turned toward Cass as Baron froze, his nose high in the air. Although she considered herself in good shape, she was breathing heavily. She noticed that Cass wasn't breathing hard at all.

"Cass?" she said uncertainly. "Why are we stopping?"

"It's the water," Cass replied. "It's slowing him down."

"Then it's all over?" Deep despair washed over her. "He can't track in the water?"

"Actually he can," Cass assured her. "Dogs can scent *over* the water. Twister's found victims in waterlogged areas before. He's even located missing swimmers—from a boat.''

"He was searching from a boat?" She looked at Baron again. His head was swiveling everywhere, his nose lifted, and he sniffed in rapid noisy inhalations.

"Yes. Rescue dogs even found a missing airplane that crashed in the Everglades. Twister wasn't in on that rescue, but he could have been. He has the nose for it.''

"But, Cass, the weather's so bad..." Mercedes looked up. If the black clouds were any indication, the light rain threatened to become a downpour.

"Labs have an incredible sense of smell, and Twister's is better than most. If Jake can be found, he'll do it.''

Mercedes twisted the leash around her hand as she waited for the dog to move on. "How will I know?"

"When Twister—Baron—wants to alert you, he'll point at the general vicinity if he can't get to Jake. If he's really close, he'll freeze and bark. If we can't see the victim, if the location is hidden, then we watch his tail.''

"His tail?"

"Yeah. If it wags fast, we've got a live find. If it wags slow, we've got an injured or dying find. And if it doesn't wag at all..."

"The victim is dead?" she asked bluntly.

"Yes."

Mercedes suddenly remembered something Nina had asked Cass. "What about the alligators?" she asked. "Were you telling the truth about them? That they don't attack people?"

"Alligators only hunt prey in certain size ranges. Adults exceed that size range. There *is* a danger to small children," Cass replied. "But rain makes it much harder for them to hunt. I'm more worried about the fact that Jake can't swim. This marsh empties directly into the ocean.''

Mercedes swallowed painfully, her eyes tracing the outline of Baron's black bushy tail as she prayed for it to start wagging furiously.

"What about the other rescue dogs? Where are they?"

"I don't know. Maybe the storm held them up."

"Oh, no. You mean there's just Baron?"

Suddenly she felt Cass's hand on her shoulder, his fingers gently kneading her back. "One dog is all we need. Give him a little encouragement, Mercedes," he said. "Just have a little faith in him, and he'll work wonders."

She nodded, feeling unaccountably better at his touch. "Come on, Baron," she said in a soft voice. "You can do it, Baron. Seek, boy, seek!"

Baron slogged through the deeper water, his nose high in the air, before he abruptly backtracked into the ankle-deep area again. He led them off on another track just as the rain started to fall in earnest.

Within minutes her hair was soaked, despite her windbreaker's hood. The wind had grown stronger; that and the sound of the rain prevented any more talk. The cloud-obscured sun started to set, and Mercedes felt her spirits sink, too.

We'll never find him, she thought with despair as Cass stopped to accept a flashlight from someone. He lit her way through the thickening darkness. One nasty blade of saw-toothed grass sliced right through the material of her jeans. The stinging pain of the razor-sharp edge caught her by surprise, and she stumbled. Again Cass was there to grab her arm and steady her. Only this time he didn't release her after she'd regained her footing.

His hand slipped down from her elbow to her fingers and held on tight. His other hand reached for the dog's leash. He took it from her, transferring the painful jerking of the dog's forward momentum from her aching shoulder to his.

Mercedes gasped with relief. Baron checked his rapid pace, turning around at the interruption. He hesitated, but at Mercedes's urging, he continued.

Mercedes glanced at Cass. She wanted to tell him how much she appreciated his help, but the noise of the rain had increased. Just the same, she mouthed a thank-you to him. When he squeezed her fingers and nodded, she knew he'd understood.

They went on, Baron leading the way in a zigzagging path. His black body was barely visible now, and the rescuers behind them could only follow Cass's flashlight beam. Baron and Cass half dragged, half led Mercedes through the hampering grass and murky waters of the marsh's edge.

Mercedes had no idea where they were, or even how much time had passed. A sharp pain stabbed at her side, and the cuts from the grass throbbed. The footing became more precarious as the wind and rain churned up rotting vegetation from the bottom of the marsh. She slipped and stumbled forward, Cass still supporting her.

"Take a breather!" he ordered, checking Baron's forward pace. Mercedes shook her head, thinking of that little boy, but Cass's arm was strong. He grabbed her waist and forced her to stop.

"You can't help Jake by collapsing yourself. We need you, Mercedes! There's no one else to work the dog."

Mercedes looked over her shoulder. She pushed her sodden hair back into her hood and shivered, suddenly aware of how cold she was. Lightning flashed, followed by the cracking report of thunder and another flash of lightning. It briefly illuminated the wet muddy rescuers behind them. Mercedes noticed that both parents had come along on the search. The swamp waters boiled around their knees from the downpour. Everyone stood there, waiting for her and Baron to continue.

It's hopeless, Mercedes wanted to cry. And it would be all her fault. She was no match for swamps, the storm, her own physical weakness. But then another flash of lightning illuminated Cass, who stood beside her, his arm fast around her waist. He was scanning the area, taking full advantage of the brief flashes. His face showed none of the panic Mercedes was feeling. Mercedes couldn't believe it. He actually looked confident!

She was grateful for that. She drew on his strength and made it her own. When he turned back toward her, much of her panic had subsided.

"Ready?" he asked easily, as if they weren't in the middle of a raging storm.

Mercedes nodded. His hand slipped from her waist to grasp her hand again. He gave her a reassuring smile and a quick kiss on the cheek. His touch melted some of the icy fear in her chest, and for the very first time since she'd left the cabin, Mercedes dared to hope.

The water got deeper with the rain, but Baron stayed near the shallower areas of the swamp. Suddenly his pace slowed, his body froze, and he barked. The leash went slack in Cass's hand. Another flash of lightning lit the rain dripping off the dog's thick black coat.

Mercedes held her breath, and watched as Cass shone his flashlight in a straight line beyond the dog's alert body. Other beams merged with his to show a child's air mattress bobbing on the water.

The boy's mother screamed, and Mercedes flinched at the sound. Suddenly she was back on that snowy mountainside, desperately waiting for news of Gilles....

Mercedes swayed when the others swam out into the deeper waters. Her knees buckled, and Cass caught her. She felt his fingers stroking the nape of her neck, his voice comforting, soothing.

She closed her eyes, refusing to watch as the searchers retrieved the tiny passenger on the mattress. She didn't need to watch, because she'd recognized that mother's scream.

It was a cry of joy.

CHAPTER ELEVEN

CASS HELD Mercedes's waist firmly. The walk back through the muddy marshes to Fred's cabin was fairly direct. It wouldn't take nearly as long as the hike out, but Cass was still worried about the woman next to him. Mercedes looked ready to drop.

He'd insisted she rest while Jake was reunited with his parents. The police had radioed for additional help, and since the storm was moving out to sea, boat traffic was again permissible. One of the Coast Guard crews had arrived with a swamp craft. It was barely large enough for the driver, Jake, a medic and his parents.

There was certainly no room for Mercedes, but if the boat hadn't already left, Cass would have insisted she take the father's place. Even some of the policemen had noticed Mercedes's exhaustion, and offered to make a human chair to carry her back. She'd refused.

Even now, she slogged back through the marsh under her own power, Baron at her side. Cass had expected her to collapse, but Mercedes continued to surprise him. She had reserves of strength, both physical and emotional, that amazed him.

For an untrained woman to take on a dangerous search-and-rescue mission in the middle of a raging storm was brave enough. But the fact that she stuck it out to the end, despite her own painful history with rescues, revealed courage that affected him deeply.

When the frightened, cold, but uninjured child had been loaded onto the boat, Mercedes had actually managed to smile. She'd accepted Jake's parents' profuse thanks, as if she'd been doing rescues all her life.

Her only complaint—if you could call it that—came after the rain had finally let up. Baron was shivering on the hike back, and Mercedes wondered why no one had thought to leave a blanket for him. "After all, he's an old dog. Nina would never forgive me if he got sick."

Someone located a soggy towel and Mercedes had graciously thanked the donor, wrung it out and dried Baron as best she could. Then she'd resumed the trek.

The rain had stopped completely by the time they reached Fred's cabin. One of the officers gave them—and Baron— a ride back to Cass's place.

"You three made our job easier tonight, especially since the other dogs were so late showing up." The muddy policeman exited the squad car to open Mercedes's door. She and Baron climbed out, followed by Cass. "Thanks for the help. And the happy ending."

Mercedes smiled weakly when the young officer bent down to scratch Baron's ears. Baron responded by shaking his ears, then thoroughly shaking the rest of his body. Water flew everywhere, and the policeman laughed as he got back into his car.

The girls were waiting wide-eyed at the front window. The minute Cass, Mercedes and Baron stepped onto the porch, the door banged open and the girls flew out.

Cass couldn't follow Nina's rapid Spanish as she fired off question after question. Even the reticent April was begging to know what had happened. He immediately put an end to their suspense.

"We found Jake, and yes, he's going to be fine. The rest of your questions will have to wait. Nina, you go with your mother. Grab her some extra towels, then bring me her muddy clothes when she gets into the bathtub, please.''

He reluctantly released Mercedes. "Will you be okay?'' he asked. Her face was even whiter in the starkness of the porch light.

Mercedes nodded. After commanding the dog to stay, she went inside.

"April, grab me some towels, too, would you? And some shampoo for me and the dog. He and I might as well wash up out here.''

April hurried in, her nightgown flapping around her knees. Cass was stripped down to his swim trunks when she reappeared. He shampooed the dog quickly and efficiently. Baron was so tired he didn't resist; he even allowed April to dry him on the porch while Cass turned the hose on himself for an impromptu shower. April let herself and Baron into the cabin, but came back with a clean pair of jeans and a fresh T-shirt for her father.

"Thanks, sweetheart,'' Cass said. "Go on inside while I change. I'll join you in a few minutes.''

Mercedes was seated on the couch when he came in, April beside her. Nina sat on the floor at her mother's feet, Baron's head in her lap.

"The girls made us something to eat,'' Mercedes said, gesturing toward the tray on the coffee table.

"I did the soup,'' Nina announced. "April made the hot chocolate.''

"We used the microwave, Dad,'' April added quickly, "not the stove.''

"Thanks, girls. I appreciate it.''

The cold marsh water and even colder hose water hadn't exactly been body warmers. Cass sat down in the recliner and gratefully took a big swallow of soup, but not before checking on Mercedes. At least the color was back in her cheeks, he saw with satisfaction. Her long hair was now clean, damp and spread loosely over the shoulders of her modest pair of summer pajamas.

"Feeling better?" he asked, pleased to see she'd waited for him to join her before eating.

"Much. I was just telling the girls what happened."

Nina's eyes were wide. "Baron was a hero."

Baron didn't raise his head from Nina's lap at the sound of his name. His tail thumped only twice before he wearily lowered it to the floor again. Cass frowned. First his concern for Jake, then Mercedes, had blinded him to just how exhausted the dog really was.

"Your mother was the hero, Nina," Cass managed to say calmly. "Baron wouldn't listen to me, but he did listen to her."

April blinked. "Dad! You called Twister *Baron!*"

"I know." Cass hadn't meant to bring up the subject of the dog tonight. But since he had, he chose his next words carefully. "Twister responds best to his new name, April. And his new family. The rescue proved that."

April was incredulous. "He wouldn't listen to *you?* Not even on a rescue?"

"No. I'm sorry, kiddo, but I'm afraid Twister is more their dog than ours now."

"I guess he'll be going home with Nina then," April said immediately. "That's okay. You still have Buddy."

Cass was completely bewildered. He'd expected April to be wearing that anxious look; instead, she seemed happy with his answer. But he merely said, "That's right. We still have Buddy."

Nina squealed with delight and clapped her hands, but it wasn't Nina's response Cass was watching. He set down his mug, left the chair and went to sit next to April, hoping to decipher her strange reaction.

April didn't respond to his hug or his presence—as usual. She stiffened in his arms and slid even closer to Mercedes.

Cass sighed, then withdrew to kneel down on the floor next to Baron and Nina. He caressed the dog's damp head, seeing the heavy sprinkling of gray beneath the lower jaw, hearing the heavy breathing, feeling the ribs laboriously rise and fall.

He met Mercedes's gaze, suddenly ashamed of himself. "You were right," he said. "Baron *is* too old to be doing rescues anymore." He pulled a spare comforter from the couch and wrapped it gently around the dog. For once, Nina allowed him near her pet, her eyes sparkling with joy.

"You take good care of him for me, Nina. This old dog and I have been through a lot." Cass tousled Nina's hair, then wished Nina's responding smile had been April's. "April, are you sure you're all right with this?"

April nodded. "I'm glad Twister will have such a good home." To Cass's continued confusion, April wasn't disturbed in the least. In fact, she was humming as she stood up and took Mercedes's empty soup bowl and tray to the kitchen.

"Go help her clean up, Nina," Mercedes suggested.

"Aw, Mom!"

"Come on, honey, it's late. Take this, too." Mercedes gave Nina her hot chocolate mug. "Then I think you should go straight to bed."

"Tell April to go with you," Cass added. "We'll come say good-night in a few minutes, then we're going to bed ourselves."

Nina took the mug and left, but not before giving the dog one final pat. She even graced Cass with another sunny smile.

"Well, Nina's certainly happy about this. Although I expected April to be more upset." Cass shook his head.

"No, Cass. April doesn't want any part of rescue work, and I can see why." Mercedes shivered, despite the snug warmth of the cabin. "It's very frightening."

"I suppose it would seem that way to some people."

Mercedes slanted him a curious look. "Aren't you ever frightened?"

"Of the search?"

She nodded.

"No. The scariest part is the waiting."

"I know about waiting," Mercedes said softly.

"I guess we both do."

There was a long silence. "Cass, tell me about your wife. About the night she died."

"You don't want to hear this," he warned. "Tonight was enough of a strain for you, what with Gilles's ..."

"Forget about Gilles, Cass. Tell me about your wife."

He looked up and saw the solemn expression in her eyes. He thought back to the night almost twelve years ago that had changed his life....

That Christmas Eve should have been a night of joy and goodwill. To Cass Montgomery, it was anything but.

The swaddled infant in his arms had cried herself to sleep. Thanks to the fury of a Wyoming blizzard, the log cabin's electrical power was out. The last of the gasoline for the backup generator had just been used.

"I'd better go out to the woodpile," Cass had said. He sat in the rocking chair, his new daughter well blanketed and cradled in his arms. "This storm is getting worse by the minute."

"I'll go." His young wife rose gracefully from her seat by the hearth. "It's the least I can do. This whole miserable trip was a bad idea from the start. I should have listened to my parents and stayed in town."

The troubled look on Marian's face wouldn't do, Cass thought. She should be smiling. It was Christmas Eve—their infant daughter's *first* Christmas Eve. He caught Marian's arm as she passed by, drew her wrist to his lips and kissed the soft inner surface.

"It hasn't been that bad," Cass insisted. "At least we've had some time alone. Since April was born, we haven't had a moment to ourselves."

Marian sighed. "She *is* the first grandchild on both sides."

"How could I forget? I've heard it at least twenty times a day from all four of her grandparents." Cass tenderly adjusted his daughter, then just as tenderly pulled Marian onto one knee. "They've all been constantly dropping in—not to mention aunts, uncles, friends.... You've been exhausted and cranky, and April's been off her schedule. But just look at her now."

Cass pushed back the blankets around his daughter's perfect little face. "Since we left town, she's been much happier. So have you."

Marian smiled down at her daughter, although the expression in her eyes was still troubled. "It's Christmas, Cass. My parents were heartbroken when they heard we wouldn't be spending it in Cheyenne with them. So were yours."

"You were stressed, and April wasn't nursing well." Cass deliberately made his tone gentle, hiding his irritation at four grandbaby-crazed adults. "The doctor said if things didn't improve, we'd have to put April on formula. You told me you wanted to nurse April for at least six months. That's why you took a leave of absence from work, remember?"

"I remember."

Cass pressed his advantage. "Well, you and April haven't had any problems here. She's eating well, and you've lost those shadows under your eyes." *And I haven't had to show pushy relatives to the door over and over again at all hours of the day and night.*

"I know we all needed some peace and quiet, but still..." Marian pulled her hand away from his grasp to rise and cross over to the window. "I don't know, Cass. The weather's awful and the power's out. Our vacation cabin wasn't built for babies."

"It was built for Wyoming winters," he assured her. "The cabin walls are good and thick. April's warm, fed and sleeping comfortably. We have plenty of food, and I chopped tons of wood. There's enough to keep a fire going until New Year's, if need be."

Marian was silent.

"Look, if it'll make you feel better, not only will I get the wood, I'll bring in a double load."

That got a response.

"No, I'll go. You two look so comfortable."

"It's awfully cold out," Cass warned her.

"I'm a Wyoming native, too. A little snow won't kill me."

"Maybe not, but that wind..." He listened for a moment. "It's definitely picked up. Come here and take April."

Marian shook her head. "You don't want to wake her up, do you?"

"Visibility's terrible out there." Cass hesitated. "At least take some rope for a lead," he said after a moment. "There's a coil in the kitchen under the sink."

Marian grinned. "Really, Cass, you've been watching too many old movies. I'm just going to pop out to the woodpile." She reached for her sweater and gloves, ignoring her heavy coat and boots. "Wait here. I'll be right back."

Only she hadn't come back. Not then, not that whole terrible night.

And a tortured Cass, tending the fire to keep a two-month-old infant warm, was reduced to frantic calls for help on the cabin's still-working telephone lines. But although he quickly reached the Rocky Mountain Rangers, help was slow in coming.

The sudden blizzard was one of the worst on record, even for an area used to massive amounts of snow. Other victims were missing, too, they told him. The search-and-rescue teams were in short supply. And those with the special rescue dogs trained to track humans in all conditions were even rarer. "We don't know when we can get someone out to you," they'd said.

"You don't understand! Marian was just outside the door," Cass begged above the howling wind. "She can't have wandered far! I've searched as much ground as I can, but I can't bring my daughter with me and I can't leave her alone for long. The power's out, and there's no one else to tend the fire! For God's sake, can't you hurry?"

But the blizzard was vicious and they couldn't. Roads were closed, choppers couldn't fly, and even ski and snowmobile travel was impossible on the rough wooded terrain. Once the wind died down enough for the special rescue-dog-and-handler team to finally arrive, it was too late.

Marian was found almost a mile from the house—first her sense of direction, then her life, taken by the swirling snow. A numb Cass had stood outside in the morning calm of Christmas Day, his daughter in his arms. He watched the tears run down the face of the dog handler. His own wouldn't come until much, much later....

"I'm so sorry," the middle-aged woman managed to choke out. Her gloved fingers were trembling as she stroked her dog, a massive golden retriever with a thick silky coat. "We came as fast as we could, but the roads were bad, and we had to find a missing little boy first, and..."

The woman had to draw a deep breath before she was able to finish. "There just aren't enough of us to go around, Mr. Montgomery. I'm so sorry," she repeated, and started to walk away.

"Wait!" Cass called.

She paused and pivoted, the retriever at her side faithfully mirroring her motions.

"About your dog..." Cass said.

The woman's lips parted in confusion. "Champ?"

"Yes. Where could I find a rescue dog like that?"

"You can't find them. You have to teach them."

Cass had a sudden driving urge to know more. "How?"

"My husband and I both belong to a national search-and-rescue team. They helped train us and our dog."

"So you work for them?"

"We're volunteers. We all pitch in whenever we can. I only wish—"

She broke off as April started whimpering with hunger. A medic approached with a warm bottle from the ambulance. Cass carefully uncovered his daughter's face to feed her, then his eyes were back on the rescuer.

"Thank you for finding my wife."

"But we didn't... I mean..." The woman didn't finish. She was obviously deeply distressed. Cass hurried to reassure her.

"You did your best. That means a lot to me." Cass gave her a ghost of a smile. "I'm very glad you found her. I—"

Cass stopped as April spit out the strange-tasting rubber nipple and whimpered again. The helpful medic tried to take her from his arms. Cass shook his head. He readjusted April's heavy woolen blankets and patiently inserted the nipple again. It wasn't until April took it that he asked, "About your rescue organization—would you write down their address? I want to send them a letter. You know—tell them how grateful I am."

"That's okay, sir. You really don't need to do that."

"*I want to,*" Cass said fiercely, so fiercely that after a moment of stunned surprise, the dog handler followed him into the cabin.

A few minutes later, Cass carefully slid the paper into his coat pocket. "Thank you."

The woman nodded, and Cass walked her to the door.

"I apologize for taking you away from home on Christmas Eve, but I hope you and your husband have a real nice Christmas Day."

He hugged April to his chest with one arm, reached down to pat the dog's head with the other hand, then held it out to the handler.

"Thank you again, both of you."

The woman choked on a sob, squeezed his hand instead of shaking it, then left.

And after the funeral, so did Cass. He left behind his thriving law practice and the nursery Marian had furnished with such loving hands. He left his bitter unforgiving in-laws and his own well-meaning parents, who vehemently insisted April would be better off with them.

Except for his motherless baby, Cass left behind everything he'd ever known and loved. And slowly, eventually, the healing process began.

It was his daughter who kept him going. But it was his new search-and-rescue dog, Twister, who kept him sane....

CHAPTER TWELVE

"OH, CASS, I'm so sorry."

"It's all right, Mercedes. It was a long time ago." Cass left his place on the floor and joined her on the couch. "But now do you understand what I mean? As long as I'm not waiting, as long as I'm actively searching like tonight, I'm not afraid."

"But I *was* afraid, Cass, and I was searching, too. I'm such a coward."

Cass shook his head. His hand rose to stroke her cheek. He lifted a strand of her hair and tucked it behind her ear. "You're a very courageous woman, Mercedes."

Then, as he had on the beach, he cupped her face in his hands. But now he had time to pull her close, time to leisurely kiss her, time to savor the taste of her lips.

She said his name, a feeble attempt at a protest neither of them took seriously. She said his name again, and suddenly he found himself wondering how quickly that cool voice would heat up in the throes of passion. The thought was so enticing Cass actually trembled.

Yes, he'd dated from time to time, but as a single parent, he'd had little time or energy for anything other than casual friendships. Mercedes evoked urges he hadn't experienced so strongly since his wife died.

And those urges wanted fulfillment. He could tell she felt the change in his kiss. This time when she pulled away in protest, Cass knew he'd gone too far. He let her retreat.

They stared at each other for a long moment. Mercedes spoke first.

"It's been a wild night," she said, her head lowered, her words shaky.

Cass smiled. "Not many people I know could do what you did."

"You're the one who was brave. I couldn't have managed without you there. The dog's incredible—I hadn't realized. And you know just what to do. I wish..." She lifted her eyes to his.

"What, Mercedes?"

"I wish you and Baron had been there to look for Gilles. Maybe Nina would still have her father."

His hand dropped from her cheek. Cass felt his gut wrench.

"Cass?" Mercedes asked hesitantly. "Did I say something wrong?"

"I wish I'd been there too, Mercedes," he replied bluntly. "Maybe then you could get on with the business of living."

"*Me?*"

He heard her soft gasp, but refused to back down.

"You. You're one raw open wound that bleeds and bleeds and bleeds—not only for Gilles now, but for Nina. My God, Mercedes, that isn't life! That's death! It's such a waste. How can you do it?"

"Do what?"

"Be so strong one minute and so weak the next. You're hurting your daughter by allowing her to wait for Gilles!"

"I'm not allow—"

"You are! You cater to Nina's every whim. Your every waking thought is on her. No wonder she hasn't faced her father's death. You've made it possible for her *not* to."

Mercedes's hands flew to her mouth. "How can you say that?"

The pain in her eyes tore at him, but he couldn't stop. Wouldn't stop.

"You've wrapped Nina in a protective cocoon. You've sheltered her so much she can't heal. So she just suffers silently, waiting. And we both know how deadly that kind of waiting can be."

"She's doing better," Mercedes insisted.

"She's doing worse. I can see it in just the short time she's been with me. I know all about people hurting. I deal with it year in and year out. Nina's hurting and she's getting worse. And your being Nina's safety net isn't helping. This is one fall she's going to have to take alone. For God's sake, Mercedes, let her hurt and be done with it!"

"I have no intention of abandoning my daughter," Mercedes flung back. "I suggest you concentrate on your own daughter's problems and leave Nina to me."

"I would, but I can't. I've tried. No one's been able to reach April in the past three years except you. I honestly believe you're the very last chance my daughter has to be happy. April and Nina both need your strength. So face the facts."

Mercedes's anger grew. "Whose version of the facts, Cass? Yours?"

"The only version there is! Your husband is dead, Mercedes. He's never coming back. And if you don't force Nina to see the truth, she'll be waiting for him until she's old and gray. And it'll be your fault."

The words hung in the air, stark, cutting and undeniable.

"You're cruel." Mercedes' voice dropped to a whisper. "I never thought you could be so cruel."

"Life is cruel," he retorted. "My wife is dead, and my daughter might as well be, because she's dead inside. And the one woman—*the one woman*—who could possibly help April is too busy propping up her own daughter's sick fantasies. Well, I'm not going to stand by and watch *my* daughter drift farther and farther away from me. Or watch Nina cry in my arms because she doesn't dare cry in yours!"

"What . . . what are you talking about?"

"Nina asked me if I thought her father was dead."

Mercedes anger was furious and immediate. "I told you not to talk about that to her!"

"I didn't bring up the subject—Nina did. But this is exactly what I'm talking about! You're so busy trying to avoid upsetting Nina that she's become more confused than ever. *Let* Nina get upset. Let her rant and rave, but let her face the truth. Is that so hard to do? Or are you so wrapped up in your own grief that you just don't care?"

"I don't have to explain myself—or my daughter—to some stranger the courts threw at me!"

"I'm not giving you a choice, lady. I'm not going to watch your child suffer any longer. Someone's got to help Nina face the facts, because if her fantasies and rebellious behavior isn't a cry for help, I don't know what is."

"I'm doing all I can!"

"It's not enough." His brutal words battered and wounded, and still he continued. "If you're brave enough to trek through an alligator-filled swamp to rescue a child you don't even know, you're brave enough to save your own daughter. And mine, too, damn it! Mine, too!"

There was another long silence. When Mercedes spoke, he saw something in her face he'd never seen before.

Hatred. Her next words confirmed it.

"I wish to God I'd never met you."

He rose to his feet. "That makes two of us. And if it wasn't for April, I'd cheerfully wish you back in Phoenix. Because at least then I wouldn't . . ."

"Go ahead, say it. You've said just about everything else. You wish I was back in Phoenix because . . ."

Her harsh tone pushed him over the edge.

"Because then I wouldn't have to look at the stranger April trusts more than her father."

There was a terrible stillness.

"That can't be true, Cass," she finally said. "April trusts you."

"Open your eyes, Mercedes. Better yet, just leave me alone."

"Cass—"

"Shut up, Mercedes."

Cass leaned his head against the couch back, damning himself—and her—a million times over.

They remained silent on the couch, while the blanketed dog at their feet slept on. No one noticed the girls peering around the corner of their bedroom door.

"Mom said to go to bed!" Nina pulled at April's nightgown sleeve.

April yanked her arm free and gave the younger girl a little shove. "Be quiet! I can't hear what they're saying!"

"That's because they aren't talking anymore, stupid." Nina climbed back into bed and pulled up the covers. "Close the door. The light's shining in my eyes."

"This is my room, and I want the door open."

"Aaaa-priiil!" Nina protested. "I can't sleep with the light in my eyes!"

April gritted her teeth. How such a nice lady like Mercedes could have such a bratty daughter was beyond her. "Then pull the covers over your head, you big baby, because I'm not closing the door!"

To April's relief, Nina did. April again concentrated on listening carefully. She hoped she hadn't missed anything. She waited a long time, but there were no more words. She waited even longer. Still nothing. April had almost concluded that both adults had fallen asleep on the couch. She started to go back to bed.

But wait, her father was talking again. What was he saying now?

"Mercedes, I'm sorry."

Sorry for what?

"For what?" Mercedes echoed April's thoughts. "Telling me to shut up? Or telling me what a terrible mother I am?"

"I don't want to talk about that right now."

Cass's conciliatory tone had become angry again. Darn that Nina, April thought with annoyance. She *had* missed something!

"When?" Mercedes was demanding. She sounded upset, too.

"When you come to your senses," her father replied. Her dad's voice sounded strange, thought April, almost like he wasn't her dad at all. "Since I doubt that's going to be any time soon, I'm going to go to bed. I suggest you do the same."

April shivered. Dad was using his I'm-really-angry voice. What was wrong? What had Nina's mother done? What if he was sending Mercedes home tomorrow?

What if she never saw Mercedes again?

For an awful moment April thought she might be sick. The queasy feeling that Mercedes's presence usually chased away returned with a vengeance. April grabbed at her stomach with one hand, put the other on the wall to steady herself and crept a little farther into the hallway. She watched her father head for the kitchen, returning with a forgotten piece of silverware. Mercedes followed.

"What am I supposed to do?" she asked. "Pretend this whole conversation never happened? In one breath you say I'm doing a bad job with Nina and in the next you expect me to work miracles with April."

"Right now, I don't expect a damn thing," Cass said. "I'm tired. I'm going to bed."

"But—"

"Go, Mercedes."

April shook her head in confusion. Work miracles with her? What was going on?

There was another pause. Then she heard Mercedes again. "Do you think Baron'll be all right?"

"He just needs a good night's sleep. I'll take him to the vet first thing tomorrow if he hasn't bounced back. I wouldn't want you flying home with a sick animal."

But the judge said we had to spend two weeks in Arizona! Unless that doesn't count anymore. Is Mercedes going to leave without me? April felt her stomach lurch again. She almost ran for the bathroom, but swallowed hard instead and kept listening.

"We can leave the day after tomorrow," Cass announced. "I'll make reservations in the morning."

We're still going to Arizona? April held her breath.

"But you gave Nina the dog! And after everything that's happened, you still want to come back with us?" Mercedes said incredulously.

"We had a deal, remember? So we all go to Phoenix. Don't try to get out of it."

April nearly fainted with relief. That was Dad's I-said-what-I-meant-and-I-meant-what-I-said tone. Even Mrs. Borden never argued when Dad talked like that.

"If Baron checks out okay, I see no reason we can't all leave at the end of the week," her father went on.

There was the sound of water running in the kitchen. Her father must be rinsing off the dishes. It was a few minutes before April heard the adults enter the living room again. She retreated down the hall where she wouldn't be seen.

"I should sleep out here and keep an eye on Baron," Mercedes was saying.

"I'll do that."

"But you said Baron's our dog now. I can't expect you to take care of him."

"Must you argue? You're as exhausted as the dog." April noticed that the hard edge in her father's voice was gone. He suddenly sounded very, very tired. April wondered if he should let Mercedes stay with Twister, after all.

"Go to bed, Mercedes."

April tensed, uncertain whether to go back to bed herself or to head for the bathroom. Her stomach still felt iffy, but she didn't want to be caught sneaking around. Neither did she want to miss anything. She remained where she was to hear Mercedes say,

"He's one heck of a dog." It sounded as if Mercedes was stalling, the way April stalled when she didn't want to go to bed. April watched her bend to pet Twister. "Thank God he was here."

"When I think of the past three years," her father replied, "and all the people Baron could have helped and didn't..."

Because I turned him loose. April started to shake.

"One great thing about Baron—he almost always makes live finds. I can't say the same about Buddy."

Buddy finds more dead bodies than live ones. She's not as good as Twister. No dog is.

"At least one family had a happy ending tonight," Mercedes said, sounding almost as strange as her father.

Those other families didn't. And it's all my fault.

"Somehow, someday, I'm going to find out the name of that idiot who turned Baron loose at the airport—there's no way that cage could've opened on its own. And when I do, I'll file a lawsuit so fast it'll break records—if I don't break his murdering neck first."

A *murderer?* Was *that* what she was? April gasped audibly. She barely heard her father's, "Who's out of bed?" as the hall seemed to tilt and spin.

"April, is that you, honey?"

April didn't answer. Her eyes rolled back and she fell to the floor in a motionless heap, her hands clutching her stomach.

CHAPTER THIRTEEN

"ARE YOU SURE she'll be all right?" Cass anxiously asked April's pediatrician.

The next morning found them both at the doctor's office, instead of the vet's. Baron had risen fit and fine. He'd eaten a hearty breakfast, played in the sand with Nina, then contently curled up for a late-morning nap at the foot of Nina's bed.

April, on the other hand, had spent much of her night in the bathroom throwing up. Even when the last of the spasms had finally passed, she looked so ill that Cass wanted to take her to the emergency room.

Mercedes stopped him.

"Cass, it would just make things worse," she objected. She was sitting on the closed toilet, April in her lap, and sponging the girl's white clammy face. "I don't think this is anything clinical."

"Then what exactly would you call it? She's never passed out before!" Cass's words were rough with worry. The sight of April motionless on the floor had absolutely terrified him. He hadn't felt so shaken since the night Marian had disappeared. "She needs to go to the hospital right now!"

April whimpered at his words and held tightly on to Mercedes. Cass watched as Mercedes dropped the washcloth into the sink. She gathered the child even closer, reached for a brush and calmly stroked the short tangled hair.

"I took her temperature, Cass. It's normal." She looked up, her soft brown eyes meeting his. "I think...this is all nerves from the rescue."

"You think? You aren't a doctor!"

"No, I'm not. But I do know that if you take April to the emergency room, she'll be stripped, poked, prodded and sent home, anyway. It'll just add to the trauma. Let her stay here with us. They can't do anything for her that we aren't already doing."

Cass hesitated, something he rarely did. Usually he was so confident, so decisive, but now he felt like a rookie out on his first rescue. He knelt, his face close to his child's. "April, sweetheart, tell Daddy how you're feeling. How's your tummy?"

No answer.

"Does it still hurt? How about your head? Do you have a headache?"

Still no answer.

"Do you want me to take you to the hospital?"

That got a response. April shook her head.

"Are you sure?"

April nodded. Cass touched April's forehead to smooth back the sweat-soaked bangs, but April immediately shied away. He stood there in the bathroom, watching his daughter's suffering, yet powerless to help. He was forced to let an outsider hold her and dispense the comfort that should have been his to give.

The next morning the pediatrician concurred with Mercedes's diagnosis.

"Physically she's fine, Mr. Montgomery," the pediatrician assured him from her office while April dressed in the examining room. "Keep an eye on her, though. If she isn't eating well or sleeping through the night, give me a call. You might want to have her talk to her psychologist again. Your rescue work is obviously very stressful for April."

Cass nodded, collected April and headed back to the cabin. But this time he took the back roads instead of the highway, wanting the extra time alone with April.

"If your stomach's up to it, shall we stop and grab an early lunch?" Cass asked. "You hardly touched your breakfast. How does some soup sound?"

"Nah." April continued to look out the window. "I'm not hungry."

"How about a drink?"

She shook her head, and Cass sighed. As usual, April was being uncooperative. However, in the car she was a captive audience, so he might as well take the plunge.

"I have something I want to say, April. I owe you an apology."

His daughter actually looked at him then. "Me? For what?"

"For scaring you. For not realizing how much rescue work frightens you. April, you don't have to have anything to do with rescue work anymore."

"I don't?" Her mouth remained open in amazement.

"No. From now on, you stay home."

"I ... I don't have to help anymore? Not even with the puppies?"

"Not even with the puppies," he said. "I really thought you liked being with me and training the dogs. I was wrong. It's obvious now that you don't."

"I used to. But when I started thinking about it..."

Cass held his breath as she paused, afraid she'd clam up again if he pressed. He reminded himself to be patient, to wait. Finally April spoke again.

"Those puppies will end up finding dead bodies, too. Just like my mother's. I don't want to see someone's dead mom."

"Oh, sweetheart, of course you don't! No one ever does."

"But *you* do it! I thought you wanted me to be a rescuer, too. You know...because of Mom."

Cass flinched at her words. "April, I would never force anyone to do what I do, especially a girl your age."

"You always brought me along."

"Only to the training sessions, April. And only because I thought you enjoyed it—and because I enjoyed your company. I swear I wasn't trying to turn you into a...a miniature version of myself." Cass shook his head. How could he have failed to see just how deep April's unhappiness ran? And why had she hidden it for so long?

"I hate it." A lone tear traveled down her cheek. Cass swore as more tears followed her first. He pulled over to the side of the road and slowed the car to a stop.

"Why didn't you tell me this sooner?" he asked as he unfastened his seat belt and slid over, his arm going around her shaking shoulders.

"I tried," she whispered, "but I was too scared."

"You were frightened? Of what, April?"

No answer. Cass reached for her, sick with worry at the hopeless expression on her face. "Were you afraid of *me?*"

"I thought you wouldn't love me anymore if I told you."

"April, that will never, ever happen!" he vowed. "I'm your father. No matter what, I'll always love you."

"No, you won't."

April shook off his arm and abruptly pulled away. There was an alarming silence in the car. This was no childish tantrum, he realized. Cass took a deep breath, forcing himself to remain calm. "Tell me, April. Why do you think I wouldn't love you?"

"Just...because."

"Because?" he gently prompted.

"Because I'm a bad person." The words were so soft Cass had to strain to hear them.

"You're a *good* person, April. Not wanting to do rescue work does not make you a bad person."

"That's not why." He saw April swallow hard. "It's something else. Something I did."

"Go on."

April clenched her hands into fists and said nothing.

"Nothing can be *that* bad, pumpkin," he said, trying to inject both comfort and reassurance into his answer.

"It is. It *is.*"

"*How* bad?"

"When I die I won't go to heaven. I'll never get to be with you or my mother." She looked straight at him, her expression as bleak as her words. "Ever."

Truly frightened, Cass reached for her again, but this time April actually hit his hand away. He made himself withdraw, even as his heart bled at her rejection.

"You're wrong," he said forcefully. "I'm your father, and believe me when I tell you this. You *will* go to heaven."

Silence.

"When that day comes I expect you'll be old and gray. In the meantime I want you to tell me what's making you so unhappy."

She turned away from him.

"April, please," he begged. "I promise I won't be angry. I promise to do everything I can to help. But I can't do a damn thing if you won't talk to me."

April shook her head over and over again as she hugged herself hard. Her pain and anxiety was almost palpable, and finally Cass couldn't bring himself to prolong it.

"It's all right. You don't have to tell me if you don't want."

April stopped shaking her head began to and shiver. Cass rested his hand on daughter's shoulder; this time she didn't shove him away. Her skin was ice-cold.

"If you won't talk to me, promise you'll talk to Mercedes."

She didn't agree. But to Cass's relief, she didn't disagree, either.

"You don't even have to promise," he amended. "No pressure. Just...think about it, okay? Let me know you'll at least do that."

April nodded her head, just one short jerky nod. If it wasn't for that motion, that tiny ray of hope, Cass didn't know if he could have made the drive home. He sat there awhile, trying to calm himself, ignoring the passing traffic. But when a large truck blared its horn, Cass reached for his seat belt and fastened it.

"It's awfully close to lunch," he said, sounding as normal as possible for April's sake. "And we have to pack, too. I guess we should be getting back."

April said nothing. But once he was on the road, Cass reached for her cold hand and held it tight. He vowed to get the four of them on Thursday's flight for Phoenix.

NINA WANDERED up and down the aisle on the plane, one hand outstretched and slapping every seat she passed as she sang various selections from *Camelot*. Nina made certain to slap April's seat especially hard.

"Dad!" April protested. "Make her stop. That's the third time already!"

Nina smiled angelically and kept singing. At her mother's "Nina, sit down!" she headed back toward her seat in the plane's first-class section—which fortunately was again empty. Only this time, she didn't sit next to Mercedes. She sat next to April, who immediately moved three rows ahead. Once again, Nina moved to sit next to her.

"Nina..." Her mother warned.

"I'm just trying to be friendly," Nina replied in her sweetest, most innocent voice. Mercedes wasn't fooled one bit, nor did Nina expect her to be. Her mother could be awfully smart about some things—and awfully blind about others. Like about April. And April's father.

The Montgomerys want my mother, pure and simple. Any idiot can see that. And April was particularly pathetic about it. But Nina was in no mood to share her mother with anyone except her father. She had her dog, and she was all set to go home—*without* two Montgomerys in tow.

Nina ignored Mercedes's frown and stayed beside April, still singing "If Ever I Would Leave You." She thought the verses appropriate. Maybe April would get the hint.

"I'm sick of that song," April complained. "Go sit somewhere else. There's lots of empty seats."

Nina immediately switched into a rousing version of "Oklahoma," making a point of increasing her volume just enough to annoy April even more, but not enough to attract the attention of the two adults behind them.

"Don't you ever shut up?" April grumbled.

Nina grinned again and continued singing. This was too easy. April Montgomery was an only child, not used to the rough-and-tumble ways of numerous cousins fighting for territorial rights. Nina had been scrapping for her place in the Delacruz pecking order ever since she'd been in diapers and an older cousin had first swiped her favorite teething ring.

Nina had learned fast that territory was won, not awarded, in large extended families. And there were lots of things to fight for—like who got the extra drumstick, the wishbone or the very last cherry Popsicle. Or who went first on the swings and the slide, who played with the newest toys and who got a window seat in the car.

There were a hundred serious issues to be decided if life was to progress smoothly, and Nina knew all the rules. She'd had to learn them thoroughly, for only a few cousins had outright advantages. The very oldest had their size. The very youngest had the adults' protection. The children in between had only their wits. Fortunately Nina thought fast and acted even faster. And she knew when to retreat. Consequently, in any group of children, she could hold her own and then some.

April, on the other hand, was the proverbial sitting duck. Nina knew she wouldn't stand a chance with *any* Delacruz child over the age of three—even over a cherry Popsicle, let alone such an important prize as Baron. *Or Mercedes.*

Nina almost, *almost* felt sorry for her opponent. Then, to compensate for that feeling of weakness, Nina sang two more verses of "Oklahoma" with nonsense words before shutting up. She turned toward her opponent and waited to see what April would say.

"I hate you," April announced.

Nina rolled her eyes. She'd given up on that strategy in kindergarten. It never worked on anyone, not even on her great-grandma Delacruz, and she was the softest touch around.

"I'm telling Mom you said that." Nina flipped her long hair, à la Vivien Leigh's Scarlett. "She won't take you on any more shopping trips. She won't even want to talk to you."

"That... that's not true!"

"You'll see." Nina watched April nervously chew on her lower lip and added, "After all, I'm her daughter. You're just a stranger."

"Am not!"

Nina sighed. Five-year-old Julio Delacruz could do better. She might as well finish this off right now. The rules said you could annihilate any opponent, but you had to do it quickly with the weak ones.

"Mom is *my* mother, not yours. She doesn't need another daughter. She has *me.*"

"If I had you for a daughter, *I'd* want another one!" was the sharp retort.

Nina's eyes narrowed. That wasn't much of a retaliation as far as the Delacruz rules of war went, but for April, it was almost a full-fledged volley.

"Then take out a classified ad," Nina responded, borrowing from fifteen-year-old Constanza Delacruz's repertoire. "But Mom *doesn't* want you around. Or your dad, either. Tell him to go home and take you with him."

April's smile this time was almost as sweet as Nina's earlier one. "My dad likes her. *I* like her. And *she* likes us both. That's three against one. Or can't you count?"

Nina inhaled sharply. Well, well, well! It appeared she'd underestimated her opponent. Nina decided to bring out the heavy artillery.

"What about Baron? Your Dad fought and fought to keep him, but who won that one? *Me.*"

"I never wanted Twister back in the first place," April spat.

"Right," Nina retorted.

"I didn't! You only got Twister because I let you have him!"

Nina blinked, confused by this latest volley. April's words had the ring of truth. "You gave away your own dog?"

"That's right. You ruined him, anyway. You...you made him almost bite me."

Nina's radar beeped. April might have told the truth about not wanting Twister, but she was lying about *why* she hadn't wanted him. Nina filed away this piece of information for future scrutiny and went back to her original attack. "Find someone else for a mother. Your dad can't marry mine, because she's taken."

"Your dad's dead, so she's *not!*"

Nina's mouth dropped open in shock. This one-sided contest wasn't so one-sided anymore. The last punch had been a direct hit. It took a few seconds to recoup her losses.

"My dad's still alive!" Nina insisted loudly.

"*My* father says *your* father is dead, and he should know! He's been doing rescues for years!"

"Dad's alive," Nina repeated. Her anger flowed white-hot. It required the greatest restraint not to smash April's lying mouth. She searched for and found a punishing retaliatory blow. If she wasn't so angry, she would have smiled.

"And when I tell Mom what you said, she'll really hate you then!"

Nina watched April turned white, then bury her face in her hands. Suddenly Nina didn't feel so good about the victory she was positive she'd just won.

"April... are you all right?"

"Go away and leave me alone."

Nina couldn't believe it. The girl was actually crying! That was against the rules! All the Delacruz children knew arguments weren't meant to cause tears—they were simply there to resolve problems. Unless, of course, you were very young. The older kids always had to give in to the babies when they cried. It was a strict rule enforced by children and adults alike. Crying constituted weakness, and you had to protect the weak among the family.

But April wasn't a baby *or* a member of the family. And she'd said her father was dead, so she deserved to lose! Still, Nina found herself in unknown waters. She wished Constanza was around to tell her what to do. Or maybe one of her aunts. Or better yet...

I wish my dad were here.

"April—"

"Go away and leave me alone!" April faced the window, but she couldn't disguise her sobs. Nina was reminded of her baby cousins, instead of an older girl. Suddenly she realized April was as helpless as any of them. Nina was surprised, then angry, then resigned. It appeared she'd have to let April have her way. "Look, I'm sorry. I won't tell Mom what you said, okay?"

"Really? You promise?"

"Cross my heart." Nina even added the physical gesture so desperate did April look. "There. Feel better?"

Nina didn't wait for an answer. Instead, she reached for the seat pocket and cocktail napkin she'd wrapped around her unopened bag of peanuts. "Here. You look gross." She pushed the napkin into April's hand. "Wipe your nose."

April did with one hand. The other still held her stomach.

"You want me to call your dad?"

"No!"

"Are you getting sick again like the other night?"

April didn't answer, but Nina grabbed the airsickness bag and passed it over, anyway. "Here, hold this, just in case. I'll get us some sodas. You like ginger ale? Mom says ginger ale is good for upset stomachs."

As she reached for the bell, she saw that her mother was watching them closely. For once Nina was hard put to respond with a smile. She was used to normal happy children. April Montgomery wasn't either of those.

What a mess! Nina thought. When the flight attendant arrived she asked politely, "Could we have two ginger ales, please?" even as she wished the Montgomerys far, far away.

Life was so confusing when people didn't play by the rules....

MERCEDES WATCHED the girls carefully. "Do you think April's all right?" she asked Cass. "Nina can be quite a handful."

The two of them had tacitly chosen seats in the same row—Cass in the end seat on the right side of the aisle, Mercedes on the left next to the window.

"If April was having problems, she'd move again," Cass replied. "Look, they've both ordered sodas from the flight attendant. They must have declared a truce."

"For now. I just wish April wouldn't let Nina push her around. Her cousins are an active bunch, and Nina's used to scrapping with them."

"It's nice she has them," Cass remarked.

Although she waited, Cass had nothing else to add. Mercedes felt restless, confused and depressed. Jake's rescue had certainly taken its toll on everyone except, perhaps, Nina. Cass's confirmation that Baron was indeed Nina's dog had certainly put Nina in high spirits...until she found out that April and Cass were still coming to Arizona with them.

Nina had made her feelings about that idea quite plain. As for Mercedes—she didn't know what to think. Just the thought of having Cass in her house sent her adrenaline, and her desire, into overdrive. She craved his company even more than she craved his body, and that craving was powerful enough. The realization horrified her. She was a widow who wanted to remain that way. Or was she?

Mercedes stole a quick glance at him when he went back to scanning the in-flight magazines. Watching Cass in action during the rescue had shown her more than just his strength and courage. He was an expert in so many things she'd never even thought about. He'd found his way in and out of a swamp in the dark of a storm. Dog or no dog, she couldn't have done that. He'd read Baron's reactions under the same poor conditions. He knew when to hurry, when to rest, when to push and, most of all, when to hope.

There was no doubt about it. Cass Montgomery was an expert in what he did. And he had no problem admitting when he was wrong. He'd trusted her judgment with April, hadn't he? Even when he'd found his daughter unconscious on the floor—a nightmarish situation for any parent—he'd bowed to her instincts, her decisions.

So why couldn't she do the same and listen to his suggestions about Nina? She honestly felt she was doing the best she could for her daughter. Battering her only child over the head with harsh reality couldn't be right, could it? Mercedes wanted Nina to accept the truth in her own good time. Not forcing it on her didn't make Mercedes a coward. She *wasn't* a bad parent. So why was she so angry—and so afraid?

Was she afraid Cass might be right?

Was she afraid to think about the future, a future that included not just Nina, but a connection with Cass and April?

Mercedes closed her eyes and rubbed her temples with her fingers. Loneliness must be catching up with her. Gilles had been gone for so very long. . . .

"Are you okay?"

Mercedes blinked, experiencing a feeling of déjà vu. "This is where we came in, isn't it?"

"I suppose it is."

"Well, I don't want any aspirin or a drink. This time I just want—" She broke off.

"What, Mercedes? What do you want?"

Mercedes looked at him. For once, his expression was as enigmatic as his daughter's as he waited for her answer.

"I guess I want everything to go back to the way it was— so Nina would have her father."

"That means everything would go back for you and Gilles, too. Is that what you want, Mercedes?" He continued to hold her gaze.

"I . . ." Mercedes fought against her sudden rising panic. "But what about Nina? What's going to happen when she finally realizes Gilles is dead?"

"I believe that ultimately Nina's a survivor, Mercedes. She'll come to terms with it." He shook his head. "She's not the one I'm worried about."

"Oh. You mean April."

"April—and you."

And despite the long flight to Phoenix, Cass refused to say another word.

CHAPTER FOURTEEN

"ARE YOU TWO MAD at each other?" Nina asked suspiciously. "Or are you mad at us?"

Cass didn't appreciate the question. The four of them were finishing their breakfast in Mercedes's Phoenix home, with Baron under the table. The meal had been a tense silent affair. So far their first full day in Arizona was off to a rocky start, made even rockier by Nina's question. "Mad" was hardly the word to describe Mercedes's reaction to his accusation that she was preventing Nina from accepting her father's death.

Judging by Mercedes's behavior ever since the night of Jake's rescue, "betrayed" was more the word. Whatever progress he'd made with her was gone. Right now, she didn't trust him any more than April did.

"I'm not angry, Nina," Mercedes replied. "I don't think the Montgomerys are, either."

"Maybe they don't like our food. We didn't like theirs. We'll have to give Baron the leftovers."

"I like everything," April said quickly. "It's great." To prove it, she popped a piece of melon into her mouth.

Nina wasn't convinced. "Maybe you're all jet-lagged. My dad always gets cranky when he flies. I never do," she added smugly. "And I've flown to Quebec lots of times."

Cass gritted his teeth at Nina's mention of Gilles St. Clair, then quickly glanced at Mercedes to see if she would correct Nina. Damn, he thought, taking in her pained expression, she wasn't going to even try.

The tension was so thick that Nina tried a new tack. "Is everything all right, Mom?"

"Just eat your breakfast, Nina," was all Mercedes said.

Cass busied himself buttering a piece of whole-wheat toast, wondering if Mercedes would ever make Nina confront the truth, discard the fantasy of her father's return. It was a heavy burden for a ten-year-old child. And the sad thing was that allowing Nina to maintain the fantasy wasn't helping either mother or child.

Then and there, Cass resolved to do for Nina what Mercedes was doing for April. Mercedes was too confused to help her own daughter, but he wasn't. And after all, he and Nina were two of a kind. They were both survivors. Unfortunately Nina's misguided efforts to deal with her loss were making the family situation worse, instead of better. It was time to take the blinders off. If she'd let him....

It wouldn't be easy. Nina was quick, Nina was tough and Nina had the instincts of an alley cat when it came to defending her turf. She'd made it clear she didn't want any Montgomerys near her dog, her mother or herself. But that didn't matter. Cass should be able to get through Nina's defenses. Ironically enough, he might not understand his own daughter, but Nina he could read.

He watched Nina finish her cereal, then slip Baron a bread crust, despite a house rule forbidding it. Nina caught his gaze. She defiantly lifted her chin, daring him to comment. Cass knew better. Nina wasn't above pitting Cass against Mercedes when it came to tests of loyalty, tests Cass knew he would definitely fail. After a few seconds, she deliberately fed Baron another crust, her eyes on him the whole time.

That didn't take long, he thought. *One meal in the Delacruz home, and the battle lines are already drawn.*

As Cass made no outward response, Nina went back to her meal. So did Cass. When breakfast was over he asked Mercedes, "What are your plans for today?"

"Well . . . I have to unpack and do laundry. Then I have to go through my mail and pay the bills. That should take most of the morning."

Cass cleared his own dishes as Mercedes put the milk and jam away. "And after that?"

"I'll fix you all lunch, then I'll swing by the museum. I want to check my messages—and my boss wants me back out to the ruins by tomorrow."

"So soon? You just got home. You haven't even had a chance to settle in."

Mercedes paused, her hand still on the handle of the refrigerator door. "I don't mean to be rude, Cass, but the museum wasn't happy about this...vacation. I've got a field study I have to finish. It'll take a couple days at least, maybe more."

"Isn't there someone else who can do it?"

Mercedes shook her head. "No. For this project, we're shorthanded as it is." She started wiping the counters. "We've had some pottery pieces, stone tools and jewelry turn up lately. They aren't authentic. All field archaeologists, myself included, are involved in tracking down the forgeries."

"There are always going to be unscrupulous people trying to sell forgeries. Why the sudden urgency?"

Mercedes paused, the wet dishrag motionless over a splash of strawberry jam. "We think someone's stealing materials from the ruins to create these phony antiquities."

"They're looting the ruins?"

"Uh-huh. Not only are they vandalizing our sites, they're making big money selling the fakes as genuine artifacts. There's a huge private market for antiquities in the Four Corners area," she said, referring to the junction of Arizona, Colorado, Utah and New Mexico. "Also in Europe. Lots of museums—even my museum—have been fooled into paying for them. They're that good. The masonry and rocks are especially popular with the thieves. They keep turning up as stone axes, hammers *manos* and *metates*."

"Mortars and pestals for corn?"

Mercedes nodded. "And some of the ancient adobe bricks have been fashioned into crude pottery shards. It's hard to tell the fakes from the real things."

"Why haven't the police and rangers been able to track down the culprits?"

"Because Arizona has thousands of archaeological ruins. We can't possibly guard them all." Mercedes scrubbed at the jam, taking out her frustration. "That's why I've been assigned to check out certain sites. Other museum workers are doing the same thing."

"So this is a statewide effort?"

"Yes. If we can pinpoint the location of the looting, the police and park rangers can set up surveillance teams. Maybe then we can put an end to both the fraudulent sales and the destruction of the ruins."

A chill ran through his veins. "Mercedes, I don't like the thought of you out there alone. What if you run head-on into these people? It could be dangerous. And if Nina's with you..."

Mercedes actually stopped her attack on the counter. "Cass Montgomery, I would never endanger my daughter!"

"But you just said—"

"Look, the particular ruin I've been assigned, Montezuma Castle, is probably the least likely site for looting."

The chill in his blood remained. "How do you know? What makes this place immune?"

"The structure has remained almost completely intact. Any structural theft would be immediately obvious. All five stories of it are still standing. You see, most ruins are in various states of decay. Some have crumbled so much that only the foundation outlines are left. Not at the Castle. We're talking complete preservation of the walls, floors, everything."

Cass whistled. "Even taking into account the desert climate, that's hard to believe."

"Yes, but Montezuma Castle is one hundred and twenty feet off the ground and built in a limestone recess. Also, the original builders, the Sinagua Indians, were skilled masons. So the location and construction have kept the Castle in a great state of preservation."

Cass said, "I think I remembered reading about it in the museum magazine."

Mercedes nodded. "Montezuma Castle is one of Arizona's more high-profile ruins. It's very popular with tourists, especially since it's easily accessible."

"How accessible?"

"It's only three miles off the interstate, and unlike most sites, has modern facilities. I'd say its popularity would make looting much harder than at some of the more isolated areas."

Cass could feel the icy chill drain from his body. As an added relief, Mercedes hadn't bristled at his concern.

"However," she continued, "this statewide search isn't going to be of any help if we don't check out *all* the ruins. My boss believes visual checks are mandatory. Plus, I have some other work to do out there—which is why I can't stay home and play hostess."

"I understand." He watched as she finished with the dishrag and rinsed it out in the sink. "Well, since there's no danger involved to the girls, the four of us can make a little expedition of it."

"Are you sure?" Mercedes asked uneasily. "I need at least a full day, Cass, maybe two. And this is the desert we're talking about. We hit the high nineties and one hundreds this time of year. Nina and I are used to desert heat—you and April aren't."

"You said Montezuma Castle had modern facilities," Cass reminded her. "Just let me know where April and I can rent camping gear. We won't get in your way. We can either give you a hand or sightsee on our own, whichever you prefer."

"Cass, camping isn't allowed at the park. I'm allowed to stay because of my job, and they don't mind if Nina comes along."

"Then we could all stay at a motel. Or just April and I could. You said the ruins were right off the interstate."

"I don't know..."

He deliberately ignored the unhappy look on her face, just as he ignored the fact that she obviously didn't want him along. "We'll be ready to leave whenever you are, first thing in the morning if need be."

You aren't getting rid of me that easily, Mercedes. Not by a long shot.

SATURDAY MORNING started well before the hot Phoenix sun rose. Mercedes had decided they would all book a motel and spend the weekend at the site. They loaded her Jeep with a couple of changes of clothing, water and food for the site. Her tools, camera and notebooks were stashed alongside the bag of dog food and the backpacks. The party was under way just as the first streaks of gray pushed up from the eastern horizon.

Predawn traffic was light. Mercedes had no problem entering the merge lane of Interstate 17, the major north-south highway. They were headed toward the Verde Valley, almost ninety miles north of Phoenix. It was there that Montezuma Castle overlooked the valley's Beaver Creek.

"If we're so close, why such an early start?" Cass asked as they set off.

"I like to take advantage of the cool mornings. And I can get a lot of work done before the visitors show up. Also, the drive is slow in places because the highway has some sheer drop-offs and sharp turns."

"I've never been to a desert before," April said from her seat in the back. She was peering anxiously out her window. "What if we see a rattlesnake? Or a scorpion? And I read there's tarantulas and Gila monsters here, too."

Nina rolled her eyes. "They hardly ever bite anyone. You sound just like a dumb *torista*, April."

From the rearview mirror, Mercedes saw April flush. "Nina . . ." she rebuked.

"Well, she does!" Nina replied crossly.

"Please excuse my daughter, April. She tends to be cranky when she has to get up early." Mercedes tossed Nina a pillow from the front seat. "Nina, apologize, then put your head down and close your eyes."

For a change, Nina didn't argue. "I'm sorry, April. Make sure you wake me for breakfast, Mom."

"Snakes and scorpions love the shade here," Mercedes told April in a reassuring tone, "just like your snakes in Florida. If you're careful around the shady areas, you'll be fine. And Nina's right. Gila monsters are very rare, and they and most Arizona scorpions aren't fatal to humans. That goes for tarantulas, too."

"But the snakes . . ."

"They prefer to conserve their venom for prey. That's why rattlesnakes usually shake their rattles when they're surprised by a human. They're giving you a chance to retreat. They'd prefer not to bite people. Venom production is a slow process."

"But someone could still get hurt," April fretted.

"I always carry antivenin in the cooler," Mercedes assured her. "But trust me, we won't need it."

"People go their whole lives in warm climates without getting bitten." Cass twisted around in the front seat to face his daughter. "Most of them never even see a poisonous snake."

"That's right," Mercedes seconded. "Believe it or not, the biggest danger to people out in the desert is the sun and the heat. But, April, we have plenty of water, and there are drinking fountains at the Castle. We won't have any problems."

April nodded, still frowning a little.

"Why don't you close your eyes, too?" Mercedes suggested. "We've got almost a two-hour drive ahead of us. There's another pillow in the back, if Nina hasn't stolen it."

"I'm not sleepy," April insisted. "I want to look at the cactus."

The sun had risen enough so that the towering saguaro and smaller branching ocotillo cacti could be seen.

"You really should take a nap. You too, Cass. Both of you are still on East Coast time."

"Actually I'd rather stay awake—if you don't mind conversation while you're driving."

Mercedes darted a quick look his way. He could see her defenses rising immediately, and her next words confirmed it. "As long as we keep to neutral subjects."

He refused to be intimidated by her warning. But with April awake in the back seat, he couldn't say anything other than, "Tell us a bit more about this ruin we're going to see."

Mercedes nodded, her attention back on the road. "Montezuma Castle is more than just a ruin. It's one of the country's earliest national monuments."

"How early?" April piped up.

"The park was established in 1906. The ruins themselves date back to the twelfth century." Mercedes gave Cass another quick glance. "You're familiar with the Southwest's cliff-dweller ruins?"

"I've read about the pueblos in your magazine. In fact, there was an article in that issue with the picture of you and Twister."

"I remember the picture," was her tart response.

Cass ignored it. "The article had some information about Montezuma Castle. It's one of the smaller ruins, isn't it?"

"Uh-huh. It's nowhere near as large as other major sites such as Mesa Verde in Colorado, which originally had over eight hundred rooms. Montezuma Castle only has nineteen."

"Who lived there?" April asked. "Who built it?"

"Well, the Verde Valley was once a rich floodplain. The Hohokam people were the first settlers of the area."

"Ho...what?"

"Hohokam. Accent's on the middle syllable. It's Pima Indian for 'those who have gone.' The farmlands in the Verde Valley were overfarmed and not fertile anyone, so the Hohokam migrated north, which left the valley free for the Sinagua Indians to move in."

"And they built Montezuma Castle?" April asked.

"Yes, but not right away. They originally dug pits in the ground and built houses over those holes. At first they were dry farmers—that is, they didn't irrigate, but relied on the rain to water their crops. Sinagua is Spanish for 'without water.' But then the culture began to change. They began to adopt the Hohokam methods of farming and began to irrigate, using Beaver Creek. And around 1150 they abandoned their pit houses and began building large pueblos on hilltops or in cliffs."

"Why?" April was leaning forward in her seat, taking in every word.

"The valley was once again becoming overpopulated. The big game in the bottoms was being overhunted, and farms were being raided."

"They were stealing the crops? How mean!" April exclaimed.

"Cliff dwellings provided a safer place for the Sinagua and their food supplies, at least for a time. But when the overfarming was coupled with a major drought, the valley couldn't support life anymore. In the early 1400s, the Sinagua Indians abandoned the whole valley, Castle and all."

"Where did they go?"

"Probably north, where the land was still fertile. You see, April, crop rotation and modern methods of agriculture weren't known back then."

"How sad."

"In a way it is. But the valley did come back in later years. The drought ended and the soil renewed itself. And the government decided to protect the ruins the Sinagua had abandoned—Montezuma Castle, which is the largest. And there's an old pit house excavation on display, along with Montezuma Well."

April put her hand on the back of Mercedes's seat. "What kind of a well? One with a wooden bucket?"

"No, not that kind. This is actually a limestone sink. The small lake down at the bottom was created by underground springs. The Well is four hundred and seventy feet in diameter, and there's a good seventy-foot drop below the Well rim."

"That's awfully big," April marveled.

"There are cliff dwellings on the inside just below the rim of the Well, and a few more right at the edge of the water, too. There's a tiny shore along the bottom of the path."

"Can we see them?" April's question echoed the one in Cass's mind.

"Sure. There are steps going all the way down to the bottom of the Well, because looking up is the best way to see the cliff dwellings inside."

"I want to go there!" April said.

"Count me in," Cass added.

"I'd love to take you. It's a shame more people don't visit the other two sites, but the Castle is where the ranger station, gift shop and exhibits are located. And the paved roads."

"Gift shops?" April exclaimed eagerly. "I brought my money."

"The gift shop is quite small, April," Mercedes warned. "Postcards, books, that kind of thing. This isn't Disney World."

"That's okay. I love to look."

Mercedes smiled at April's enthusiasm as she concentrated on passing some slower highway traffic.

"Is the Well water drinkable?" Cass wondered.

"No, there's too much limestone dissolved in it. But both the Hohokam and the Sinagua found it adequate for irrigation. In fact, even today the inside of the Well is a desert oasis. Which means it's full of vegetation because the Well is continuously fed by underground springs."

"But what about the Indians? Where'd they drink?"

Mercedes gave April a glance from her rearview mirror. "They drank from Beaver Creek. The water's clear and aerated, unlike the Well water." Mercedes shook her head. "I doubt anyone's been able to see into that black ooze for a long time. It's full of algae and limestone."

"Yuck," April said, making a face. "They should have named it Disgusting Well, instead of Montezuma Well."

"Montezuma Castle certainly doesn't sound like a Sinagua name," Cass remarked.

"Blame the early Arizona settlers. They thought the cliff dwellings had been built by the Aztecs. Hence the error."

"If it's wrong, why didn't they change it?" April asked, stifling a yawn.

Mercedes shrugged. "I'd guess because people used it for so long."

"Whatever it's called, I can't wait to see it."

"We've got quite a ways to go, April," Mercedes said with a smile. "You might want to take that nap, after all."

April didn't answer, but in a few more miles, she'd succumbed to sleep.

"It's nice to see April so enthusiastic," Mercedes observed. "I'm surprised she *can* sleep."

"It'll take more than April's enthusiasm to carry us through the next two weeks," Cass said quietly.

"It's a start. You could at least try to make the best of a bad situation."

"Spare me the clichés, Mercedes. You've been angry with me ever since we left Florida, and we both know why." He watched Mercedes's cheeks flush. "Don't think April's not going to pick up on it. Or Nina."

"Maybe if you'd concentrate on April, instead of Nina and how I raise her, you might keep April's spirits up!" Mercedes retorted.

"Do you really expect a few Indian ruins and a trip to the gift shop to wipe out April's problems? I still haven't been able to nail down what's bothering her. It has something to do with rescue work, but that's as far as we've gotten. Your anger isn't making things easier."

"I promised to find out what I could," Mercedes reminded him.

Cass took a deep calming breath, but it didn't dilute the harshness of his words. "That was before I knew how mixed-up you were, Mercedes. I don't know who's more confused, you, April or Nina."

There was a long silence before Mercedes spoke again. "I see. So does this mean I'm still the world's worst mother?"

Cass didn't like the way the conversation had changed. He should have stuck to chatting about the ruins. "Give it a rest, Mercedes. I never said that."

She refused to retreat. "You might as well have. You have a few things to answer for yourself—starting with those kisses in Florida to keep me around for April. Since I've fallen from my lofty pedestal, I guess I don't have to worry about you using *that* old ploy again."

"Pull over." His voice was white-hot with anger.

"What?"

"Pull this car over right now, or I swear I'll do it myself."

Mercedes took one look at his face and realized he was deadly serious. Fortunately, they weren't deep into the rocky mountainous area yet. She pulled over at the next wide patch of shoulder.

"Get out."

"Cass—"

"Get out or I'll drag you out."

He stepped outside and strode purposely around the front of the car toward the driver's side. Mercedes unfastened her seat belt and switched off the ignition. She hurried outside, keys still in her hand. Cass closed the door behind her. When he pivoted her way, his face was a study in controlled fury.

"I've tried to be patient, Mercedes. I know this isn't an easy situation for anyone, and you've got the worst of it. But get one thing straight. I wouldn't want any woman I had to bribe, beg or seduce near my daughter! And I wouldn't want any woman who even *thinks* that way! So if that's what you believe those kisses were, you can turn this car around and head straight for the airport!"

Mercedes stood up to his anger. "I'm sorry. I shouldn't have said that."

"Damn right, you shouldn't! But the insult wasn't half as bad as the motive behind it. You wanted to get back at me for what I said about you and Nina, and you didn't care how you did it. Well, congratulations, lady, your shot hit the mark."

He glared at her. "But it's not going to change a thing. It wouldn't matter to me if you were my most cherished lover or my most hated enemy. I'd still tell you the exact same thing. Gilles St. Clair is dead, and Nina will never face that loss unless you get tough with her. But you refuse to listen to reason! Breakfast this morning was a perfect example. You could have said something then, but no, you ignored it, as always."

"I didn't want to upset her meal!"

"You don't want to upset her, period!"

"Cass..." Mercedes backed away from him, her own uncertain suspicion that he was telling the truth frightening her even more than his wrath.

"Don't 'Cass' me. You can go to hell, Mercedes. Straight to hell with my blessing. But when you do, don't take your daughter along for company."

Mercedes was stung out of her shocked state. "What's that supposed to mean?"

"You really don't get it, do you?" Cass ran a hand through his hair. "Can't you see? It's what I tried to explain before—making things easier for Nina is only making things worse for Nina! In her own way, she's just as miserable, just as disturbed as April."

"That's a lie!" she spat. "Nina's confused, not disturbed."

"She's desperately unhappy!"

"How do you know? You're not a mind reader!"

"I know, because she told me so herself."

Mercedes's knees almost buckled. For a moment, the ground swayed under her feet, then she rallied. "When?"

"When you took April shopping and I had Nina for the day."

"I don't believe you! Nina would come to me before she'd ever confide in you!"

"You think so? And why is that, Mercedes?"

"Because I'm her mother."

"Then for God's sake, act like one!" Cass spun on the ball of his foot, the gravel underneath crunching as he made his way back to the car.

Mercedes stood motionless. After all the pain she'd experienced since Gilles's disappearance, she couldn't believe she was capable of feeling more. Could Nina actually have confided in Cass?

He couldn't be telling the truth, could he? she asked herself over and over again. Cars zoomed past her on the highway as she stood there. She felt cold and lifeless, even in the rapidly heating air of the desert morning. She didn't know what to think, what to do, where to go. She hardly noticed when Cass turned around and came back to her.

She stared at him, trying to understand the expression on his face and her own turbulent feelings. But nothing made any sense at all.

He put an arm around her waist, then gently propelled her to the passenger side of the Jeep. He helped her in, fastened her seat belt, then took the car keys from her hand.

"I'll drive," he told her. She didn't argue. He started the engine, and she felt his eyes on her. She turned toward the window. After a moment, Cass pulled out into the traffic, timing his entry to coincide with the opening left by a beat-up brown pickup truck.

He glanced curiously at the two men inside—both as disreputable-looking as their truck—then returned his attention to the road.

CHAPTER FIFTEEN

"MOM...MOM! Answer me!"

Mercedes looked up at her daughter from the outdoor bench where she was seated. Nina stood between her and the steep-walled creek bed that housed Montezuma Castle. The desert sun shone down fiercely, continuing to bleach the buff-colored cliffs in a centuries-old process.

"Aren't you hot, Mom?"

Despite the blazing heat that sent the living scurrying for shade, despite the killing temperatures that heated the black asphalt in the parking lot to a sticky spongy surface, Mercedes was cold. Cass's words had sent her back to that Alaskan mountainside. Thoughts of Gilles and death had chilled her thoroughly. She was cold on the inside, cold on the outside, cold through and through. She didn't think she'd ever get warm again.

"Not really, Nina."

"You should be. Everyone else is. We left Baron inside the building with one of the rangers."

"With Mitch?" Mitch was a particular favorite of Baron's.

"Yep. He gave him some water and let him lie down under his desk." Nina glanced up ahead at the path, where Cass and April were waiting beneath some trees. "I think you should get into the shade," she said urgently.

"In a minute. Right now I want you to take Cass and April around the loop and show them the ruins."

Nina scowled. "They don't need me. They can go without me. You can't get lost, and it's not a long walk."

That was true; the park service had paved a trail that led from the entrance building straight out to Montezuma Castle. Along the walk signs were posted describing the cultural and natural history of the area. The path traveled from the ruins to the old crop beds, creek and irrigation troughs, then looped around through the desert scrub and trees to bring visitors back to the entrance and exhibit building.

"They could," said Mercedes, "but since they're our guests, I want you to go with them."

"You come, too." Nina said stubbornly. "We'll wait."

Mercedes shook her head. "No, Nina. I want to stay here for a few minutes. Then I'm going to check out the ruins alone. You know you can't come with me for that."

Nina shifted her weight from one foot to the other. "At least wear your hat."

Mercedes picked up her khaki-colored safari hat and put it on.

"And have another drink," Nina ordered. She uncapped her canteen and handed it to Mercedes. "Here."

Mercedes took a swallow, then passed it back. "Thank you."

"Why can't we all walk to the ruin together? April wanted to watch you climb the side of the cliff."

"She can watch me later."

"Okay. You got a full canteen? And new batteries in your flashlight?" Nina pointed to the two items Mercedes had attached to her belt in the parking lot.

"I'm all set."

Nina hesitated. "Are you all right, Mom?" she asked.

Mercedes wasn't about to tell Nina about the earlier argument outside the Jeep—the argument both she and April had fortunately slept through.

"Sweetheart, I just want some time alone." She turned away from her daughter, away from Cass and his daughter, her eyes on the distant cliffs. "Go on, Nina. They're waiting for you."

Nina bit her lip, then set off. She waved, and Mercedes managed a small smile, but as soon as Nina's back was turned, the smile faded. The desert sun and the hot breeze gave way to old memories, and she was back in Alaska again.

Gilles hadn't come home. Friends and professional rescuers alike had searched in vain. Her life had frozen solid in that moment, as solid as the granite mountain Gilles had attempted to climb. She'd spent the time since then waiting for Nina to laugh again, waiting for both their hearts to heal.

But Nina hadn't healed, and Mercedes's heart had remained cold. The man of the snowy mountains who had brought those brief moments of happiness to her life was gone. It had been a man of the sun, instead, who'd begun to thaw her icy shield. Mercedes knew she'd shied away from that warmth, afraid of feeling again, of taking a risk again. It hurt too much.

She watched Nina and April going down the path, Cass behind them. He turned around once to try to catch her gaze, but Mercedes's face was obscured by her sunglasses and hat. He stopped for a moment and looked as if he was going to come after her, but she deliberately looked away. When she had enough courage to look toward them again, he and the girls were gone. The trees and winding twists of the path had taken them from view.

Mercedes felt more alone than ever. Gilles was gone, Gilles who'd loved his adventures and his mountains more than he'd loved his family. He'd been content to love her and Nina from afar. And Mercedes, who'd loved him despite everything, had learned to live with his frequent absences. She'd worked hard to make a stable home for Nina and accepted Gilles's passion for climbing. But she'd never understood it.

Unlike Gilles, she could no more have left Nina behind for months at a time than she could have cut out her own heart. Yes, she knew others lived like that. The families of men and woman in the military, of doctors and nurses with long hospital shifts, of people who traveled all over the world on business—they all grew accustomed to long separations. But Mercedes never had.

In her weaker moments, when she was alone at night and Gilles was away, she'd wish for a man who preferred his wife's warm bed to a cold sleeping bag on a mountainside. A man who'd be home for Nina's school plays and Nina's Girl Scout awards and Nina's birthdays. A man who'd stay home long enough for Mercedes to give Nina a brother or sister....

If only she'd fallen in love with a man like Cass, instead of a man like Gilles.

The thought pushed itself to the surface with a force that left her trembling. Mercedes actually rose to her feet, hurrying away from the birthplace of that thought as if she could actually leave it behind.

The Castle's path was deserted as she strode ahead. Although noon was still a few hours away, the sun blasted down through the clear turquoise sky. Mercedes found herself directly below the ruins, their primitive shapes illuminated and bathed in a primitive heat. Mercedes grasped a shaded portion of the iron railing that kept curious visitors on the path, and tilted back her head. As she studied the five-story structure, she wondered about the thoughts and emotions of the people who'd lived there.

She slipped under the iron railing, headed toward the modern combination ladders and ancient, carved toeholds that would take her up the face of the cliffs, and began to climb. The higher she climbed, the more civilization seemed to fall away. The sun beat down on her back just as it had on other women centuries earlier.

Those Indian women never had to worry about their men risking life and limb for the personal challenge and glory of climbing a mountain, Mercedes found herself thinking. Such craziness would be unheard of. The men protected their women and children. They didn't leave them alone at home without a very good reason—driving away against enemies or gathering food or assisting a needy member of the tribe, like an injured hunter or a lost child.

Suddenly the mental picture of an ancient Sinagua warrior made way for one of Cass searching the swamps for a lost little boy. And finding him. Shock knifed through her.

Was she falling in love with Cass Montgomery?

Mercedes rested her cheek against the sheer cliff wall and closed her eyes. She wasn't ready for this. She didn't want this. Being Gilles's wife had worn her out. Being Gilles's widow had drained her dry. She barely had the strength left to try to help Nina, let alone make a fresh start with another man. Except that this man swore he could help her daughter, and he believed she could help his.

It was too much. It was all too much.

Her whole world was falling apart. She was trying so hard to cope, yet understood nothing but the obvious. Like the way her cheek was scorched by the heated cliffside, or her sunglasses scraped against the sheer wall, dislodging a loose piece of rock. It fell onto her bare knee, then bumped against her boot. That rock she could identify; its actions she could deal with. But as for anything else ...

Mercedes began to climb again.

Finally she reached the lower front structure of the first story. She stepped inside an ancient room. The quiet coolness spread over her, but somehow it wasn't a welcome change. This was the cold of the past, of the long-ago dead.

The thick clay walls muffled sounds, dimmed the sunlight and cooled the air. Even the echo of her footsteps couldn't shake the tomblike feeling. Mercedes shivered. She reached for her flashlight, flipped on the switch and carefully began her inspection.

Room by room, level by level, Mercedes searched. The minutes passed into one hour, then two... three. Yet no matter how carefully she looked, no matter how many nooks and crannies she inspected, she found nothing out of order. Every wall was intact, every brick in place. The whole structure was as solid as ever.

She emerged into the desert sun again, one hand braced against the stone for balance. For a moment she stood blinking, the creek bed one huge blur while her eyes adjusted to the blazing light. She pulled her sunglasses out of her shirt pocket and soon her vision began to clear. There, far below, was Cass. She could feel his eyes on her, even as she felt the chill leave her skin. For a moment it almost seemed as if it was his presence, rather than the sun that warmed her blood.

But then Nina waved, and that strange spell-like notion was broken. Mercedes waved back, refastened her flashlight to her belt and began the slow, careful climb down. Cass, Nina and April watched her progress until she was finally on the ground again and once more in their midst.

"Weren't you afraid to climb those ladders?" an awe-struck April asked as Mercedes slid under the iron railing and stepped back onto the visitors' path.

Mercedes smiled at her. Nina had ceased to be impressed with Mercedes's cliff-climbing abilities years ago, and April's wide-eyed admiration was a welcome diversion from the silent brooding man at her side. Cass's gaze hadn't left her yet. Discomfited, Mercedes deliberately centered her conversation on the girls.

"No, April, I wasn't."

"She's had lots of practice," Nina added impatiently. "Come on, Mom, let's go inside. It's hot."

"Can't we stay a little longer?" April begged. "It's pretty neat here."

Mercedes managed another smile. "So you like our ruins, then."

April nodded vigorously. "I've never seen anything like this before."

"Well, I have—a zillion times—and I want a drink," Nina complained. "My canteen's empty."

Cass finally spoke. "It is awfully warm. We could all do with a drink. And you missed lunch, Mercedes. If your inspection's finished, maybe we should head back to the entrance building."

"There's not a brick out of place, so I'm ready. How about you two?"

She inspected the girls. Despite the straw hat Nina had lent her, April's cheeks were flushed. "Did you put sun block on?" she asked her.

"Uh-huh. And Dad made me and Nina drink from our canteens, but the water's warm." April grimaced. "I'm glad we went back to the Jeep to eat lunch. At least the sodas were cold."

"Too bad the air isn't," Nina complained.

Mercedes pulled Nina close, and kissed her forehead, then frowned. Even Nina seemed unusually warm.

"Head for the building, ladies. Mercedes can decide what she wants to do with the rest of the afternoon while we cool off."

"Sounds good to me." Mercedes clasped Nina's hand and gave it an encouraging squeeze. She held out her other hand, and April immediately took it. Cass was left to trail behind. Mercedes felt a sudden pang at her unintentional snub, then decided not to let it bother her. The four of them hurried back to the small entrance building as quickly as the heat would allow. Inside the air-conditioned room, April perked up. She wandered among the scorpion exhibit, squeaking over the "grossness" of the preserved specimens.

Nina had seen it before, however, and stayed at Mercedes's side. Her cheeks were still red with heat, and Mercedes noticed that she looked worse than before. She didn't even speak to Baron, who came out from his nap spot to greet them.

"Nina, honey, I want you to go to the ladies' room and splash some water on your face. I'll be there in a minute, okay?"

Her daughter listlessly did as she suggested. That left Mercedes and Cass alone, except for the dog.

"How did the girls do while I was gone?" Mercedes asked.

"We didn't go all the way around the path," Cass replied. He headed for the water fountain outside the rest rooms, Mercedes right behind him. "It was way too hot." He began to fill his canteen. "After the girls ran out of water, I had them go back to the Jeep. I turned the car on and ran the air-conditioning while we ate lunch. Hope you don't mind."

"No, not at all." Mercedes suddenly felt uncomfortable, remembering how and why he'd ended up with her keys.

"How are you doing?" he asked, finishing with his canteen and gesturing for hers.

"Me?" For the life of her, Mercedes didn't know how to answer that question. She fumbled at her belt.

"You missed lunch, and you were outside in the heat all day."

"Oh, that." She almost stammered with relief. "It's nice and cool inside the ruins. As for lunch, I wasn't very hungry."

"I'm not surprised. I didn't have much of an appetite, either." His face was expressionless, and suddenly the awkwardness of earlier returned full-fledged.

"I . . . I'm going to check on Nina. Baron, stay."

Nina was still in the ladies' room, bent over the sink and sponging water on her face with a paper towel.

"Feeling better, *bambina?*" she asked, smoothing back the loose strands of hair that had worked their way out of Nina's braid.

"*Sí*, Mama." Nina shut off the water.

Mercedes tidied Nina's appearance. "Maybe you should get your hair cut like April's. Short hair would be cooler."

"Forget it," Nina said with a trace of her old spirit. "Besides, you never cut *your* hair."

Mercedes bit her lip. Despite the inconvenience, Gilles had liked her hair long. When she freed it from the tie she usually wore, it stretched below her waist. She might as well get it cut, she thought. There was no one to object now.

"And," Nina continued, "*South Pacific* tryouts are coming up this summer. I want to go for the part of Ngana."

"Who?" Mercedes deliberately pushed away thoughts of Gilles toying with her hair late at night in their bed.

"Ngana. She's the lead actor's kid. I need long hair to look Polynesian." Nina dried her face and tossed the paper towel away. Then she entered one of the stalls.

"Do you want me to wait for you?" Mercedes asked, for Nina still looked uncharacteristically flushed.

"Mom, I'm not a baby!"

No, but you're all I've got.

"I'll be out in a minute." Nina firmly closed the stall door between them.

"Okay, but make sure you wash your hands when—"

"Mo-ther!"

Mercedes sighed loudly and left. Cass was waiting as she walked back into the lobby area.

"Is she okay?"

"She sounds better. But if the heat's bothering everyone, maybe we should call it a day. Excuse me a moment—I'll be right back." She walked toward the entrance counter, Baron in tow, where one of the two rangers manning the building was at the cash register. "Mitch, what's the temperature?"

"It's 101—about normal for here."

Mercedes shook her head in dismay, a gesture that didn't go unnoticed by Mitch. "The heat's never bothered you before, Mercedes."

"No, but I never had out-of-town guests with me, either. And even Nina's complaining today. I guess it's because they don't get to work inside the ruins where it's cool, like I do."

"Maybe you should call it quits."

"I'm way ahead of you. I might as well go find a motel now and pick up where I left off first thing Monday."

"Why wait until Monday?" Mitch asked. "Why don't you just come back tomorrow?"

"But the monument will be closed. Usually I wouldn't mind working here on a Sunday without facilities, and of course Nina's a little trooper, but I can't ask my company to rough it."

"No problem. I can let you have a spare key to the building for tomorrow. We can leave the air on for you."

Mercedes hesitated as the still-flushed Nina fanned herself with her hand in the distance. "Are you sure?"

The ranger followed her gaze. "Yep. I'll phone the main office, officially clear it with them and you'll be all set." He grinned. "We know where to find you if any exhibits disappear."

"If you really don't mind . . ."

Mitch shook his head.

"It *would* make things easier for me. Thanks, Mitch. I just got back from vacation, and I have a lot of catching up to do."

"Then take this." He opened the desk and passed her a spare key. "Just lock up and slide it through the mail slot when you're done. I'll get it when the place reopens on Monday."

"I really appreciate this. And thanks for watching Baron today, too."

He waved her off with a smile, then went to assist a young couple waiting to pay their admission fee. Mercedes returned to the girls and Cass, Baron at her heels.

"I think the four of us should head out and get to a motel now," she said, then told them the gist of her conversation with Mitch.

"Can we get one with a pool? And can we come back tomorrow?" April begged.

"Yes, and yes."

"Oh, good! I want to see the Well." April clapped her hands enthusiastically.

"I'd like to see it myself," Cass said. He draped his arm around his daughter's shoulders, and for once she didn't shrug it off, Mercedes noticed with approval

"We can come back early in the morning. I'm pretty well finished at the Castle, so the four of us can drive down to Montezuma Well." Mercedes forced herself to look at Cass with a calm expression. "If that's okay with you."

"Sure is."

"Then let's hit the parking lot."

"Dinner's on me," Cass announced as they made their way outside. "What are you ladies hungry for?"

"Pizza!" April shouted.

"Mercedes? Nina?" Cass asked.

Nina nodded as Mercedes said, "Pizza's fine. Maybe we can get a few salads, too."

Cass unlocked the Jeep door and held it open. Baron jumped in first, followed by April and a lagging Nina.

Mercedes got into the front passenger seat when Cass indicated he'd still be glad to drive.

"Can we have a pool party?" April begged. "Please, Mercedes, please?"

Mercedes ignored Cass's raised eyebrow. If April wanted to call her Mercedes, she didn't mind. "It's okay with me if it's okay with your father."

"I don't see why not," Cass replied, climbing in behind the wheel.

April clapped her hands. "It'll be fun!"

Fun? Mercedes thought. Life with the Montgomerys was a lot of things, but so far, fun hadn't been one of them.

CHAPTER SIXTEEN

THE POOL PARTY at the motel was actually a success, Mercedes thought—at least as far as April was concerned.

Not only was she a strong swimmer, she was a good diver. Nina, who was merely competent, refused to be left behind. The diving contest between the girls was one-sided, but for once Nina gracefully conceded defeat. That left the way open for them to clown around in the water, squealing and giggling as only young girls can.

When the sun started to set, the adults finally sent their tired children inside for the night. Their rooms were on ground level, right at poolside, so Mercedes and Cass, still wearing swimsuits, remained behind. Even Baron had abandoned them to stretch out on the cool tile floor of the bathroom in the room Mercedes was sharing with the two girls.

"Make sure you rinse your suits out," Mercedes called after them. Nina kept walking, but April turned around to give Mercedes a smile and a big wave of acknowledgment.

"I haven't seen April this animated since, well, since that day with you and Nina at the beach," Cass said, watching his daughter with a tender expression. "It appears that April, water and the Delacruz women are a lively combination. Thank you, Mercedes."

Then, before she could reply, Cass rose to start cleaning up the napkins, soda cans and remnants of two large pizzas. Cass was determined to stick with safe subjects and was rewarded when a grateful Mercedes rose to give him a hand.

"She's an excellent swimmer and diver, Cass. But then, I'm not surprised. She's so very graceful. She'd probably do well at any physical activity."

"Her mother loved the water. She was a top collegiate swimmer." Cass tossed the last of the paper plates into the trash. "There's a lot of Marian in April."

"I can't say the same about me and Nina. She's her father's daughter all the way. Just as stubborn as Gilles, too. Once she sets her mind to something, she'll do it or die trying."

Cass saw Mercedes freeze as she suddenly realized what she'd said. He paused also, a dented soda can in his hand. So much for keeping to safe subjects, he thought.

Her voice was trembling when she spoke again. "Well. I guess that's something Nina and I will have to work on."

Cass reached for her. His broad hand descended onto her shoulder, a comforting touch she could have easily shaken off if she wanted.

Cass took her into his arms and held her close. The can clattered to the ground as she rested her head on his shoulder and drew on his strength. He stood quietly, letting her choose her own time to pull away.

When she did, it was because of the desire flooding through them. He felt it, and he knew she felt it, too. He was positive she hadn't wanted to feel this way, nor was he doing anything to encourage it. But the fierce pull of physical and emotional attraction was as vital, as real, as the heat from the desert sun. And in the silence of the Arizona twilight, it screamed for fulfillment.

"I should go check on the girls," was her excuse for drawing away.

"You can't run forever, Mercedes," Cass said.

"From what?" she said impatiently. "Not this again!"

He stood just a few paces away from her. "You need help with Nina. I could be that help—if you'd let me."

"Why? Because you've had lots of practice? Because we're your latest rescue victims?" she snapped.

"Because I care about you."

The simple words hung in the air as he waited for her reaction. It wasn't what he'd hoped for, although it was no more than he'd expected.

"Tell me, Cass. Do you turn the lives of everyone you *care about* upside down? Or are Nina and I the exception?"

Cass refused to back down. "I could be good for Nina—if you'd give me the chance. I understand her—and you."

"Don't give me that 'I'm the perfect family man' line, Cass. I'm not buying it. Not after everything that's happened, starting with the fact that you sued me for custody of Baron."

"I gave you the dog, Mercedes," he reminded her.

"For a price. And only after upsetting Nina." Mercedes ran her fingers through her hair distractedly. "At least you didn't insult me by declaring undying love and throwing flowers at my feet."

Cass took one look at her crossed arms, her rigid shoulders. She didn't want to have this conversation. Still, he pressed on. "And if I had?"

"I'd have thrown them right back." Her eyes narrowed. "You just want a mother figure for April. And you want me in your bed."

Cass looked her straight in the eye. "That, too."

Mercedes gasped, obviously taken off guard.

"I want you for April," he said quietly. "I want you for myself even more."

Mercedes paused. She seemed to be thinking, steeling herself. Again, her response was not what he'd hoped for.

"Even if I wanted to remarry, I'd never settle for someone who's prepared to risk his life day in and day out. In your own way, you're as much of a thrill-seeker as Gilles was. The only difference is that you have a dead wife to use as your excuse. Well, Nina deserves better!''

Cass felt the blood drain from his face at the blow she'd inflicted. Mercedes had twisted his words and used them against him. If it wasn't for April—and Nina—he would have turned his back on her right then and walked away. But he had two girls to fight for first.

''Don't you hide behind Nina,'' Cass warned. ''This is between you and me.''

''This *does* concern Nina, because you want me to replace one poor-risk father with another!''

''If nothing else, I'd be home for her, which is a hell of a lot more than you could ever say for Gilles St. Clair!''

It was Mercedes's turn to go white.

''And don't expect me to apologize, either. I refuse to be lumped in the same category as that . . . that overgrown boy you married.''

Something flickered in her eyes. ''At least Gilles married me because he *loved* me, not because I was convenient.''

''Are you really sure of that?''

Silence.

''Tell me I'm wrong.''

Cass waited, but she didn't deny his accusation.

''You're a coward, Mercedes Delacruz. You married the wrong man, and now you're afraid to take a chance with me. And you're afraid I'll succeed with Nina where you've failed. Because you *have* failed with her. Why don't you just admit it? I have with April.''

''Fine, I'll admit it. I've failed my daughter.'' Her voice shook. ''There, are you happy?''

''Happy?'' His eyes filled with bitterness. ''Hardly that, Mercedes. Try desperate. And if you had any sense at all when it comes to Nina, you would be, too.'' His words had the harsh, cheerless knell of reality.

"Save the speech. Yes, I made a big mistake marrying Gilles. But I don't regret it—because I have Nina. And you're wrong about one thing. I'm not afraid of you. I don't *want* you."

He shouldn't ask. He knew deep down that he shouldn't ask. But he had to know. "Why not?" His voice sounded like someone else's.

"Because I loved Gilles St. Clair. I don't love you."

"Doesn't matter," he lied. *And oh, what a lie. It matters terribly, painfully, desperately.* "Because I'm here for Nina. And Gilles is not."

Cass bent over to retrieve the dropped soda can, his face as stiff as his motions. When he straightened, she'd hurried to her room.

Cass crushed the can in his hand before he finally threw it away. He methodically gathered up the towels, then headed back to his empty room. But instead of showering and changing for the night, he lay down on one of the two beds, without bothering to change out his swimsuit.

He closed his eyes, threw one arm over his face, and wished for impossible dreams to come true. Then he swore. He was a realist. He usually knew better than to believe wishes could come true. Cass groaned and swore again. Things couldn't possibly get any worse than they were right now.

He was wrong.

A knock on the adjoining room door surprised him. Had there been a problem with the sleeping arrangements? He hoped not. Mercedes and Nina were sharing one double bed, with April in the other.

The knock sounded again.

"Come in. It's not locked."

Cass lifted his head and looked up. It was Mercedes. She'd changed into some lounging pajamas. He let his head sink back onto the pillows.

"Go away, Mercedes," he said wearily. "I'm not in the mood for company."

He saw her hesitate. "It's about April, Cass."

"Tell April to go to bed. And go yourself." He flung his arm back over his face. He hadn't felt this bruised, this battered, since Marian's death.

"Cass, maybe April should come in here with you. Nina's sick."

"Sick?" He sat up. "What's wrong?"

"She says her throat hurts, and she's got a fever. Remember how she was feeling poorly at the ruins? I think she's coming down with something." Mercedes twirled a long strand of hair around her forefinger. It was the first truly nervous gesture he'd ever seen her make. It made her seem very young.

"I thought I should tell you," she continued hesitantly. "April's asleep, but maybe you should move her into your other bed. She might catch Nina's bug."

Cass reached for his jeans and a shirt. "I'll throw on some clothes and be right with you."

He was as good as his word.

"Hey, kiddo, hear you're not feeling well," he said to Nina upon entering the adjoining room.

Nina coughed, nodded miserably, then coughed again. Baron was at her side, his nose nuzzling her dangling hand. "My throat hurts. I want a drink."

"I tried to give her some water, but she wouldn't take it," Mercedes explained, a full glass in her hand.

"I hate water." Nina kicked fretfully at the covers.

"Nina, honey, you need fluids," Mercedes said. "You have a fever. Please sit up and take this."

"No! I want a soda!"

Cass placed his hand on Nina's forehead. The girl's forehead felt clammy.

"I gave her some children's chewable tablets, but they haven't had time to kick in yet." Mercedes sat on the edge of the bed, trying to coax Nina into compliance. "Please drink this for Mommy, sweetheart."

"I want a root beer! If Daddy was here, he'd get me one."

It was clear from the stubborn look on Nina's face that she wasn't going to cooperate. "How about if I hurry down to the office and the soda machine? I'll bring you back a root beer if you sip on the water until I come back."

Nina reluctantly sat up and took a token sip.

"Good girl. Mercedes, would you like anything?"

"If you could grab some extra sodas for later..." Her voice trailed off. For once Mercedes looked unequal to the demands of motherhood. The hand holding the glass wasn't steady, and she seemed almost as miserable as Nina. Obviously he wasn't the only one suffering from the aftereffects of that conversation by the pool.

He grabbed the ice bucket. "Will do."

"Do you need any change?"

"No. I'll be right back."

Cass slipped out and purchased two root beers and three ginger ales. He was gone only a few minutes, but by the time he returned, April was awake. "Nina's sick!" she said as soon as he stepped back in the room. She was sitting up in bed, a frown on her face. "And she's not faking this time, either!"

"I know."

"Do we have to go back to Phoenix?"

"Maybe." Cass set the ice bucket on the dresser. He removed a root beer, popped open the can and handed it to Nina. "Drink up, you."

"But, Dad, I didn't get to see the Well!" April protested. "Mercedes was going to take me!"

"Nina has a fever, April. We have to think about her needs first."

"But Mercedes promised! It's not fair!"

"It's not my fault I got sick," Nina said crossly, her feverish cheeks flushing even more.

"But we'll be going home soon! I'll never get another chance to see Montezuma Well!"

"April, please..." Mercedes said. She was still sitting on the edge of Nina's bed.

April ignored Mercedes's soft plea and continued to argue with Nina. Baron started barking as Nina argued back, which started her coughing. She coughed so hard she dropped the root beer. The full can spilled all over her nightgown and the bed sheets, barely missing Mercedes in the process.

"April, you idiot! See what you made me do!" Nina yelled in Spanish.

April didn't understand all the words, but she understood the hostility behind them. "Shut up!" she yelled back.

And in the midst of all the chaos, Mercedes buried her face in her hands and began to cry.

Her harsh sobs immediately rendered both girls speechless—and tore at Cass's heart. At first he didn't know what to do, what to say. But the two girls immediately turned to him for guidance. Then he sprang into action. He rummaged through Nina's suitcase, found her a clean nightgown and handed it to April.

"You go with Nina into the bathroom in my room and help her clean up. Here." He handed April a replacement soda can. "Make sure she drinks all of this. Then I want both of you to climb into bed there. April, you take my bed. Nina can take the other. Now move it. I don't want to hear one more complaint out of you."

"Yes, Dad." With one last wide-eyed look at the still-crying Mercedes, April got to her feet.

"Nina, do you need any help walking?" Cass asked. "Are you dizzy?"

Nina shook her head, for once as silent as April.

"Then go clean up. Let April help, okay?"

"What about Mom?"

"I'll clean up the bed and take care of your mother, then come check on you."

Nina slid off the bed, her wet nightgown sticking to her. She briefly rested her hand on her mother's shoulder as she passed, then slowly followed Nina through the adjoining door. As soon as Cass heard it close, he approached Mercedes.

He tried to talk to her. She wouldn't answer. He tried to sit next to her. She wouldn't let him. He tried to put his arms around her. She pushed him away.

"Mercedes, please . . ."

His chest hurt as he said her name a second time. He stood awkwardly beside the bed, watching her cry into her hands. But when he tried to hand her a tissue, she moved from the wet bed to the other one to avoid him.

Cass didn't try again. He busied himself stripping off the soiled sheets, then damp-dried the bare mattress. After stuffing the wet towels and soiled sheets into the motel laundry bag, he folded up the comforter, which for the most part had been miraculously spared being splashed by the sticky liquid, and placed it at the foot of the mattress. Mercedes continued to cry throughout it all. Cass silently wished Gilles St. Clair alive for just five minutes so he could break his neck.

Finally he shooed Baron into the bathroom and closed the door. The dog was whining, disturbed by all the tension apparently; he still whined in the bathroom, but at least he wasn't underfoot anymore.

"Mercedes, I'm going to check on Nina, okay?"

He received no response, nor did he expect one. Cass set the box of tissues beside her and left for the next room. Nina was clean and in bed, and so was April. But neither girl was sleeping.

Nina spoke first. "What's wrong with Mom?" she asked as Cass laid his hand on her forehead again. Nina did have a fever, but it didn't feel quite as high. Perhaps the tablets were working.

"She's tired and sad. It's been a rough day—and she hasn't had your father around to help."

"She misses him?" April asked from the other bed.

"Yes."

"Is she . . . is she still crying?" Nina asked.

"Yes."

Both girls fell silent. Then April said in a small voice, "Tell her I don't mind if we go home tomorrow, Dad. I don't need to see Montezuma Well."

"Thank you, April. I'm sure that'll make her feel a little better."

"Tell her I drank all my soda, and I'm sorry I spilled the first one," Nina added, not to be outdone.

"I will." Cass pulled down the blanket, leaving Nina only the sheet. "No heavy covers. We want to keep you cool tonight. Now close your eyes."

"I can't sleep. My skin's all achy."

"That's the fever. But close your eyes, anyway."

After a few moments, Nina did, and Cass turned toward April.

"Do you think we should take Nina home tonight, Dad?"

"Neither Nina nor Mercedes is up to a long drive. We couldn't see a doctor until tomorrow, anyway."

Cass sat down on the bed. He smoothed back his daughter's hair, something she rarely let him do. Then he kissed her on the cheek and adjusted her covers. "Thank you for taking care of Nina," he said. "I'm sure Mercedes appreciates it."

April nodded. "Can you make her feel better?"

"I'm working on it." Cass stood and, under April's watchful gaze, turned off all the lights except one small one.

"Sometimes it's hard for sad people to feel better," April revealed abruptly. "No matter what you do, they still feel sad."

"Then you should say your prayers," Nina replied in a prim little voice before Cass could respond.

"No." April shook her head. "Prayers never work for me."

Nina didn't argue. Cass couldn't. He kissed his daughter one last time and left the room.

MERCEDES HADN'T MOVED from her spot on the bed when he'd returned, but at least those terrible racking sobs had stopped. Several crumpled tissues were scattered at her feet.

"Nina's in bed. She's all cleaned up, and she drank a fresh soda." Cass sat down on the unmade bed across from her. "I told her we'd spend the night here and drive home first thing in the morning."

Mercedes nodded.

"I'm sure Nina would like you to kiss her good-night. April, too. Maybe you can go in a while later. They were both worried."

Mercedes nodded again. She hadn't looked at him once, Cass realized. Her eyes were downcast, her hands clasped in her lap.

"Is there anyone I can call for you? Maybe your mother or one of your sisters?"

She shook her head.

"Then you should probably get some rest," he said briskly. "Why don't you lie down? I'll stay up with Nina— check on her and make sure she drinks. If you want, I can give her two more tablets in four hours if her temperature doesn't go down. Just tell me where they are."

She lifted one listless hand to point at her purse. Cass found the tablet tin right on top.

"Got it. Now, why don't you close your eyes for a few minutes?"

Mercedes hesitated.

"I've left the adjoining door wide open, and I promise to wake you if Nina's worse. I think she's just coming down with a cold," he said, gently pressing her shoulders onto the bed. Her skin felt chilled, so he pulled the comforter up over her. Then he dimmed the lights. "You want a drink or something?"

She shook her head again.

"Okay. I'll be right here if you need anything." Cass sat on the stripped bed, leaning against the pillows. He turned on the TV with the remote, muted the sound so he could hear Nina and tuned in a baseball game—not that he felt like watching. But it was better than staring at the walls, since Mercedes refused to make eye contact. As the minutes of the night ticked away, the innings played on the silent TV. From time to time he rose to check on everyone. Nina had fallen asleep almost immediately. Cass was surprised how much he missed her energetic personality. It seemed strange to see the child so motionless. April had taken a little longer to fall asleep, but a full day at the ruins and the motel pool had finally taken their toll. He'd sat next to his daughter for the longest time, wondering what had gone wrong in her life and wishing he could help.

Nina's and Mercedes's problems, bad as they were, were out in the open. If only he knew what April's dragons were, he might be able to slay them. But he couldn't fight the unknown.

When he went back to check on Mercedes, her eyes were closed. He plumped up his pillows and watched the final inning. His team lost. It wasn't until he reached for the remote and snapped off the game that he heard her soft voice in the dark.

"How's Nina?"

"She's sleeping. Her fever's gone down some. I sponged her face a few times and gave her a couple more tablets. She should be okay for the night, but I'll keep checking on her."

"Thank you."

"No problem."

He lay there in the dark, wishing he could see Mercedes's face.

"I can stay up with her if you change your mind. She's my child, and you're probably tired."

"It's okay, Mercedes. I can't sleep, anyway," he said.

"I know why," Mercedes said wearily. "You can't sleep because you're angry. I'm surprised you can stand being in the same room with me after all the horrible things I said."

Cass shook his head, his hair rustling against the pillows. Then he remembered she couldn't see him. "The only person I'm angry with is myself, Mercedes. Not you. I could have picked a better time to say what I did. It's just that, well, April and I leave soon, and time isn't exactly on our side here. Tonight's fiasco is my fault."

"No. It's mine. I didn't mean to—"

Cass interrupted her. "Look, you don't owe me any explanations. Just close your eyes. Try to rest, okay? Nina will need you in the morning."

"And April," she added. "I hope I didn't upset her too much, going to pieces like that."

"She said to tell you she doesn't mind skipping the Well tomorrow. She'll be okay."

"No, she won't. Maybe I can get up before sunrise, take April and zip out to the Well. I could do my inspection, give April a quick tour and be back before Nina's even awake. Then we'll head home." A pause. "If that's all right with you, and if Nina's just coming down with a cold and not the flu. Or strep," she qualified.

"April would like that."

Cass couldn't help loving her for her concern for his child, even as he couldn't help longing for that same generosity toward him. He wondered if it would ever happen, if she would ever fight for happiness for herself the way she fought for her daughter. And his. That thought made him ask, "Are you going to be all right?"

A long pause.

"I don't know.... I hate Gilles for what he's done to Nina. If he'd spent more time with her when he was alive, if his long absences weren't so normal, she'd know he was dead. But all too often Gilles couldn't be bothered with Nina— even though she adored him." Another pause. "I can't forgive him. I never thought I'd ever hate someone I loved so much, but I do."

He heard her heavy sigh, the sound filling every corner of the room with sadness.

"And what about me, Mercedes?"

"I hate seeing Nina so confused. I hate myself for not being able to help. But... I can't hate someone who's merely told me the truth."

But could you love that someone?

The question went unasked.

CHAPTER SEVENTEEN

"APRIL, IT'S MERCEDES. Wake up, honey."

Mercedes watched April open her eyes. "Huh?"

"Quiet. We don't want to wake Nina."

"Is it time to get up?" she whispered.

"Yes, if you want to see Montezuma Well. Your dad said I could take you out to the ruins this morning. It'll only be a short visit, but if you hurry, we can be out and back before Nina gets up."

April sat straight up in bed with excitement. "Really?"

"Shh! Yes, really. Now hurry and get dressed. I'll be outside waiting."

"That was quick," Mercedes said as April joined her not ten minutes later. April had put on a pair of jean shorts, a durable cotton shirt, socks and sneakers, and carried both her hat and canteen. Mercedes was similarly outfitted, although she was wearing steel-toed boots. "Nina usually takes forever."

"How is Nina?" April asked.

"The fever's gone, but she sounds pretty congested. I think your dad's right—she's coming down with a cold."

"What time is it? It's still pretty dark."

"Five-thirty. We'll have to miss breakfast. The motel restaurant's not open yet."

"That's okay. We can eat later," April said eagerly, waiting for Mercedes to unlock the Jeep. "Let's go!"

Mercedes smiled at her enthusiasm. "All right. But don't get in yet. First let me write a note for your father."

She reached into her backpack for pen and paper, scribbled down their destination and concluded the note with, "I plan to be back no later than eight. April and I will eat breakfast here before we all head home. Please have Nina drink more fluids if she wakes up. Thanks." She signed it with a simple "M" and handed it to April.

"Here. Put this where your dad will see it. And please don't let Baron out of the bathroom. I don't feel like bringing him along, and I don't want him pestering Nina."

April nodded. She hurried inside and was back again in a flash.

Her excitement remained high all the way to the ruins.

"This is *great!*" she said a half hour later as they peered over the wooden barrier of the pit-house excavation. Her eyes darted this way and that. "The diagram shows what goes in all these holes. I can really see a Sinagua pit house in my head."

Mercedes rested her arm lightly around April's shoulders. The deep holes had once contained support poles for the mud-and-stick sides and roofs. April insisted on studying each one of them.

"Actually this pit house is Hohokam," Mercedes replied. "It's from an earlier settlement—before the Sinagua."

"But why were there so many people? There's no water here, not like at the Castle." April moved to a new spot at the restraining barriers for a better look.

"But long, long ago the Verde Valley *wasn't* a desert," Mercedes explained. "It was a grassland complete with freshwater marshes. The grasslands are gone, but many of the water sources remained. That's why there are so many ruins in this area."

"Oh, I wish I could spend all day here," April sighed, leaning even farther over the wooden barrier. Her shadow fell through the open space to the dirt floor of the pit-house excavation.

"I wish you could, too, but we'd better get going," Mercedes said gently. "We've got another short drive and then a hike."

April reluctantly left the pit house, but her enthusiasm soon returned as they reached the dirt parking lot marked Montezuma Well. "Where is it?" she asked.

"You can't see anything from here. We have to hike to the top of this hill. The Well is a sinkhole inside the center. Looking down, you'll be able to see plenty of ancient homes."

"I can't wait!"

"Then grab your hat and canteen, and we'll get started." Mercedes pulled out her own hat and canteen, plus her camera bag from the back of the Jeep.

"Isn't there a gift shop and ranger cabin here?" April asked as Mercedes locked the Jeep and they began climbing the hill's pathway. "All I see is *those.*" April wrinkled her nose at the outhouses lined up at the far edge of the parking lot.

"This is it, April. There's no regular ranger service here, no building, no facilities, no paved roads. Except for the signs, this is pretty much how Montezuma Well looked years ago."

April's gaze swiveled all around. "At least there were people back then. It's almost like a ghost town now."

Mercedes stopped her upward progress at the nervous note in April's voice. "This *is* a ghost town, April. Only instead of having old abandoned buildings of wood, like most ghost towns in the West, we have abandoned rock-and-adobe ones. The desert can be a very lonely place if you aren't used to it. And the ruins are closed today, remember?"

"It's kind of creepy. It's so *quiet.*"

"Well, as long as you're with me, nothing can hurt you," Mercedes said briskly. "But if you've changed your mind, we can go back to the car."

April shook her head. "I'm not scared. I'm just not used to it yet. And I really do want to see the Well."

"I'm glad." When April's hand slipped into hers, Mercedes gave it a reassuring squeeze and the two of them resumed their ascent. "We'll have a good time. I know my way around, plus we have water and a full tank of gas. There's nothing to worry about."

CASS WAS AWAKENED by a high annoying whine. He groaned and tried to go back to sleep. But the whine persisted, rousing him to full consciousness. This time he recognized the sound as distinctly canine.

"Twister, lie down," he said. His command was followed by two sharp barks, and Nina's words in Spanish from the other room.

"Mama, let the dog out!"

Cass rubbed his eyes and sat up. He could have gone for a few more hours' sleep, minus the jeans he was still wearing, but Nina's coughing and Baron's barking forced him to his feet.

"Just a minute, Nina," he called.

He stumbled to the bathroom and let out the dog. Baron immediately dashed into the adjoining room and jumped on Nina's bed. Cass ran the water at the sink, intending to bring Nina a drink, when he saw Mercedes's note. He read it, then carried the glass of water to the next room.

"Morning, Nina. Want a drink?"

She nodded and took a swallow. Her voice was hoarse when she asked, "Where's Mom?"

"At the ruins with April."

"Without me?"

"Afraid so. How are you feeling?"

"It's just a stuffy nose. Mom should have taken me," Nina fretted, then coughed. Baron snuggled closer to her.

"It's more than that, I'm afraid. Drink some more water, and don't worry, your mother will be back in time for breakfast. By eight, she said." He took the glass back when she'd finished, then felt Nina's forehead. "Your fever's gone, she'll be happy to hear."

"Did anyone feed Baron?" Nina asked.

"I don't think so. How about if I get his food and tie him outside while you get dressed? Are you up to that on your own?"

"Yeah. But I hate being sick." Nina coughed again and sniffed as she slid out of bed. "This is such a pain."

"THIS IS SO NEAT! I'm done taking pictures of this ruin. Let's go on to the next one!" April scrambled down the path of the circular sink that was Montezuma Well. The lower they went, the more ruins they could see in the pockets above their heads.

"Hold on!" Mercedes ordered. "I'm not finished searching inside *this* one yet. Wait for me, April," she ordered.

She'd combined April's tour with her inspection. Trouble was April wanted to move much faster than Mercedes did, so she'd let the girl use her camera to slow her down. Even then April was everywhere at once.

"Oh, look! From here I can see another ruin way up top!" April tipped her neck back and pointed the camera toward one of the ruins far above their heads near the rim of the Well. "This is so cool!" April snapped more pictures.

"Uh-oh," she murmured after another five minutes.

"What?"

"Um... I think I'm out of film. Do you have more? Can I look in your pack?"

Despite the interruption to her work and the emotional strain of the past few days, Mercedes wasn't angry. April had shown more liveliness in two days at the ruins than in the past three weeks. Mercedes climbed out from under the protective shade of the ruins, under the metal retaining bar and back onto the concrete path. Her pack was at April's feet. Mercedes never wore one inside a ruin, afraid its bulk might hit a delicate wall in the close quarters and cause damage.

"I do have one more roll of film here, but let me load it for you," she said as she rummaged around in her backpack.

"Wait'll I show Dad! Can we get these developed right away?"

"I can use an overnight service instead of the museum lab," Mercedes offered. The price would be higher, but since April actually wanted to share something with her father, she didn't mind. "And you might want to go a little easier on the shutter this time," Mercedes suggested. "I've only got a few more places to inspect, but the rest of my film is in the car."

"Okay," April said cheerfully. "But won't we be climbing up there?" She pointed to the highest of the ruins.

"Those ruins are inaccessible from the main path."

"Can't we take the steps back up to the top and climb down from the rim?"

"No. The sink walls are limestone, which isn't the strongest rock. And, April, the ruins themselves are fragile. It's best to stay off them."

"They aren't safe?"

"Not really." She opened the film pack and popped it into the camera where it automatically loaded. "Even if they were, it's best to keep some things from the public."

"Why?"

"Come on, I'll show you." Mercedes lifted the pack with one hand, gave April the freshly loaded camera with the other, and led her farther down the path to one of the more traveled areas.

"Look inside this room," she said.

April gasped. "Someone's spray-painted the walls!" Names and dates in big ugly black streaks marred the simplicity of ancient Sinagua design. "There's all kinds of food wrappers in there. And empty drink cans, too!"

"Pretty sad, isn't it?" Mercedes climbed over the retaining wall to retrieve the litter. She shook away the insects from the wrappings and the still-shiny cans before saying, "Here. Toss these in my pack. We'll throw them away on our way out."

April shook her head in disgust. "What kind of person would trash a place like this?"

"Uneducated people. And they were here pretty recently. Well, at least the ants got a free meal." Mercedes frowned, then pulled off her hat to wipe her dripping forehead.

"Getting hot?"

April nodded. "Hungry, too." They were back on the trail in the full sunlight and had almost reached the bottom of the Well, only a few feet above the waterline.

"I'm almost finished here. We'll be back at the motel in no time. In the meantime, why don't you drink more water?"

"It's all gone."

"Have some of mine." Mercedes passed April her canteen.

April shook it and frowned. "It's almost empty. Are you sure?"

"Yes, finish it off. I have more in the Jeep."

April needed no more urging. "Thanks, Mercedes. But I'll leave you some, okay?"

"Okay." Mercedes waited until April was through, then started to hook the canteen back on her belt. "I only have one more spot to check, then we're all done."

April busied herself studying the ruins again. "Hey, look, someone's here!"

"It's not your father, is it?" Mercedes asked, wrestling with one particularly difficult hook. She doubted that Nina was suddenly well enough for Cass to bring her here. But who else could it be this early? She finished with her canteen and looked up to see two men standing at the very top of the path.

"No, and there's another man with him," April replied. "I guess they're early birds, too."

"Too early," Mercedes said, her eyes narrowed. "The ruins aren't opened today." This could explain the litter in the cave, she thought, and felt a prickle of anxiety.

"Maybe they're rangers."

Mercedes shook her head. "No uniforms."

"Maybe they're from a museum like you."

"I don't think so." Mercedes lifted a hand and waved it in a friendly greeting. There was no answering wave, and she felt suddenly uneasy. She didn't like this.

She didn't like it at all.

"They didn't wave back. I guess they aren't friends of yours." April said. She went back to studying the ruins.

A nasty, nagging feeling trickled down Mercedes's spine. Something was very wrong here. Who were these men, and why were they here? Montezuma Castle was a popular ruin with easy access. That was why she hadn't worried about bringing Nina and the Montgomerys along on this trip. But Montezuma Well wasn't as popular, wasn't as accessible, and this was Sunday.

Worst of all, the two men hadn't waved back. Tourists didn't mind waving back, and local desert dwellers considered a wave a distress signal. Either way, there should have been *some* response.

Instead, there was nothing except the motionless figures of the men at the Well's only exit. It made Mercedes nervous.

What better ruin to loot than Montezuma Well, and what better time than a Sunday? Why hadn't she thought of this before?

She didn't want to panic. By the same token, she couldn't ignore the hairs prickling on the back of her neck, either. Mercedes bit her lip and made her decision.

"April, honey, I've changed my mind. You've been such a good helper I'm going to take you to one of the higher ruins, after all."

"Really?" April gasped. "I get to see one of the special ones?"

"That's right." Mercedes deliberately made her words light. "I want to show you how the ancient Indians used them as fortresses. But first I need to know if you're a good climber."

"Oh, I'm a great climber. I climb trees back home. I'm not afraid of heights."

"Not even if we climbed all the way up there?" She motioned with her chin to a small ledge almost sixty feet above them that sheltered a small pueblo. Its single room was propped right on the edge of the sheer sides and would give them some margin of safety.

"I can do that," April said excitedly. "No problem."

Mercedes prayed she wasn't exaggerating. "Good." She casually threw her arm around April's shoulders and guided her off the visitors' path. "Let's get going. No time like the present."

"Mercedes," April said, "You left your pack on the sidewalk."

"I know." Mercedes ducked under the path's pipe barriers, pulled April after her and picked up the pace.

"Wait! I'll go back and get it for you," April volunteered, but Mercedes tightened her grip on April's hand and jerked her back to her side.

"Leave it," she said harshly.

"But my film's inside!"

"We can't climb with heavy camera gear," Mercedes said in a more controlled voice.

"We should put it someplace safe, then. Maybe one of the shady rooms where people can't see it."

"It'll be fine where it is. Come on, here's where the way up starts."

"My pictures..." April gave one last regretful glance at the backpack, but Mercedes was already giving her a boost up to the first set of hand- and footholds.

"Just put your hands in the smaller holes. Then your feet in the bigger ones. They're pretty easy to see. If you aren't sure where to put them, ask me. I'll be right behind you, April. Up you go."

April was still reluctant. "Cameras are expensive! What if someone steals it?"

"Forget the damn camera. Now climb!"

CHAPTER EIGHTEEN

OH, GOD, NO....

Mercedes watched as one of the men circled the top of the rim, while the other raced down the concrete path. And unless she was mistaken, the man above had a gun in his hand.

Dear Lord, how could I have been so stupid?

"How are you doing, April?" she asked.

"Good. Only everything's getting kind of crumbly up here. Oops, sorry." April's foot dislodged some dirt. Mercedes closed her eyes against the shower of dust.

"That's okay. Easy does it, April. Take your time, and keep your eyes on the footholds," she said.

April nodded and continued upward; Mercedes checked on the progress of the two men. The man at the rim wasn't hurrying. Fortunately for her and April, the pocketed sides of the Well didn't allow him a clear shot. He'd have to lie on his stomach and lean over the edge of the sinkhole.

Unfortunately the man on the bottom was already following them, using the same footholds they'd used. And he climbed quickly and easily, as if he'd done this before; he climbed as well as Mercedes herself did—and as novice April couldn't. The look on their pursuer's face, even from their higher vantage, wasn't pleasant. Mercedes murmured a brief prayer as she gave April's bottom another boost.

We had a good head start, but will it be enough?

"AREN'T YOU GOING to eat your breakfast?" Cass asked.

Nina shook her head mournfully.

He'd ordered room service for the two of them, but even though they'd been at the room's little breakfast table for the past twenty minutes, Nina's plate was untouched.

"Not hungry?"

"I always eat breakfast with Mom. I thought she'd be back by now." Nina poked at her scrambled eggs. "Cass..."

Cass looked up from his coffee. It was the first time Nina had used his Christian name. That, and the trembling emotion on her face had his full attention.

"What is it, Nina?"

"Mom's never late."

Cass glanced at his watch. "It's not that late. It's not even eight-thirty."

"She said *by* eight. And I'm sick. Mom always fusses when I'm sick."

Cass frowned. Mercedes was extremely protective of Nina. She'd never stay away unless she'd encountered an unforseen problem. Car trouble? Or worse, an accident? He knew she'd never have kept his own daughter out longer without his permission. Maybe something *was* wrong.

Panic gripped his heart, even as adrenaline dumped into his veins. But he forced himself to be calm for Nina's sake. "It's probably just a flat tire or something."

"But the Jeep has new tires and a spare. And Mom knows how to change them super-quick. Something's happened. What if she gets lost like my dad did?" Tears formed in Nina's eyes and ran down her cheeks.

"Hey... hey! Don't do that." Cass pushed away his own half-eaten breakfast and reached for Nina's hand. "No tears. And no jumping to conclusions, okay? I'll tell you what. We'll check things out. Does this town have a taxi service?"

Nina sniffed and nodded. "There're lots of tourists here."

"Okay, we'll go out to the Well and check on them our-selves. Wash your face while I call us a cab. Here. Use my napkin."

Nina managed a watery smile. "Can we take Baron?"

"Yep. Get his leash, okay?" He helped Nina to her feet and gave her a quick reassuring hug before making the call. A few minutes later a taxi beeped outside their door.

"Come on, Nina. Let's go."

"MERCEDES, STOP PUSHING me!" April said nervously as Mercedes again boosted the girl's behind with her palm. "I don't want to fall!"

"You heard the little girl, Mercedes," a male voice mocked from below. "You wouldn't wanna fall, now."

"Who was that?" April tried to see, and she paled.

"Don't look down!" Mercedes ordered. In a conven-tional building they would have been at least five stories high. While their pursuer was a good two stories behind them he was gaining steadily. And Mercedes and April still had ten more feet to go to reach the ledge. "Keep climb-ing!"

April froze, but Mercedes swatted her bottom. "Move it!"

It wasn't until April was climbing again that Mercedes turned around and yelled to the ugly face below her. "Who are you? What do you want?"

"Well, I thought I wanted some more arty-fax for my pa to sell. But I decided I wanted a little company, too. A little *female* company."

It was Mercedes's turn to freeze. He brazenly admitted being a looter—and worse. His claims made her sick.

And she had April with her!

"Leave us alone!" she screamed as she started climbing again. "Take your bricks and go away!"

"My name's Chuckie," he replied with a grimace that was meant to be a smile. "And I will, but you're coming with me."

Fury swept through Mercedes as April whimpered. That leering male face and the frightened child's cry made her desperate. She reached for a loose limestone rock off to the side and dropped it on the man below. One of them hit the target. "Chuckie" roared with pain.

Then everything happened at once. Chuckie flew up the Well's side with a speed even Mercedes had never attempted. April panicked—she slipped and screamed Mercedes's name. Mercedes grabbed at the teetering child with one arm, then both of them swayed precariously as two sets of hands and feet occupied holds carved for only one. By the time she'd resecured April's balance and her own, Chuckie was just below her.

And his dirty ugly hand was wrapped around April's ankle.

April gasped, then fell deathly silent. So did Mercedes.

"You got two choices here, Miz Mer-say-deez." His use of her name mocked her, even as it threatened her. "You can start climbing down with me nice and peaceable. Or you can watch me throw this little girl into her own personal swimming pool."

Mercedes stared at the jagged limestone rocks piercing the green-black surface of the sinkhole water fifty feet below, and shivered. "If I come with you, what happens to April?"

"I hold on to her until you reach bottom. Then I let her go."

"You'll let her go?" Mercedes asked as she tightened her grip. One of her arms was wrapped around April's waist. Her free hand had grabbed the security of a rock-dwelling desert bush. Its tough thorns drew blood, but its root held fast.

"Yep. She can stay in one of these rooms until you and I are done partyin'."

"You promise you won't hurt her?"

Chuckie shook his head. "My solemn word of honor, ma'am."

Mercedes closed her eyes. She didn't believe him. And there was no way she was leaving Cass's child alone in the desert, never mind with this piece of filth. Even if Mercedes trusted him, which she didn't, April was trembling so hard Mercedes doubted the child could make it to the ledge above without help.

"Don't go, Mercedes," April begged. "Please don't leave me."

"You come with me or the kid's coyote food, Mer-say-deez." Chuckie's fingers tightened even more cruelly on April's ankle.

Hatred flowed furiously through her veins, hatred Mercedes made sure she kept hidden. "All right, Chuckie. I'll come with you," she said in her sweetest voice. She even managed a smile. "Only please let me kiss April goodbye."

Chuckie nodded. "One kiss, and then down we go."

Mercedes bent as if to kiss April's temple. But in a sudden move, she dropped her weight and kicked with every ounce of strength she had at Chuckie's face. Steel-toed hiking boots smashed squarely into his nose.

Chuckie's anguished scream mixed with April's high-pitched one. Before he could recover, Mercedes again kicked at his head. Chuckie's free hand flew off the rocks, but his other was still around April's ankle, dragging both woman and child down.

"Let her go!" Mercedes screamed, smashing her boot into his face once again. *"Let her go!"*

The thorns ripped her palm, puncturing it, as the extra weight of a full-grown male started pulling the plant loose. Frantically, Mercedes made one last mighty effort at a kick, but this time she aimed for the wrist grasping April's ankle. The hand released its hold and the man was falling, falling, falling....

His crooked wrist and outstretched fingers were the last thing Mercedes saw as Chuckie bounced off the rocks and sank beneath the murky water. But the screaming continued from the other man up on the rim. And his screams frightened Mercedes even more than Chuckie's had. Because *this* man was still alive. *And he had the gun.*

Mercedes yanked her hand from the bush, hardly feeling the pain. "Climb, April," Mercedes ordered with a ruthlessness she barely recognized as her own. *"Climb!"*

"WHAT DO YOU MEAN, this is as far as you can go?" Cass demanded from the back seat. The cab had stopped just outside the dirt-road entrance to Montezuma Well. "Is this a cab-for-hire or not?"

The driver, a college student, tried to be patient. "Please, sir," he said politely. "I looked the other way when you insisted on bringing along the pooch. My boss says no animals. But a few hairs on the seat is nothing compared to broken shocks. No way this cab can drive that desert road."

"Try it, anyway!"

"I can't, sir. Sorry."

Cass silently swore.

"Why don't you wait until Montezuma Castle reopens Monday? That road's paved, and any cab in town can get you there."

Cass swore once—out loud and in front of Nina, no less. Nina stared at him with big eyes, her arms tightly around Baron's neck. That look made him regain control.

"What's your name?" Cass asked more calmly.

"William Baker. You can call me Will, though."

"Okay, Will, here's the situation. This little girl's mother works for the Native American Musuem in Phoenix. She and my daughter have the Jeep, and they were supposed to be back at the hotel for breakfast. They never showed up."

"Did you call the police?"

"We want to check things out and make sure it's nothing serious before we call them. They haven't been missing that long. But we're worried. The lady is never late."

"I can understand, sir. Radiators can boil over, and those cactus and rocks can puncture any tire. That's not counting soft sandy spots that can mire you down good. I know. I've been stuck in them myself. Can't you rent a car?"

"I don't have time to rent a car! I want you to take me in *this* car!"

Will shook his head. "The last guy who drove his cab on an unpaved desert road got fired. I can't pay my college tuition this fall if I get fired, and there aren't that many jobs in this town."

Cass saw Nina bite her lip. Her eyes were filled with desperation, her little body braced for disappointment. Only he wasn't going to disappoint her.

"How much is your tuition?" Cass asked.

"Too much." Will sighed. "You should see all the overtime I have to put in."

"How much?"

Will shrugged, and named the figure.

"Give me your pen," Cass ordered. He pulled a blank check from his wallet and wrote in an amount.

"Here's your tuition. Take it."

Will took one look at the check and hesitated. "Paper bounces easily, sir. A lot easier than finding a boss who lets me schedule my hours around my classes."

Cass wrote again, this time on the back of a deposit slip, and passed it forward. "Here are my driver's license and bar-association number. I'm a lawyer. Only an idiot would risk disbarment over a bounced check."

Hopeful, Nina lifted her head from Baron's neck. Cass gave her a tiny nod of reassurance.

"Now, Will, you have two choices. One, you take the check and drive this cab down that road. Or two, I take back the check, throw you out of the car, and *I* drive this cab down that road. What's it going to be?"

Will folded the check and slid it carefully into his shirt pocket. "I hear the Well's really nice this time of year, sir," he said, and shifted the cab into drive.

"Is THAT MAN coming back to get us?"

April's whispers carried across the darkness of the single-room cliff dwelling. She was huddled against a wall, her knees drawn up to her chest, her chin trembling.

"No, April. He isn't coming back."

Mercedes had placed April far back from the ledge. With her good hand she was adding to the pile of rocks and stray building materials she'd amassed. The injured hand, which she'd wrapped in her bandanna, wasn't much use. It was bleeding and swollen, and one of her fingers wasn't working right. How she'd ever climb down five stories—let alone help April down, was beyond her.

April's ankle was badly bruised from Chuckie's fingers and Mercedes's kick. She could barely walk.

"He's dead, isn't he?" she whispered.

"Yes, April, I think he is."

Both of them had seen Chuckie fall, so Mercedes didn't bother to lie. But she did stop what she was doing to give April a hug. She cuddled the girl in her arms and blessed the ancient adobe walls that blocked the sun's glare and shielded them from a gunman's targeting eye.

"What about the other man?" April asked. "Is he still out there?"

"I watched him hike to the bottom. But he hasn't tried to climb the walls yet," she said.

Unfortunately he hadn't left, either. Their dwelling had a clear view of the single exit at the top of the rim. She'd been watching that exit. Their lofty hideaway gave them a perfect bird's-eye view, but so far Chuckie's partner was still below.

"Are you going to get in trouble for looting these buildings?" April asked nervously.

Mercedes almost smiled at the absurdity of the question. "We're not exactly looting them, more like rearranging them, and no, sweetheart, I won't."

April shivered. "You . . . won't let that other man get me, will you?"

"Not a chance, not as long as I'm here," Mercedes reassured her. She kissed the child in her arms, then silently began to assess their situation.

Obviously there was some kind of bond between the dead man and his partner. Brothers, perhaps? Chuckie had referred to his "pa." In any event, the stalker below refused to leave. She guessed he was evaluating the situation, just as she was. Mercedes might have the advantage over him while it was light, but once darkness fell, that advantage greatly lessened.

And what would happen if other people showed up? What if Cass showed up to look for her? What if Nina was with him?

She couldn't bear the thought of danger to Nina any more than she could bear the thought of harm coming to April—or Cass. And it would be her fault. She'd come out to the Well and walked right into the midst of a pair of looters, all because she'd made a foolish error in judgment. She'd assumed that since the Castle was such an unlikely site for looting, the Well was equally safe. That thoughtless assumption might cost her more than her life. It might cost April's, too.

Now she might die without ever telling Cass she was sorry. About the things she'd said—and the things she hadn't said. She might die without telling Cass she loved him.... She started to tremble.

"Mercedes?" April asked from her lap. "Are you okay?"

"My hand's just a little sore," she replied, her arms still around the girl. "How are you?"

"My stomach hurts."

"When we get back to the motel, I'll buy you the biggest breakfast they have," Mercedes promised in what she hoped was a confident voice. "Or the biggest lunch, whatever you want."

April shook her head. "It's not that kind of hurt."

Mercedes gathered the girl closer and leaned back against the adobe wall. Even in the shady dark it felt hot against her back. The air was stifling, and she was sweating from the heat. Or from fear...

"What kind of pain is it?"

April took a long time to answer. "The kind of pain when you've hurt someone."

"April Montgomery, you listen to me," Mercedes said immediately. "You didn't hurt that terrible man. I did. You were *not* to blame."

"I didn't mean him." Mercedes had to strain to hear her next sentence. "It was someone else..."

Mercedes mind reeled. She'd just killed a man. She couldn't deal with that now. She'd had no choice, no choice at all, but she knew she'd always remember how it felt to push another human being to his death. But at the moment she had a more pressing concern—she was frantically worried about her safety and that of three other people. Yet Mercedes lovingly stroked April's hair as she searched for the right words. Obviously April believed what she was saying. Mercedes had to take her claim seriously.

"If you've hurt someone, you must have had a good reason," Mercedes said quietly. "I had a good reason to fight earlier. I was defending myself—defending you. Was it something like that?"

April shook her head, then buried her face in her hands.

"Tell me your reason, April," Mercedes coaxed softly. "Whatever it is, I'll listen. I want to help."

April lifted her head. "You won't yell at me?"

"No."

"You...you won't tell Dad?"

"Not without your permission."

April grabbed handfuls of Mercedes sweat-soaked shirt. "You have to *promise*."

"I promise."

It took a few moments before April released her shirt, but she still didn't speak.

"It's okay, sweetheart. You can talk to me."

Still nothing. Mercedes had almost given up hope of getting a straight answer when she heard April's soft tremulous admission.

"Twister got hit by that car because of me...."

CHAPTER NINETEEN

MERCEDES COULDN'T PREVENT the next words from tumbling out. "You, April?"

"But I didn't mean to! It was an accident!"

Mercedes took a deep breath and strove for calmness. "Tell me what happened."

"We...we were on vacation. Only then Dad had to go on a rescue. He said we had to go home early."

"So you were angry?"

"Yes, and scared. I didn't want to go on a rescue."

"But your father never takes you on rescues."

"He might as well. All he does is talk about them and train dogs for them. I know he wants me to be like him. But I don't want to find people, live ones or...dead ones."

April shivered, and Mercedes remembered back to Florida, when April had confessed to being terrified at the thought of dead bodies.

"I wanted it all to stop," April whispered. "I wanted us to have our vacation. So I turned Twister loose."

Mercedes shook her head in confusion. "But how, April? Didn't your father notice?"

"No. He was in line trying to get our boarding passes. Twister was with the luggage. I...I told Dad I had to go to the bathroom. He wanted to walk me to the ladies' room, but it was so close. And the ticket line was long. I told him I'd be right back. Then, when he wasn't looking, I ran to where the luggage was and got Twister."

Mercedes couldn't believe her ears. "The baggage handler let you do that?"

"He was busy and Dad was in that long line. Nobody said anything."

"So you ran outside with Baron?"

April nodded miserably.

Mercedes pictured Phoenix's airport. It was a smallish airport, with parking lots right next to the loading zone. The loading zone led straight to the ticket counters inside. Nina could easily have run in and out without Cass noticing her absence.

"First I took off his tags and threw them away. Then I found a shady spot in the parking lot close to the sidewalk and I tied him to a post." Her voice trembled. "Twister's the sweetest dog. I was sure some nice family would take him home."

"And then your father would stop working rescues?" Mercedes was beginning to understand. "And stop making you a part of his work?"

"Yes. But..."

Mercedes held April tighter. "But?"

"Twister saw me leave, and he started barking. He was pulling and pulling at his leash when I left, but I tied him good. It must have broken after I went inside. And then a car must have come and hit him—but I didn't know that...and...and... I didn't mean for Twister to get hurt, Mercedes! I really didn't!" She started to cry. "Twister thinks I did it on purpose. He hates me."

"Oh, April, how terrible for you," she consoled. She remembered Baron's menacing growl when April and the dog were first reunited. She remembered how the dog had steadfastly refused to leave Nina's side for April. Dogs had long memories for some things, and obviously this tragic abandonment was one of them.

But her thoughts were interrupted by April's next hoarsely spoken words. "It's all my fault, Mercedes. All those dead people are my fault, too."

"What dead people?"

She had to strain to hear April's response.

"The ones Dad and Buddy didn't find in time. The ones Twister would have found. They died because of me."

"April, you didn't kill them!" Mercedes held the trembling girl even closer.

"Dad said Twister was a better rescue dog than Buddy," April sobbed. "Dad said the person who lost Twister was a murderer."

"He would never say that."

"But I heard him! He said it when we were at the beach cabin—the time my stomach hurt so bad."

Mercedes suddenly remembered the night April had passed out. Cass *had* said something along those lines. And then she remembered how white April's face was, how her little hands were wrapped around her belly—just like they were now. A horrible suspicion swept through Mercedes.

"Honey, you weren't responsible for anyone's deaths. You weren't! But I want to know something. How long have you *believed* you were?"

April wouldn't answer, wouldn't even look at her.

"Since you heard your father say that at the cabin?"

The girl buried her head against Mercedes's shoulder.

Mercedes tried another tack. "How long has your stomach been bothering you?"

"A long time," came the muffled answer.

"A few weeks? A few months?"

"Longer."

Mercedes's heart ached. She didn't want to ask the next question, but knew she had to. "Ever since you turned the dog free?"

A slight nod.

"Oh, April..." Mercedes could barely talk, so tight was her throat at the suffering April had gone through. She set the child back from her a bit. "Look at me, sweetheart. Come on, it's okay," she whispered. "Why didn't you tell anyone?"

"I was scared. I didn't want Dad to hate me."

Mercedes chose her next words carefully. "You told me, April. And I don't hate you."

"You don't?"

"No. I only feel bad for you."

April put her head back on Mercedes's shoulder and wound both arms around her neck. Mercedes began to rock April back and forth, her own eyes now as wet as the girl's. "You're not a killer, April. What you did to your dog was very wrong, but his disappearance has nothing to do with those poor people who died."

"You're just saying that," April said, the despair in her eyes breaking Mercedes's heart.

"No, I'm not. You can't predict the future, April. No one can. Who's to say Baron could have found them any faster than Buddy? The dog's getting old. He's slowing down. A younger dog like Buddy *is* faster than Baron and probably has been for some time."

"But Dad said—"

"Adults say lots of things to help them deal with bad times," Mercedes interrupted. "Your father doesn't believe you're a murderer. That was just his anger talking—he was angry at me that night, not you. And if you were to talk to him about this..."

"You can't tell him! You promised you wouldn't tell him!"

"I know, and I won't. But I think it's time you told him yourself."

"I can't!" April wailed.

Mercedes steeled her heart against April's pain—the way she should have steeled her heart against Nina's pain. That was what Cass had told her. Sometimes a parent had to be tough, even heartless, to be effective, and this was one of those times. Mercedes was not going to back down now.

"You have to. Because this secret is hurting you. Just like Nina's refusal to accept her father's death is hurting her."

April lifted her head at that. "But Nina thinks—"

"Nina's wrong. She's hiding from the bad things, and I'm letting her. But we can't hide forever. It hurts us, and it hurts others who love us."

Like Nina. And Cass.

"You have to talk to your father," she said again.

"I can't do it! Please don't make me."

"You can, and you must. You have no choice in this, April." Mercedes smoothed back the short blond hair with her good hand. "Tell you what. I promise to talk to Nina again if you promise to tell your dad about Baron."

"Will you . . . will you come with me?"

She nodded. "You and me, side by side. Then you can get the bad stuff out in the open, deal with it and start fresh. Nina, too. Just as soon as we get out of here."

If we ever get out of here . . .

"CAN'T YOU GO any faster?" Cass asked impatiently. "I could walk faster than you're driving!"

"That's exactly what you'll be doing if I rip out the undercarriage on these rocks, sir."

"Go around them!"

"I am, but I have to be careful to stay off the shoulder," Will replied.

"What's wrong with the shoulder?"

"It's too sandy. We'll mire down good." Will took a quick peek at Cass from his rearview mirror. "You're not from around here, are you?"

"He's from Florida," Nina said.

"Really? Don't you worry about living near all those alligators?"

"That does it. Stop the car!"

"Huh?"

"You heard me, stop the car!"

When he did, Cass got out, hurried over to Will's front door and yanked it open. "Move over," he ordered.

"But—"

"I'm driving. Move over, or I'll pull you out and you can walk home."

Will reluctantly made room for Cass, although he continued to protest.

"You aren't going to drive too fast, are you?" he asked nervously.

"You bet I am."

"But that's suicide on these roads! You'll wreck the car!"

"I have to look for this child's mother, and I can't spend all day waiting for you to find the gas pedal. Or listening to your stupid questions."

"I just wanted to know about the alligators," Will said in a hurt voice.

"Alligators are the least of your problems. Put your seat belt on. Nina, tighten yours and hold on to the dog. Will here is going to see how fast a Florida driver can go."

"Um, I changed my mind. I think I'll walk after all."

"Too late." Cass fastened his own seat belt—and floored it.

"I'M GOING TO TAKE another look outside, April. You stay put and rest that ankle, okay?"

"Be careful," April whispered.

"You bet I will." *Especially since he has a gun,* a fact she intended to keep from April as long as possible.

Mercedes carefully inched up to the window to peer out. What she saw made her heart run cold, and she gasped.

"What is it?"

"The second man." She grabbed a rock from her pile. "He's coming up the wall."

April wailed again, but Mercedes knew this was no time for coddling.

"Listen to me, April. I'm going to throw rocks at this guy until I knock him down," she explained. "If something happens to me and I can't throw anymore..."

"Why? What's going to happen to you?" April's voice was almost hysterical.

"Like if my hand gets tired, then you take over. Pretend you're a Sinagua girl defending your home against invaders. Keep throwing those rocks. The window's at a bad angle, so you'll have to use the doorway. But *don't* let the enemy see you."

"Why?"

Now's the time to tell her, Mercedes thought. "Because I think he has a gun."

April grabbed at her stomach and started crying.

"Shut up, April!" Mercedes hissed. "Don't make noise—it'll give away our position! Do you want to stay alive or not?"

April abruptly stopped crying, then slumped over in trembling fear. Mercedes's heart twisted, but she didn't dare leave her post. The enemy was getting closer all the time, and the pile of mortar and adobe at her feet suddenly looked pitifully small. She picked up the biggest chunk in the stack and hefted it in her good hand.

Dear Lord, please don't let him near us. And please, please keep him away from Nina and Cass.

She took one last breath, stuck her arm and head out the narrow doorway and threw, just as the waiting motionless man took aim and pulled the trigger. The bullet missed her.

But the sound reverberated against the circular walls of the well, bouncing off the limestone and echoing everywhere. Mercedes dropped to the dirt floor and threw her body over April, covering her ears.

There was a second shot, and its report mingled with the echoes of the first. The front wall of their room, already weakened by age and its trespassers, trembled at the sound wave's onslaught for one shivering second...

...and collapsed onto the woman, the child and the man far below.

CASS HEARD THE REPORT. Fear ran icy in his heart as he yelled, "What was that?"

"What?" Will yelled back above the racket of the bumping speeding car.

"That noise! It sounded like—" Cass never finished his sentence. An even louder noise blasted just below them. The cab skewed and fishtailed, then yawed to a stop on the side of the road.

"A flat tire?" Will said helpfully.

Cass slammed a fist down on the dashboard and swore.

MERCEDES SLOWLY, slowly came back to consciousness. Someone was patting her cheek and calling her name over and over. She groaned, trying to tell whoever it was to go away. But her faint moans only intensified her tormentor's efforts.

"Mercedes, wake up!"

"April?"

April nodded, stroking her uninjured hand. Mercedes welcomed the touch. She was very disoriented, her side hurt terribly, and for a moment she didn't know where she was. There was adobe and mortar everywhere, and the sun beat down on top of them. "What's going on?" she managed to ask.

"The building fell on us."

"Building? What building?"

"The pueblo."

"Oh. Are you hurt?"

"Just my ankle from before."

"That's good." She closed her eyes in relief, then opened them wide again as memory flooded back. "That man! Where is he?"

"I looked for him, Mercedes. I didn't see him anywhere."

"I'd better go check and make sure." Mercedes tried to sit up. A mistake. Broken bone ends grated against each other, and she groaned in pain.

"Mercedes? *Mercedes?*"

"Just a broken rib—or two," she gasped as she carefully lay back down. She was having some difficulty breathing, too. Every word she spoke hurt, and she couldn't seem to suck in enough air. "Are you sure...he's not still try-ing...to get up here?"

"I couldn't see him anywhere. I...I think he's in the wa-ter, too."

If he isn't, let's hope his gun is. "I'm going to check."

Mercedes braced her side with one forearm and slowly eased her battered body toward the ledge, aware of aches and pains all over. Her head had escaped injury, but her back, arms and legs were sore from the falling mortar. They were lucky the wall's weight hadn't killed them both.

Mercedes peered over. What she saw was Chuckie's part-ner at the very edge of the water. From this height she couldn't tell if he was alive or not, nor could she tell where the gun was. But she could see he wasn't moving at all.

Slowly, painfully, she inched her way back into what lit-tle shade remained on the ledge. The effort exhausted her, and she had to close her eyes again.

"Mercedes, wake up!" April cried.

She immediately opened her eyes. "I'm awake."

"You aren't going to die, are you?" April asked fearfully. "I got the rocks off you as soon as I could."

"Thanks. And I'm not...going to die." She couldn't believe how hard it was to talk and breathe at the same time. "I was just...trying to figure out...a way down. I can't climb." She whispered the last words. "How about you?"

"My ankle still hurts."

"Can you...stand on it?"

"I don't know."

"Try for me. But stand...way back here." Just in case the man with the gun came to, she thought. With the front half of the adobe ruins now at their feet or in the sinkhole, she had to make sure the sun didn't reveal April to their enemy and turn her into an easy target.

The experiment was a dismal failure. "Owww!" April shrieked upon rising. Tears welled in her eyes.

"Oh, April... I shouldn't have...kicked you so hard."

"It's not your fault. That man wouldn't let go." April rubbed at her badly swollen ankle with trembling hands. "I want to go home!"

"And we will. Just as soon...as your father comes." The words came out in a gasping, ragged whisper.

April blinked. "Daddy's coming?"

"Of course. I left him a note saying...we'd be back before eight and..." She rubbed at the dirt on her wristwatch. It was after nine now. "He'll be here."

"But we have the Jeep."

"He'll be here," Mercedes repeated. *Please, Cass, come get us.* "You...be the lookout, April. If you get thirsty... drink from my canteen. I'm going to rest...just a bit, okay?"

April scooted nearer to her. "Mercedes..."

"Hmm?"

"You promise you aren't going to die?"

"Not me." Mercedes took April's hand in her own and gave it a squeeze. "Worst part's...over. All we have to do...is wait."

"WOULD YOU HURRY UP with that tire iron?" Cass ordered. "I can't wait all day!" He wiped the sweat off his forehead, then wiped his hand on his dripping shirt. The sun was beating down like a blast furnace, there wasn't any shade for miles, and he wasn't any closer to finding Mercedes and April than he'd been thirty minutes ago.

The sandy track had collapsed twice under the jacked-up cab. He'd even tried driving with a flat tire, but that only caused the cab to mire down deeper in the loose dirt. This was the third time they'd tried to jack up the car.

"Stand back, Nina, and keep your fingers crossed," Cass said as Will handed him the tire iron.

Nina crossed her fingers, but she didn't look any more hopeful than Cass felt. He started pumping the tire iron.

"Watch out!" Will yelled. "She's slipping!"

Whoof! The cab was right back in the sand and rocks again, the jack and iron thrown clear.

"This isn't going to work," Will said.

"Tell me something I don't know," Cass replied harshly. "How long did your dispatcher say it would take the police to get here?"

Will shook his head. "This is a state park. The state police have to respond, not the local sheriff. And it's a slow drive. You know what these roads can do. I wish you'd called them before you left your motel."

Cass angrily kicked at the tire. "You'd better radio for a tow truck, then. Nina, take the dog and get back in the car. At least the air-conditioning still works."

The cabbie nodded. "We can wait in comfort until help shows up."

"How far is it to the Well?"

Nina paused, her hand on the taxi door. "It's almost four miles in from the highway."

Cass's heart sank. They hadn't gone very far before blowing the tire. He doubted they'd come even a mile. "Does this road lead straight to it?"

"Yes," Nina replied, and Will incredulously asked, "You aren't going to try to *walk* in, are you?"

"Yes, I am. Will, would you mind watching Nina until I get back?"

"But it's over a hundred degrees out there! You'll fry!"

"I have water." Cass patted the canteen on his belt. He'd filled both his and Nina's before they left the hotel. "Nina, will you behave yourself for Will?"

"I'm going with you."

"No way, kid. You're staying here."

"You can't make me!"

"Nina, you're not going and that's final! Will, keep her inside the cab."

The girl gave Will a disdainful look. "He can't make me either."

"Don't argue, young lady. Get in the car," Cass ordered.

Nina's answer was to unclip Baron's leash. "Watch him, boy." She gave the command in Spanish.

Immediately the dog was on guard. Cass hadn't taken two steps in Nina's direction when Baron's lips curled in a low warning growl. Cass stopped in his tracks. He'd never tutored Baron in guard-duty skills or in Spanish, but obviously Nina had, and done a thorough job of it, too.

"Don't be foolish, Nina! Neither you nor Baron should be out in this heat."

"You're not my boss," Nina said stubbornly.

Damn it, this infuriating kid means business. "Nina. Let me take care of this. This is my responsibility, not yours."

"She's *my* mother! And I'm going!"

She headed down the dirt track, Baron keeping the two men at bay until she whistled for him. Immediately he ran to her side.

"Did you see those teeth? That's one mean dog," Will said, white-faced.

"No. That's one hell of a dog trainer." Cass couldn't help feeling impressed. And incensed. Why hadn't Mercedes taken a stronger hand with her?

"So what are we going to do now?" Will asked.

"*I'm* going after her. *You're* going to wait for the police and the tow truck. Send someone down to the Well to get us."

"You're really going to let that kid hike three miles in this heat?"

Cass took one look at the girl's determined strides, at the stiff little back, at the faithful guardian at her side.

"I don't think I have a choice, do I?"

THE SUN WAS HIGH in the sky. Its merciless rays struck every inch of the narrow ledge and heated the limestone surfaces to blistering temperatures. There was no refuge from the heat.

"It's so hot." April's voice was hoarse and dry. "Mercedes, are you sure you don't want the rest of the water?"

Mercedes shook her head just once, the rocks hard beneath her scalp. It was difficult enough to breathe, let alone talk.

"You should drink some. It's your canteen." April lifted the near-empty canteen to Mercedes's mouth, but Mercedes closed her eyes.

"Please, Mercedes, please." April was crying, but when Mercedes opened her eyes, she saw no tears on April's cheeks. They were both becoming dehydrated. She had to say something. Her words sounded faint and jerky.

"I can't breathe... when I... sit up." Being thirsty was preferable to being airless. She was sure she had a punctured lung from the broken rib, and the move to peer over the ledge had made things worse.

"Maybe I should try to climb down," April suggested hesitantly. "I could do it," she said, although she hugged her stomach at the thought.

"No!" Mercedes grabbed April's hand. "Wait... for Cass. He'll come... for you." *He's not like Gilles. He's always there for his daughter.* "He's... a rescuer... remember?"

April calmed down just a little. "You know something, Mercedes? I'm kinda glad he likes to rescue people." There was a look of surprise on her face.

"He's... a good father." *You're lucky to have him. Nina should be so lucky.*

April managed a smile. "He'll find us. Real soon, too."

"So drink... the water."

April hesitated. "I'll save you half," she promised. But she saved Mercedes much more than half.

And beneath the searing sun, hand in hand, they waited.

NINA STUMBLED, and Cass took her hand to steady her.

"You're as stubborn as your mother. You Delacruz women are the most stubborn I've ever met. If you were my daughter, I'd paddle your behind and ground you for a month," Cass declared.

Nina glared at him.

"No, a year," he corrected as he held fast to her. "And that goes for your damn dog, too."

"You could try," Nina said. But she didn't pull her hand away from his. "Cass... do you think they're all right? Will we find them?"

He looked into the dark eyes beneath that jet black hair— and saw fear mixed with trust, trust in him. He wouldn't lie to this child. She'd lived with lies—her own lies—long enough already.

"I don't know one way or the other. But I'm worried. That's why we're checking up on them, right?"

Nina nodded. She twisted the dog's leash in her hands. "But if Mom's missing and Dad's still missing, who'll take care of me?"

Cass stopped walking to gently take Nina by the shoulders. "Your father's not missing, Nina. He's dead."

Nina wound the leash even more tightly around her hand and ducked her head. Cass had to tip her chin to make her meet his eyes.

"Say it, Nina. He's dead. And I think you know it. That's why you're so worried about having someone to take care of you. And that's why you insisted on coming with me to look for your mother. Isn't it?"

Nina refused to answer. Cass hardened his heart and ignored the girl's trembling lower lip.

"Your mother's waiting for us, Nina. Your father isn't, *but she is*. And April's waiting, too. We have to concentrate on the living and put the dead to rest. Do you understand what I'm saying?"

Nina nodded.

"Then say it, too. Say, 'My father's dead and he's never coming home.'"

"I can't!" Nina wailed.

"Yes, you can."

Nina squeezed her eyes shut. "I won't."

"Fine." Cass released her. "Take Baron and go back to the cab. I don't bring babies along with me on rescues."

He deliberately turned his back and started walking away.

"Cass..."

He kept going.

"Cass, wait!"

He forced himself not to turn around at her plea.

"My dad's dead and I don't want my mom to die, too!"

Cass pivoted in the sand. There were no tears on her face, but it didn't matter. He heard the conviction in her words, saw it in the grief-stricken expression on her face.

"Please take me with you!" Nina begged. "I'll be good!"

Cass's answer was to hold out his arms. Nina hurried the few steps separating them and threw herself into his protective embrace.

"You don't have to be good," Cass whispered as he held her tight. "You just have to be honest, okay?"

Nina nodded.

"That's my brave girl. Now, new rules," Cass announced, holding her safe. "From now on, I'm in charge."

Nina nodded again. He stepped back so he could see her face, although his arms still encircled her.

"I mean it. You do *exactly* what I say. And you make Baron do what I want. I don't know why April and your mother are late. But if they're in trouble, their safety might depend on my expertise. *Mine,* not yours. You'll obey me without question—without hesitation. Do you understand?"

Nina stared down at the sandy trail in silence. The only sound was the heavy panting of the dog at their side. And then she lifted her eyes to his. "I promise."

Cass gave her a ghost of a smile. "All right, then." He adjusted her hat, made her have a drink of water, took one himself and poured some for the dog. "Now tell me—how much farther do we have to go?"

"Do you think they're getting close?" April asked.

The child's words seemed to be coming from far, far away. Mercedes could barely hear her.

"Mercedes!" April shook her, and the pain in her side jolted her awake.

"Please . . ." she gasped.

"Then stay awake!"

"I...can't, honey." The words came out on a gasping sigh. She was too oxygen-starved to keep her eyes open, just as she was too weak to brush away the flies crawling over her injured hand.

"You promised we'd tell Dad what I did to Twister together! Remember?"

Mercedes nodded.

"And you said you'd tell Nina about her dad, too."

Mercedes struggled to find the air to speak. The pain seared her chest; the hot desert air seared her throat. She might not be able to keep her promise. She could already feel her strength being sapped, bit by inexorable bit.

"You...might have to tell him...alone," Mercedes whispered, her eyes still closed.

"No!"

"Yes. You...tell him. Tell him about...Nina's father, too."

"You promised you'd stay awake!"

"I'm...trying, April. But if I can't..." She felt the child's fingers stroking her forehead. Unlike Nina, April had a gentle touch. It reminded her of Cass. "Tell Nina...I love her. Tell your father I..."

I love him, too.

"Tell them yourself!" And April shook her again. Hard.

The pain of her broken ribs consumed her, blotting out even the fierce glare of the sun.

"Oh, God, April," Mercedes whimpered. "Please don't..."

"Then you stay awake," April said furiously. She'd positioned her body so that her shadow fell over Mercedes's face. "Keep your eyes open or I'll shake you again."

Her breath came in ragged gasps. The agony in her side and lungs made her feel sick to her stomach. But she kept her eyes open.

And they waited.

"HOW MUCH FARTHER?" Cass asked. His shirt was drenched, and despite his sunglasses, his eyes ached with the sun's glare.

"The parking lot should be just ahead," Nina said. "I think... There! I see our Jeep!"

She started to run ahead, but Cass grabbed her arm. "Wait!" he ordered. "There's another vehicle there."

"So what?"

"It's Sunday."

Nina stopped abruptly. "You... you don't think it's the looters, do you?"

"Mercedes and April were late for a reason. Until I find out what that reason is, you stay here out of sight. Go wait on the other side of that ledge with Baron."

Cass gestured toward the end of parking lot farthest away from the shabby brown truck and the outhouses.

"Wait?"

"Yes, wait." Cass handed her his wristwatch. "If I whistle for you, your mom's okay. If you don't hear me whistle in fifteen minutes, or if you see any strangers, run straight to Will and tell him. Use Baron to protect yourself if you have to."

"But Cass..." Nina was confused, and not for the first time since her father's disappearance, frightened. She didn't know what to think, what to do. But somehow, Cass looked as if he *did* know. And that confidence gave her courage.

"Fifteen minutes," Cass repeated. "Wait for my whistle."

Nina slid on his watch. It hung loosely from her small wrist.

"Yes, sir," she said.

HE WAS ALONE. Cass was in the middle of nowhere, with no one to help him. No rangers, no police, no dog. Nothing. It was like when Marian—

He refused to think about that. Refused to think about all the relatives he'd let slip away, all the friends he could have made, but didn't. There were only new dogs to train and strangers to rescue. He'd become so distanced from his own life he hadn't even been able to touch his daughter's heart and ease her pain.

Once this was over, he'd do things right by April, he promised himself. And Mercedes. *But let them be okay.*

He hurried to the parking lot and saw no one in the Jeep or the truck. Nor did he see anyone as he jogged up the path that led to the Well. There wasn't a soul in sight. But the pile of adobe bricks in the bed of the battered pickup, along with the picks and shovels, spoke volumes.

Where were April and Mercedes?

Cass increased his pace, almost running up the steep incline. His heart was pounding in his chest from heat and fear, but he didn't slow down. If anything, he ran faster.

Dear God, let them be all right.

APRIL KEPT a close eye on Mercedes. Every minute or so, she scanned the concrete viewing platform at the top entrance to the Well. "Dad will be here any minute. He's coming, Mercedes."

There was no response.

"Open your eyes!"

April had to fight back the sick feeling in her stomach. "Squeeze my hand, or I'll shake you," she warned. "I'll shake you hard." She breathed a sigh of relief as Mercedes squeezed, and continued watching across the rim.

"Dad's coming. I just know he's coming," she kept saying.

Cass stared at the huge limestone sink, at that yawning chasm. He'd seen pictures of Montezuma Well before, but the reality of the eerie silence and the murky waters far below shook him badly. Where could they be? There was a paved path with concrete steps, but the lower ruins along the path all had barricades. It would take a long time to hike down and inspect all those nooks and crannies to see if April and Mercedes were there....

"Dad's coming. I just know he's coming," April was saying over and over until Mercedes was ready to scream. She would have, if she'd had the strength. Nina used to say those very words at the airport every time they waited for Gilles to fly home.

It seemed she'd spent her whole life waiting for someone who was never there. She opened her eyes and gazed toward the entrance path to the Well, hoping against hope she'd see someone.

And then, from over the far rim, Cass appeared.

Was she imagining things? April's excitement gave her the answer.

"Daddy? Mercedes, it's Daddy!" April scrambled to stand, balanced on her one good foot and began to wave. "He's here!"

"April!" Cass yelled. His daughter's name echoed throughout the Well. "Mercedes? Where are you?"

A glint of movement caught Cass's eye. He blinked, then saw... April? He stared at his daughter's precarious perch, stared at the murky waters separating them. What was she doing in that death trap?

"April!" he yelled again as he returned her wave. "Are you all right?"

He saw her shake her head and point to her leg. Cass suddenly realized she wasn't yelling back and wondered how long it had been since she'd had something to drink.

"Where's Mercedes?" Joy at his daughter's appearance was tempered by fear. "Is she with you?"

She nodded and gestured toward her feet. Cass saw the motionless form lying prostrate on the ledge, and he gripped the iron bars of the platform's restraining fence for support. He took a deep breath.

"Is she . . ." His words came out too softly, and he tried again. "Is she okay?" The words echoed across the sink-hole.

April shook her head. Cass made two tries before he was able to get the next words out of his mouth. "Is she alive?"

April waved, and his knees buckled. "I'm coming, baby!" he shouted once his heart and lungs were working normally again. "Tell Mercedes I'm on my way."

But first, he whistled for Nina.

CHAPTER TWENTY

IT WAS NINA and Baron who found the second man's body in the rocks at the edge of the water while Cass climbed high above. And it was Nina and Baron who found Chuckie beneath the water. They were waiting at the bottom of the ledge when Cass made his first descent with April.

"Better walk this way," Nina said, protectively guiding April around the grisly sight. April missed seeing the two bodies, but Cass didn't. He stared at them, and the babbling garbled story April had told him suddenly made sense.

He started toward Nina, knowing she must have made the discovery alone while he was up on the ledge. But Nina showed no signs of hysteria.

"I'll find April some shade, and you can go help Mom, if that's okay with you."

She was actually waiting for his approval, Cass realized.

"April?" he asked. April was limping heavily. She leaned on the smaller girl, but Nina handled the load easily.

April nodded her agreement.

"I'll be down soon," he promised.

"Tell Mercedes I saved some water for her," April added, her voice so hoarse it was barely audible. "She told me to drink it all, but I didn't. I left the canteen next to her."

Cass's throat tightened. "I will."

"This way, April," Nina ordered. "Come, Baron."

Nina and April would be okay for now, Cass decided. Mercedes needed him more. He gave both girls a quick kiss, then began moving up the wall a second time, ignoring the bodies of the two men. The dead could wait, but not the living. When he'd gone up the first time, Mercedes had still been breathing, but she hadn't responded to him. April had told him to shake her, but he'd vetoed that idea, afraid of doing further damage. He'd been relieved to see that Mercedes had a steady, if somewhat weak, pulse.

"Mercedes? It's Cass," he said now as he cleared the ledge and stepped carefully around the collapsed rubble. He knelt next to her motionless body and patted her cheek. "Wake up for me, sweetheart."

This time she did. "Cass? You came..."

Her surprise, then her joy affected him deeply. "Of course I came, Mercedes," he said simply.

He watched as she gazed at him. She didn't smile. Her expression was almost one of awe. Then that disappeared and was replaced by fear. "Those men..." She grasped at his arm.

"April told me about them, Mercedes. They're both dead. And the police are on their way."

"The girls?"

"They're okay. Nina's here, sniffles and all, but she insists she's fine. April's putting weight on her ankle. I don't think it's broken. She needs fluids, but she's hanging in there. You need water, too, but I don't dare give you any, since you'll probably be going straight into surgery."

Mercedes closed her eyes again. Cass hoped it was more from relief than pain. He had to force himself to remain calm at the faintness of her voice. In the few minutes since he'd left her side, she'd weakened.

"We'll get you out of here," Cass promised, lifting her good hand to his lips and brushing a kiss on the palm. "A basket stretcher over the rim, and you'll be home free."

Mercedes's eyes opened one last time. "I'm sorry...about April. Didn't mean...for this to happen."

"It's okay, Mercedes. For now, just rest. We'll talk later."

But later was a long while coming.

Thanks to Will and his radio, the police were accompanied by the fire department and a helicopter medi-flight. Cass signed a consent form for April, and both she and Mercedes were lifted out by helicopter and flown to Phoenix's Desert Humana Hospital. Nina and Cass drove Will to the Camp Verde police station and headed back to their motel. There Cass called Mercedes's family, then checked out. With a police escort, he and Nina made the drive south to Phoenix in record time.

When they reached the hospital, Mercedes and April had already been treated, and were sharing the same room. He and Nina stopped to talk to some of Mercedes's family first and drop off Baron. All the Delacruzes had shown up in force, and at the doctor's insistence, the last of them had just left the room for the parking lot. Nina refused to go with them. She insisted on accompanying Cass to talk to the doctor.

"I'm Dr. Kachinsky," the internist introduced herself. She was an older gray-haired woman with kind eyes. "The news is good for both patients."

Cass heaved a sigh of gratitude and relief. At least he was able to listen to the doctor's next words without his heart hammering.

"How's my mom?" Nina immediately asked.

"Mrs. Delacruz has a pneumothorax—a punctured lung."

Nina bit her lip. Cass was surprised at how young Nina suddenly looked, and he slung a comforting arm around her shoulder.

"Fortunately it's easily treatable. We've put a tube in her chest and adjusted the pressure in the pleural cavity to re-expand the damaged lung."

Nina gasped. "Doesn't that hurt?"

"Yes, some," the doctor said honestly. "But it's letting your mother breathe normally. We'll take the tube out when the lung heals. She'll be here for a week to ten days."

"That long?" Nina said. For once her bravado failed her, and Cass pulled her close.

"We have her on IV antibiotics and see no problem with her recovery," the doctor added. "She'll be all right, young lady."

Nina nodded, but her face was still pinched and worried.

"What about her hand?" Cass asked.

"Again, painful, but not serious. After we got her breathing normally again, the hand surgeon used a local to repair a torn tendon and sew up the punctures. He expects no residual effects."

Nina sagged against Cass's side. He guided her to a nearby chair as he asked, "And how's my daughter?"

"She's dehydrated. We'll keep her on an IV for that. And her right ankle was badly bruised. She needs to stay off it for a few days." Dr. Kachinsky hesitated. "Mrs. Delacruz told me April has some other symptoms she wants us to look at. I'd like to run a few extra tests, but since Mrs. Delacruz isn't the child's guardian..."

"Is something else wrong with April?" Cass asked, that hard driving fear back.

"I understand she's been having stomach problems, Mr. Montgomery."

Cass exhaled with relief. "That's probably just nerves," he said.

"I'm not sure that's all it is. And as long as your daughter's admitted, it wouldn't hurt to check her out physically—and perhaps emotionally, too, considering the circumstances," Dr. Kachinsky added. "April's gone through a very traumatic event. We have an excellent child psychologist on staff, and I have the paperwork right here."

She held out the clipboard. After a moment's hesitation, Cass took it, signed and passed it back.

"Can we see them now?" Nina asked impatiently.

"Of course." The doctor gave them the room number and Nina tugged at Cass's hand.

"Let's go."

"Thank you, doctor," Cass managed to say. Then they headed for the elevators.

Mercedes was sleeping when they found the room. Like April, she had an IV. Unlike April, Mercedes was on oxygen. Pale green plastic lines were fed to a nasal inhaler. Nina would have hurried to her mother's side, but Cass stopped her just outside the door.

"Don't wake her, Nina. Let her wake up on her own. Don't jump on the bed or jostle her, either," Cass warned. "She has that tube in her chest, remember?"

Nina nodded, and the two of them walked in. Nina took the chair next to her mother's bed. Cass gently touched her shoulder before sitting down beside April. April opened her eyes when he took her hand.

"Daddy?"

Cass smiled. He leaned over and kissed his daughter on the forehead. "Hi, kiddo. How're you doing?"

His answer was the biggest hug he'd had from April in years, and the same words he'd heard earlier from Mercedes. "You came," was all she said. "You came."

"I'm your father, April." Cass lifted his trembling daughter from the bed, IV tube and all. He sat down with her in his lap, and her close. "I'll always be there when you need me. I love you."

April raised her head from his shoulder. "Mercedes told me you'd say that."

"Mercedes is a wise woman," Cass said with a lopsided smile.

April didn't smile back. "Dad, I have something to tell you."

Cass was alarmed by the look on April's face. "It can wait, honey."

"No, Dad, it can't."

And without waiting for Mercedes to wake up, in the presence of a shocked, silent Nina, April told him everything. Cass listened as April started with that day in the airport and ended with her confession to Mercedes just hours before.

By the time she'd finished she was in tears. Cass was perilously close himself.

"Please don't hate me, Daddy. I'm sorry."

"I could never hate you, sweetheart." He held his daughter closer. *The pain she must have suffered.*

"But all those people who died . . ."

Cass tilted April's chin until she met his gaze.

"Listen carefully, April. You don't know if having Twister would have made any difference. *I* don't know that."

"But you always said Twister has a better nose than Buddy."

"Yes, but Twister's an old dog now, while Buddy's young and strong. She's faster, and she lasts longer on a rescue. What Buddy lacks in the nose department, she makes up for with her willingness to search. That's just as important, April."

April was not convinced. "You're just saying that."

"Have I ever lied to you, April?"

"No, but . . ."

"But nothing. Even three years ago, Twister was slowing down. I don't think I was ready to see that yet. He was a great rescue dog in his day—and he helped me through some very bad years. Now, though, I know it's time for him to retire."

"Mercedes said that, too," was April's surprised response.

"She wouldn't lie, April. And neither would I. Believe me, *no one* died because of you. No one was ever at risk—except Twister."

April bowed her head and wrapped one arm around her stomach. His own insides knotted with pain. All this time, and he'd never known.

"Are you going to punish me for what I did?" April asked.

"No, baby."

"But—"

"Baron's injuries were an accident." Cass and April both gave a start at the sound of Mercedes's voice. "An accident caused by bad judgment. You've suffered enough, April. And so has your father. It's time to move on."

April finally raised her head, first to look at Mercedes and then at him. The desperation on his daughter's face tore at his heart.

"Dad?"

"She's right, April. Let it go. Just let it go."

April began to cry again, but now they were healing tears. Cass rocked his daughter in his arms for a long, long time. It wasn't until she was asleep that he put her back in the bed.

He tucked her in and smoothed her hair, then pulled his chair over next to Nina, who sat holding her mother's uninjured hand.

"Thank you for taking care of April today, Mercedes," he said.

"You needn't be kind, Cass," she replied wearily. "I'm the one who endangered April in the first place. I should never have taken her to the ruins with me." She sighed. "I haven't been very good with children lately. Not with April, certainly not with you, Nina."

Cass watched Mercedes's gaze swing from him to her daughter. "April and I made a promise, Nina. She promised to tell Cass about Baron, and I promised to tell you about your father."

"That he's dead, right?"

Mercedes blinked. "Yes, but...just yesterday..."

"Cass told me. I didn't want Daddy to be dead, so I just pretended he wasn't." Nina studied the tile pattern on the floor. "But then you were missing, and I was afraid you'd get lost, too. Just like Dad."

Nina broke down, and Mercedes brought Nina's hand to her heart. "Oh, Nina, I'm so sorry I wasn't there for you."

"It's okay. I shouldn't have been so stupid." Nina went on staring at the floor, bravely trying not to cry. After a long moment she lifted her head. "You know..." she said, dashing a tear from her face. Then she hesitated.

"Go on, Nina," Cass urged. "Finish what you were going to say."

"I'm glad Cass let me help look for you. And when we found you—" Nina's smile was brilliant, despite the wet eyes "—it felt good, Mom. I want to do it again—not look for *you*, I mean, but look for other people."

"Baron's too old for that," Cass said quickly, trying to forestall what he suspected was coming next. But Nina wasn't about to be diverted.

"Not with Baron, Cass. With you and Buddy! I want to do rescues! Can I, Mom? Can I?"

For a moment Cass honestly thought Mercedes would need the doctor again, she'd gone so pale. He was about to push her call button, but then she spoke. He and Nina had to strain to hear her.

"I think your father would have liked that, Nina. We'll talk about it, I promise."

"When you feel better," Nina said generously. "After you get home."

A knock sounded on the open door—it was one of Nina's aunts. "Come on, Nina," she said in Spanish. "Time to go now."

Nina looked at her mother. Mercedes nodded as Cass said, "I'll see you later, okay?"

Nina kissed her mother goodbye, waved to Cass and left. Cass and Mercedes were alone now, and the first thing he did was reach for a tissue to wipe Mercedes's cheeks.

"How are you feeling?" he asked.

"Like the lousiest parent on earth." The tears continued to fall, and Cass reached for a second tissue. "God, what a mess I've made of things."

"Hey, lighten up. We're all alive, lady. Maybe not in one piece, but still kicking." He tried to coax a smile out of her, but Mercedes wasn't responding.

"Cass, about April..."

"She'll be fine," Cass insisted. "Everyone's going to be fine."

Mercedes shook her head. "Cass, listen to me. April *isn't* fine. I think... I think April has an ulcer."

"Mercedes, really! Don't be ridiculous."

"A bleeding peptic ulcer, Cass."

"You're wrong."

Mercedes touched his arm for emphasis. "The doctor agrees with me. She told me she was going to ask your permission for more tests. Did she? And did you sign for them?"

Horrified, Cass remembered the internist's words. He turned toward his daughter, Mercedes's words floating over his shoulder. "April's very sick. That's why she's always holding her stomach. That's why she's so thin and why she fainted back in Florida. The stress of the last three years has been killing her—emotionally *and* physically."

Cass turned back toward Mercedes again, still unable to believe what he'd heard. "My God, Mercedes, she's only eleven years old!"

"It's stress that causes ulcers, not age. And she's hated herself for the past three years."

"But she never said a word! I never noticed..." His voice trailed off as guilt washed over him. "I should have noticed. You did."

"I was an objective observer, Cass. I could see that something was wrong, and out at the ruins..." Cass was shocked to see the guilt on Mercedes's face. "My dragging April out to the Well today didn't help, either. They tried to kill her, Cass! They tried to kill us both. All over a few damn adobe bricks."

For a moment he was afraid she'd start crying again. With great effort, he pulled himself together and focused on Mercedes. "Assigning blame isn't going to help April—or Nina."

He took her hand in his and tried to instill as much confidence in his words and expression as he could. "We did our best as parents. Our best may not have been good enough this time around, but it was still our best. So let's save the reproaches and concentrate on the girls. They need us, Mercedes."

Cass was pleased to see her nod. Her long black hair whispered against the starched pillowcase.

"Dr. Kachinsky recommended a psychologist for April. I think counseling might be in order for Nina again, too. *Family* counseling," he added. "There's a lot to be said for objective observers."

"You're right, of course."

"I think both girls will benefit. We'll get them whipped into shape in no time. Hey, it might even help us, too." He was amazed at how confident, even matter-of-fact he managed to sound. But judging by the hopeful look in her eyes,

Mercedes seemed to believe him, and for that, he was grateful.

"So... feeling better?" he asked once more.

"A little." Cass noticed that she was struggling to keep her eyes open, and he took the hint.

"I should go check on Nina, talk to the doctor again and give your boss a call. I'm assuming your family can help me there?"

"Yes. And I'll keep an eye on April for you. If... if you trust me to."

Cass looked at April's sleeping form just a few feet away and shivered. *Without Mercedes, who knows what would have happened to her?*

"I trust you, Mercedes. Completely. More important, April trusts you." Very carefully he leaned over and kissed his daughter. He would have liked to kiss Mercedes, but he couldn't. Not yet. There was something he had to do first.

When he straightened again, he began in a serious voice, "I know you need your rest, Mercedes. But there's something I'd like to say before I leave. About Gilles..."

He saw the pain flicker across her face, and despite the anguish he felt over April, he was still able to feel a stab of jealousy. He'd come to love this woman so much. And that love gave him the strength to say, "If you want me to find Gilles for you, I will. Buddy might not be the rescue dog Baron once was, but she does okay. And I have other friends who could help, too. I couldn't leave for Alaska right away," he qualified, "because I have to see to April first. But if finding Gilles is what you and Nina need to get on with your lives, I'll find him—no matter how long it takes."

He rested his hand on the bars of his daughter's bed, as much to steady himself as to stand guard over his only child. He, Cass Montgomery, afraid of nothing and no one, was afraid to meet this woman's eyes. And then he did it, anyway. "That's all I wanted to say, Mercedes. Except...maybe someday, when this is behind us, you can learn to trust me."

"Cass—"

"Look, you don't have to say anything," he said quickly, not wanting her pity. "I want you to know that if you and Nina ever need me to find Gilles—or for anything else—call. I'm just a thought away."

"Cass, I don't want you to try to find Gilles."

"You don't?"

"No." Her denial was a soft sigh. "They looked for Gilles for the longest time and couldn't find him. I doubt anyone else could, either. I'd rather you stayed available for the living."

She really meant it, Cass saw. Her eyes were dry, and her manner calm and steady. "But thank you, Cass. You're a generous man."

"No, Mercedes. I'm a family man who wants a mother for my daughter and a loving wife by my side."

"You're still interested in marrying me?"

He nodded, wishing he could tell more from that quiet expression on her face.

"Yes, but only if you'll let me love you and be a father to your daughter. Marriage is a partnership, Mercedes. I'd never let you carry any load alone, whether it concerned Nina or April or one of us."

All he could hear was April's gentle breathing and the hiss of Mercedes's oxygen. "You also need to know this," he continued. "I can't give up my rescue work. I've thought about it, especially knowing what I do now about April." His gaze traveled over his daughter's pale cheeks. "I intend to make sure she's far removed from that part of my life. But rescue work is what I do."

"You aren't going to quit?" There was something in her voice, not condemnation, not even surprise, but something... Respect, perhaps?

"I can't—won't—give it up. Not now. Not ever. Not even for you. But I'd always come home as soon as possible from any rescue. I'd never deliberately choose to stay away, and I'd never go if my own family needed me more."

She nodded, her face as solemn as his. There was an awkward moment, and just as he thought he couldn't stand it any longer, she spoke.

"I understand, Cass. But if we're to have any kind of a future together, you need to know something about me."

A future together? Hope beat faint butterfly wings deep inside.

"Family is important to me, too, Cass. I couldn't have survived Gilles's death without mine. If I have to live with you risking your life for strangers, if I'm to become April's mother..."

Cass's fingers gripped the rails of April's bed more tightly as he strained to hear her next words.

"I want that kind of support system for her. And not just with me or my relatives," she specified. "With *your* relatives. And Marian's, too."

Cass thought back to the bitter custody fight that had followed Marian's death.

"I've kept in touch with them for the past twelve years."

"Yes, you have. *You,* Cass, but not April. You've kept them far away from her."

"I've been well within my rights."

"No one would argue with that," Mercedes said softly. "But to an outsider, it looks as if you still don't trust them. That custody fight for April is long over, and no one's tried to take your daughter since."

"What are you saying, Mercedes?"

"I'm saying—forgive me, Cass—but maybe you haven't been as generous as you think."

Cass started to argue, then caught himself. "Go on."

"Well, if—heaven forbid—I lost Nina, then was denied all contact with her only child—" Mercedes trembled with emotion "—I don't think I could bear it."

Cass answered slowly. "I see what you mean . . ."

"Then maybe, just maybe, you should give them all another chance. You don't have to leave April alone with them, but couldn't you let them see her—see you both—in person? If it were me, it would mean so much more than the annual Christmas card and occasional phone call."

Mercedes's soft brown eyes were on him. "Do you think you could do that, Cass?"

"It's been so many years . . ." Before today, he honestly didn't know if those broken fences could ever be mended. But now . . . His heart fired with determination.

"April needs love more than she needs a psychologist," Mercedes said. "You'd be surprised at the miracles one's family can accomplish. *All* of one's family."

"It could take a long time," Cass warned, even as hope slowly grew within him.

"I'll wait, because Nina will need that time. I won't be replacing anyone in April's life, but that's not true for Nina. Of us all, it'll be hardest on her. I've hurt her enough. I won't make that mistake again."

Then Mercedes broke down completely. The tears ran down her face as Cass released the rails to take her good hand in his. He longed to hold her in his arms, against his heart, as he had done with April. He contented himself with kissing her fingers just once and gently smoothing her hair.

"Hey, none of that. It can't be good for your chest," he warned in a no-nonsense voice. "You don't want the doctor forbidding visitors, do you?"

She shook her head and blinked back the tears.

"You can have a good crying jag later. I'll schedule a day for you, say, a week from next Wednesday?"

Mercedes managed a smile. And for the first time in years, Cass felt the old memories of the past make way for something new, for the family he'd always wanted. He sat down next to her again and did what he'd told April to do with all the sadness.

His hand still in hers, he looked into Mercedes eyes and let it all go.

They stayed that way for an hour or more. Not until the hospital loudspeakers announced that visiting hours were over did Cass reluctantly rise to his feet.

"Well, I should get back to Nina. If she's feeling okay tomorrow, I'll bring her here in the morning for a visit."

"Thank you, Cass. I'd like that." And Mercedes closed her eyes.

He wanted to say more, hating to leave on such an impersonal note, but afraid it was too soon for the intimate language of lovers. He hesitated, taking in the pale face, the black hair on the pillow, then settled for a simple stroke of her cheek before going.

She smiled at his touch and left her eyes closed. The smile almost made up for the words he had to leave unsaid. He checked on the sleeping April one last time and headed for the door. He was almost out of the room before he heard Mercedes's parting words.

"I love you, too, Cass."

He'd never heard anything so damn good.

NINA SAT on her front porch, her arm slung around Baron's neck. Despite her aunt's and her grandmother's coaxing, she refused to go back inside after she'd showered and eaten.

"You have a cold, Nina. You should be inside resting."

"I want to wait for Cass."

"But you've had such a terrible day, *bambina*. And you've seen such terrible things. You need to be with family."

"I'm not coming in," she stubbornly insisted.

"Then we'll sit outside with you."

"No! Go away and leave me alone!"

In view of the strain of the day, the relatives decided to humor her, although they checked on her so often that Nina was ready to scream. *Don't people understand anything?* she wondered. She wasn't like April. She understood that death was a part of life. Lots of things died. Pretty birds and fluffy rabbits and leafy trees all died. Even her own father had died alone in the white of the arctic. Well, she hadn't *wanted* to face that, but it was true, and she finally had. So why should those terrible men be any exception?

Especially since they'd deserved to die much more than the birds or rabbits ever did. *Or her father.* After all, they'd tried to hurt her mother and April. Good riddance, Nina thought. She was glad they were gone.

It was over...or it *would* be, if everyone would stop talking about it. She'd finally figured things out. She'd admitted the truth, done what was expected of her. Was it asking too much to be left alone?

Keeping death in a living heart was foolish, Nina realized. Look how dumb April had been. Nina remembered April's words in the hospital. She'd nearly killed Baron and then made herself sick over it for three long years. It was galling to believe *she'd* been nearly as stupid as April.

Thank goodness April had been stupid twice as long as Nina, or it would be hard to hold her head up. It would be even harder living with the fact that her father was never coming back. Nina loved her mother more than anything in the world, but Gilles had been a kindred spirit. He'd understood her in a way her mother never would. Almost like Cass understood her...

Nina scratched Baron's head and blinked back sudden tears. Her mother was safe, April was safe, and she got to keep Baron, so there was no reason to cry. Only babies like April cried over things that couldn't be changed. And she was no baby. But she was worried. Those two Montgomerys...

Nina sighed. She thought about how Cass looked at her mother; it was the same way her father had looked at Mercedes. There was no mistaking that look. Nina had seen it in a hundred movies and remembered it from the happy times at home. Cass loved her mother as much as Gilles ever had. Nina had known that from the start, just as she suspected Mercedes had fallen in love with Cass. And even though Nina finally accepted that her father was dead, she was positive her mother would never marry Cass without her consent.

What to do? What would her father want her to do? It was all so confusing....

Baron wagged his tail. A few seconds later Nina heard the sound of her mother's Jeep as Cass drove into the driveway. He shut off the engine and climbed out.

"Hello, Nina." He saw her relatives peer out at them through the window. But after recognizing him, they remained inside, which was just as well. He wanted to talk to Nina alone.

"How's Mom?" she asked. "And April?"

"Both asleep. The doctor said they're doing okay." He sat down beside her on the porch, the dog nestled comfortably between them. "Why aren't you inside where it's cooler?"

Nina shrugged. Cass propped his legs on the step below and rested his hands on his knees.

"Nice sunset," he said conversationally.

"It's okay."

"Just okay?"

"I've seen them before."

Cass nodded. The purple and roses of Arizona were quite a change from Florida's orange hues, just as Mercedes had told him. They reminded him of Wyoming summer sunsets. Florida seemed awfully far away. And suddenly he was glad. There was nothing for him in Florida anymore.

"So, how're you doing?"

Nina shrugged again. "Anything you want to talk about?" he asked. "Maybe your dad?"

"Nope."

"Okay. Anything else?"

Nina looked at him after a moment. "Those two men—were there any more of them?"

"Not any longer. The police told me the two out at the Well were brothers. They just arrested the father. He's been supplying raw materials to an antiquities forger—some local artist, according to the police. The father turned state's evidence, and—"

"Turned what?" Nina interrupted.

"Told the police about the artist in exchange for a lighter criminal charge."

"He squealed?"

Cass smiled at the succinct explanation. "Yes. So we don't have to worry, Nina. They're in police custody. Your mother will be safe the next time she goes to the ruins."

Nina gave a big sigh of relief.

"Feel better?"

"Some."

Cass scratched Baron's ears. "What else is bothering you?"

She didn't answer.

"Is it me? And how I feel about your mother?"

Nina continued to stroke the dog; she wouldn't look at Cass. "You still have the hots for her, don't you?"

"It's more than just a physical attraction, Nina. I love your mother. I want to marry her. I think I could make her happy." He waited for Nina's response. There was less anger than resignation in her next words.

"I loved my dad. I don't want a new one."

"I'd still like to take care of you like I do April."

"I'm not like her. I can take care of myself."

Cass didn't argue. "Then I'd like to help you take care of your mother."

"She's so dumb sometimes. She didn't explain about Dad like you d—" Nina stopped, ashamed of her slip of the tongue, her lack of loyalty.

"She doesn't see things like we do," Cass finished for her. "Does she?"

"No. But why?"

"It's hard to say. I do know that for people like us, Nina, there's only one view of life. Everything's either right or wrong, black or white. But for people like your mother—and April—well, their views about life are full of complications. They need time to think about their lives and their decisions."

"They need to put things in perspective?"

Cass was surprised. "Yes. How did you know?"

"Something my aunt said one day."

There was silence again. Baron yawned and put his head on Nina's thigh.

"You and I make a good team, Nina. We did a great job taking care of your mother and April today, right?"

"I guess." Nina carefully stroked the black head, then toyed with the tags on Baron's collar.

"We could do it full-time if you want."

Nina considered that. April was no problem. She could deal with her. But as for Cass, that was different. He worried her. It was hard to picture her mother with anyone but her father. Still...

"I don't want to move to Florida. My grandparents and aunts and cousins are here, and I like my school."

"We could move to Arizona. I wouldn't mind, and I don't think April would, either."

Nina thought some more. "April and I wouldn't have to share a room, would we? I don't want her messing around with my stuff or wearing my clothes."

"You'd each have your own room."

"I won't change my last name," Nina warned. "I want to stay Nina Delacruz-St. Clair."

"No problem."

"I won't call you 'Dad,' either."

"I won't ask you to. 'Cass' is just fine."

He could see that Nina was running out of excuses as she desperately searched for another objection.

"April's such a baby. She gets on my nerves."

"And you get on hers. But, Nina, listen to me. The world needs sensitive souls. Our lives are enriched by them. If everyone was as practical, as down-to-earth as us, life would be pretty dull, wouldn't it?"

Nina was silent. She couldn't argue with that. She didn't know if she even *wanted* to argue anymore.

"You and April could learn from each other," Cass said. "You'd be good for each other, just like your mother and I would be good for each other. But I won't rush you. Just think about it, okay?"

Cass watched as Nina rose to her feet, Baron at her heels.

"I don't need to. I've already made up my mind."

He felt a moment's panic. "And?" he prompted.

"You better start teaching April Spanish. Because we don't speak English at home." She opened the front door wide, and Baron immediately bounded inside.

His heart expanded with relief, gratitude and the beginning of a real paternal love. Nina didn't *have* to make things this easy for him, nor would he have blamed her if she hadn't. But the daughter was as brave as her mother. Nina continued to hold the door open for him.

"Well? Are you coming in or not?"

"I'm coming in." Cass stood up as Nina's aunt and grandmother hurried to greet him in their primary tongue.

"Don't forget to speak Spanish!" Nina hissed at his side. "And this time, *try* to get the accent right!"

EPILOGUE

Five months later...

"WHERE ARE THEY? They should be here by now!" April complained. She stopped helping Mercedes sort the pottery shards just long enough to peek out the museum window overlooking the Phoenix city streets. "Traffic's not that bad!"

"Maybe they were held up at the training site," Mercedes suggested. "You know how Nina is when she gets around Baron and Buddy's puppies. She's spent her whole winter break out there with them."

"I know, Mom," April sighed. "But I want to see the wedding pictures. Dad promised he'd bring them when he came to take us to lunch, and he's late! He never used to be late in Florida. I remember when..."

Mercedes smiled and let April have her say. Mercedes's new daughter was turning into a regular chatterbox since the wedding six weeks earlier. April had also filled out some, thanks to medication and diet. She had color in her cheeks, and her gaunt look was gone. Both her doctor and her counselor had assured Cass that time and love would take care of the rest.

And it had.

Mercedes remembered applying for the wedding license. The four of them, five including Baron, had been back in the courthouse for the final custody hearing. Everyone had stood as the bailiff announced, "All rise. Civil Court of the

City of Phoenix is now in session. The Honorable Georgina B. Davis presiding.''

''Be seated.'' The judge took one look at Mercedes, Cass and the dog, and her eyebrows rushed together in irritation. ''Where is your representation, Ms. Delacruz?''

''I've released my lawyer from this case,'' Mercedes had answered.

''Please tell me you aren't going to present the rest of this case yourself.''

''I'm not, Your Honor.'' Mercedes glanced at Cass and gave him a big smile.

''At this time we wish to drop our suit and countersuit,'' Cass said.

Nina nodded vigorously; she and April petted Baron's head. The judge sighed. ''Will the plaintiff and defendant please approach the bench?''

Cass and Mercedes obeyed.

''Explanations, please,'' the judge demanded.

Cass reached for Mercedes's hand. ''We've decided to settle for joint custody, Your Honor.''

The judge was astounded. ''But you were both so determined to gain sole custody!''

''I know, Your Honor,'' Mercedes said, ''and we apologize. But the only legal action we want to pursue right now is an application for a marriage license, as well as petitions so we can adopt each other's daughter.''

''Plus my application to practice law here in Arizona,'' Cass added.

The judge leaned closer to the two of them. ''What are you saying, Mr. Montgomery? That you've used this courthouse *and* the taxpayers' money to carry on a *romance?*'' The judge's voice was loud enough to cause Baron's ears to perk up. Mercedes bit her lower lip. Cass merely grinned.

"Not intentionally... but yes, Your Honor. I suppose we have."

As the judge deliberated, Mercedes couldn't read her expression, and she experienced a tense moment. But it quickly passed. "I'll expect an invitation to the wedding." Judge Davis's eyes had twinkled for just a second, then she rapped the gavel hard. "Case dismissed. See the clerk on your way out."

And so their new life had begun. The wedding with the Canadian, Wyoming and Arizona relatives, and yes, Judge Davis, too, was a gala affair. Even Mrs. Borden and her family from Florida had been flown in to join the festivities.

"I'm glad to see you've taken an old lady's advice, Cass," Mrs. Borden had said.

"No more 'Mr. Montgomery'?" Cass had hugged her tight, kissed the wrinkled cheek she'd offered him and a few weeks later mailed her the deed to the Florida house she'd made into a home for him and April.

Despite the groups of strangers meeting each other for the first time at the wedding and the initial awkwardness between April's grandparents and the Delacruz clan, everyone had been on their best behavior. A glowing April had been so unlike her earlier self that even Nina couldn't help noticing the difference.

"You'd think *she* was getting married, instead of you," Nina had said tartly, observing April through narrowed eyes.

"Well, in a way she is," Mercedes had replied as they'd waited in the church reception hall. "For years, all April had was her father. Now she has a whole new set of relatives— eight grandparents, plus all our aunts and uncles and cousins."

"She won't learn their names posing," Nina grumbled. "What a camera hog! Just because April grew her hair out, she thinks she's a model or something."

"And who suggested that April get a new hairstyle? Who's been helping her pick out her clothes and letting her borrow her favorite earrings?" Mercedes asked with a smile.

Nina refused to admit her generosity. "Only because her ulcer was acting up. She looked terrible."

"She doesn't now. You've turned her into a regular fashion plate."

Nina rolled her eyes. "Mo-ther!"

But when Nina rejoined April, Mercedes saw that although she pestered April from time to time, she allowed no other cousins that privilege. And protecting April from the Delacruz pack was no small chore, considering the number of cousins present. Although April frequently complained about Nina's behavior to Cass and Mercedes, she refused to listen to any complaints about Nina from anyone else. The two girls might not love each other like sisters yet, but Mercedes felt their mutual loyalty was a good start.

Other bonds of loyalty were being forged, as well. April had quickly accepted Mercedes in her new role as mother. Nina had taken longer to warm up to Cass. She would always miss her father, but Cass had worked hard to find a place in Nina's heart, and the results were promising. Nina was dog-crazy, and she'd taken over April's job of helping to train young rescue dogs with the new search-and-rescue group Cass had started. And Cass had shown more enthusiasm for Nina's community theater group than Gilles ever had. Nina enjoyed Cass's company, trusted him and obeyed him better than she'd bothered to obey Gilles or Mercedes. Again, it was a start.

Mercedes was positive that, like April, Nina needed only love and time. They'd certainly worked wonders with April. She'd shyly offered to help Mercedes out during the winter school break and had subsequently proved to be such a careful, eager assistant that Mercedes's supervisor allowed April museum privileges the more rambunctious Nina was not.

And now they were all waiting to see the wedding pictures taken six weeks earlier. They'd all faced a lot of hard realities since that terrible day at the Well, Mercedes thought. Like Nina, she'd always miss Gilles in a deep secret corner of her heart. But Gilles was gone, and Cass was here with enough love and laughter for all of them. Mercedes needed that love and laughter, even as she needed Cass himself.

As Mercedes handed April another pottery shard, she remembered their wedding night. Mercedes had been nervous and shy when Cass had entered the room that had once been hers and Gilles's. When she'd purchased a brand-new bedroom set for April, she'd bought one for the master bedroom, too, but it hadn't helped. At first, she'd felt as awkward as a blushing virgin on their honeymoon. And their lovemaking had suffered.

"I'm sorry, Cass, I just can't yet," Mercedes said. She let her hair cover her embarrassed face and nervously plucked at the sexy black nightie and wrapper one of her sisters had given her for the wedding night. "I should have put this house up for sale. We should have bought a new place."

Cass shook his head. "No, we decided it would be too hard on Nina."

"A frigid bride is hardly fair to you, Cass," Mercedes moaned.

"You're hardly that." He kissed her full on the lips, then grinned as her breathing and pulse quickened. "See?"

"But, Cass, I can't make love to you in this room. It has too many memories."

Cass pulled her onto his bare chest and kissed the top of her head. "Then after the honeymoon we'll move furniture around. I could switch this room with my office. They both have baths and they're both about the same size."

Mercedes nodded. "That might work. But what about tonight?"

"Well—" Cass slowly pushed the wrapper off her shoulders "—what about the living room couch?"

"I can't. I...I should have bought a new couch, too." She broke off, embarrassed at revealing intimacies with her former husband to her present one, but Cass pretended not to notice.

"How about sleeping in one of the girl's rooms?"

"Cass! Are you crazy?"

Mercedes actually sat up at that suggestion. Cass reluctantly followed suit.

"I'll take that as a no. I guess you're more conventional than I thought."

Mercedes saw that he was actually amused.

"How can you smile about this? I *told* you we should have gone to a hotel."

"Nope. We have to get past this first hurdle while the girls are at your sister's. Once we all fly to Walt Disney World, it'll be too late. We won't be alone again for a long time." He started unbuttoning the tiny buttons on her nightie. "Unless you want to wait until we come home from Florida..."

"Cass, I'm inhibited enough! I don't want our first time to be with the girls in the house!"

"Then that leaves my office or the kitchen," he said matter-of-factly. "We can start in one or the other and work our way here."

"Not the kitchen, thank you," was Mercedes's tart response.

"That leaves the office, then. What's your preference? Desk or floor? Although I do have that big leather chair..."

"Forget it." Mercedes grabbed the front of her nightie, holding it closed as he finished with the buttons. "I've never made love in strange places and I'm not about to start now."

"Then what *do* you want?"

"I just want everything to be perfect."

There was a sudden silence, and Mercedes was appalled at what she'd just implied. But Cass had only smiled.

"Open your eyes, Mercedes." He kissed her forehead and gathered her close to his heart. *"It is."*

That kiss gave her the courage to put aside thoughts of her old life, her old mistakes, and reach out for the new. For Cass.

And the rest of the night was pure unadulterated pleasure. As were the nights that followed. And the days—they were filled with so much joy she almost couldn't believe they were real. She'd never thought she could ever feel that way again....

"Mom. *Mom!* You're not listening!" It was April. "Does my shard go in this tray or that one?"

Mercedes inspected the proffered shard and pointed to the correct bin. "That one," she said, "And lay it down easy."

"I know," April replied happily.

They were *all* so happy lately. Even Nina was smiling again. Oh, she had her sad moments, and Mercedes knew she would for years to come. But Cass could make Nina laugh, and for that, Mercedes loved him even more.

"There's the minivan!" April said suddenly. Her new pageboy swung as she hurried to the window and waved wildly. "He wants us to come out. There's no parking spaces left," she announced.

"I'm coming." Heart racing, Mercedes grabbed her keys and hurried to lock up.

"ARE THEY COMING, Cass?" Nina asked.

"Yep. April saw us. You'd better climb in the back seat

with Baron,'' he said.

"In a minute." Nina deliberately stalled by scratching Baron's ears.

Cass had to smile at Nina's stubborn streak. He fondly rumpled her hair, then grinned as she immediately checked the rearview mirror to inspect the damage. Nina carefully smoothed her tresses with an ages-old feminine gesture he'd recently seen April use, as well. April might not yet have picked up Nina's outgoing personality, but there was no doubt April had bloomed in her company.

Cass watched for his wife and daughter at the door to the museum. Mercedes had helped April in a way he never could, because Mercedes understood his daughter so much better. By the same token, he'd done for Nina what Mercedes could never do—he'd allowed Nina to stretch those strong little wings. Nina was definitely Gilles St. Clair's daughter, with a boldness and zest for life that had always frightened Mercedes, even before Gilles's death. Cass was ever-vigilant to counteract Mercedes's overprotective streak.

It was Cass who'd urged Mercedes to let Nina audition for more challenging acting parts. It was Cass who'd convinced Mercedes to let him take Nina on camping trips. But it was Nina herself who'd convinced Mercedes to let her train for search-and-rescue work. She and Cass were busy with Baron and Buddy's first litter, and already Nina was clamoring for more responsibilities. Nina needed freedom and challenges as much as April needed the safety of home and hearth. Both girls had flourished.

As had he.

Cass loved Mercedes with a passionate fierceness that made the transition to a larger blended family surprisingly easy. To everyone's initial shock, he encouraged Nina to talk about Gilles; he deliberately made the name of Gilles St. Clair welcome in his presence.

But when he was in bed with Mercedes, he knew there were just the two of them, no ghosts from the past. Their explosive passion went beyond the physical. It proclaimed their emotional want, joy and their deep fulfillment. Mercedes had turned toward him without a single sigh over the past or what might have been.

"Here they are!" Nina sang out. "Remember, you promised to take us out to dinner."

"I remember," Cass replied, but his eyes were on Mercedes. He gave her a smile as she and April hurried to the minivan.

"Hi, sweetheart," he said, kissing his wife lightly on the cheek. "Have a good time, April?"

"Tons! I got to help sort pot shards again, and I found some that matched, and—"

Nina groaned. "Spare me," she said dramatically. "Like we haven't heard *this* before."

"Nina!" Mercedes warned.

"Well, it's true!" Nina declared.

"You're rude! It's not polite to interrupt!" April flung back.

"I'm rude because you never shut up! Thank goodness your Spanish stinks or I'd never get to say *anything!*"

"Mom says my Spanish is coming along fine," April argued.

"Yeah, if you don't want anyone to understand it!"

Cass watched as Mercedes tried to play peacemaker, and kept out of it.

"Girls, please, let's drop it and concentrate on dinner. Now where do you all want to eat?"

"I want to go to McDonald's," Nina said immediately.

"That's no good," April complained. "The doctor says I can't eat fried food. We should go to the health-food place. It's right down the street."

"You *always* make us go there!" Nina protested. "I'm sick of broiled chicken and steamed veggies. I want a hamburger and fries!"

"Well, I want chicken!"

Mercedes broke in. "And I want to be alone with your father," she announced. "Cass, head for my mother's. We'll drop the girls off to eat there."

"Hey!" Nina protested.

"Sorry," Mercedes said firmly. "My decision is final. As for me—" she smiled at Cass, her eyes soft and glowing "—I want candlelight, violins and a sinfully rich dessert, Cass. Just the two of us."

"But...but..." April sputtered.

"In fact," Mercedes continued, "the girls can sleep over. Dad's been wanting to clear out the garage, and these two seem to have energy to spare. What do you think, Cass?

"Fine with me." His smile grew at the thought.

"That's not fair!"

"Oh, it's more than fair, Nina," Mercedes replied with a little smile. "After all, I'm still a newlywed. I want to be alone with my new husband."

She leaned over and, for the first time ever with the girls watching, kissed him fully, ardently, on the lips. A delighted Cass let her mouth linger, even as he let his love wash over her. It wasn't until a horn beeped behind him that he came to his senses. Cass stroked Mercedes's cheek one last time with his fingertips, then eased the minivan into the traffic.

"April, is your seat belt on? Nina, is your door locked?" he asked.

Cass heard two mumbled replies. He looked into the rearview mirror to check on his daughters and saw the aging dog wedged between them. He smiled. If it wasn't for that dog, he and April would never have met Mercedes and Nina. Twister—Baron now—had saved his sanity not once, but twice. Cass was more than just lucky.

He was blessed.